LOVING MY ALPHA MATE

RADONNA CHANDLER

BALBOA.PRESS

A DIVISION OF HAY HOUSE

Balboa Press books may be ordered through booksellers or by contacting:

Balboa Press
A Division of Hay House
1663 Liberty Drive
Bloomington, IN 47403
www.balboapress.com
844-682-1282

Because of the dynamic nature of the Internet, any web addresses or
links contained in this book may have changed since publication and
may no longer be valid. The views expressed in this work are solely those
of the author and do not necessarily reflect the views of the publisher,
and the publisher hereby disclaims any responsibility for them.

The author of this book does not dispense medical advice or prescribe the use
of any technique as a form of treatment for physical, emotional, or medical
problems without the advice of a physician, either directly or indirectly. The
intent of the author is only to offer information of a general nature to help
you in your quest for emotional and spiritual well-being. In the event you use
any of the information in this book for yourself, which is your constitutional
right, the author and the publisher assume no responsibility for your actions.

Any people depicted in stock imagery provided by Getty Images are
models, and such images are being used for illustrative purposes only.
Certain stock imagery © Getty Images.

Print information available on the last page.

ISBN: 978-1-9822-6828-2 (sc)
ISBN: 978-1-9822-6829-9 (e)

Balboa Press rev. date: 05/05/2021

CONTENTS

DEDICATION

To my son Nick who got me away from a very boring town for a while so I could help him when he needed help. That gave me time to read and get the inspiration I needed to write this book. To my daughter Kayla who of course laughed when I told her that I was going to write a book, but I know it would hurt her feelings if I did not mention her here (I love you baby girl). To my niece Sam who had read the start of a book that I was doing but never finished years ago. She said that she knew I had what it takes to write a book. I love you all and thank you for your support.

CHAPTER 1

MOVING

Hailey 🐾

I was taking another look around my room since I just got everything packed up and ready for the movers to put into the moving truck. It's going to be sad leaving the only home I have ever lived in, but mom says there is a very special reason for this move. I think it's because she is having a hard time since dad passed away. I think the memories are just to much for mom here in this house. Even though it is not the only house mom and dad have lived in, it is the only house they have lived in since I was born. Mom and dad had lived in the state of Washington, in a city called Kettle Falls. Mom says it's a very small town. That doesn't matter to me though. She says there is around 1600 people living there. I have never had an easy time making friends. I mostly spent my time alone. I had two really good friends Nikola who moved away two years ago. She is never in one place for very long because her dad is in the military. My other friend Page died from cancer. I don't understand why mom is so excited, but if it makes her happy, I will go along with it. I want the ride to our new place to be as comfortable as possible so I have on my yoga pants and my white crop top, and my Adidas. I throw my brown wavy hair into a messy bun. I don't see any point in putting on mascara, and eyeliner just to be sitting in a car going hundreds of miles away.

Hailey come on, this trip is going to take us long enough as it is. I want to get started early. My mom yell's from downstairs. As I start to walk out of my room I say goodbye small town Indiana, and as I walk out the door I say hello small town Washington. Mom looks at me and ask what? Nothing mom, I was just thinking out loud. I love my mom, but the way she had just up and decided to move drive's me crazy. She told me to look at it as the start of a great new adventure. There has got to be more to this. I have not seen my mom this happy and bouncy since months before my dad passed away. Don't misunderstand me, I love seeing her smile and happy, but it's like it happened overnight and the next thing I know we are moving.

Lauren 🐾

It is sad for me to pack up the only home we have lived in since not long after Hailey was born. We watched her grow and learn so many things in this house. I have a lot of good memories in this house. But ever since Hunter died I have been so sad. I didn't think I could live up to the promise I made him before he passed away especially since he died from that awful attack. But I did promise him that I would take Hailey back to our home town and make sure she starts training. I know that I had to snap out of it. It didn't take long for the house to sale once it was on the market. We not only got more than enough for me to buy a nice house in Kettle Falls, by what Hailey doesn't know yet is that I already bought her a car. It was supposed to be a graduation gift but since she lost her father, and because are moving I thought I would surprise her. I bought her a very nice silver Honda Accord that has black pen striping down each side. I can not wait to see her reaction. Hailey come on this trip is going to take long enough as it is. I want to get started early.

Hailey 🐾

It was getting really late and I was getting really tired. Being sixteen though I am not a small child that can just lay down in the seat while mom drive's. Besides I am sure that mom is tired too since she has been driving sixteen hours. Hey mom. Yes hun. Are we going to be stopping to sleep? Oh yes there is no way I can drive straight through. I just hope the movers are ok and that they can find the house once they get into Kettle Falls. I laugh, not at my mom but because I imagine professional movers getting lost in a town called Kettle Falls.

Would you like to get some food before we stop for the night sweetie? I was thinking we could order some pizza once we get to the room if that is ok with you mom. That would be great Hailey that way we could get to the hotel quicker.

I know kid's my age don't normally get along with their parents, but my mom is actually pretty awesome. We pull into a Holiday Inn Express, I can hear mom as she gets out of the Audi Q5 talking about how good it feels to get out, walk around, and stretch her legs.

Once inside of the room I find a list of places to eat and a list of pizza places. Mom hand's me her debit card and has me to place the order while she takes a shower and gets her pj's on.

I have always thought of my mom as a pretty person with her auburn hair and brown eyes. Most people I have seen with any shade of red hair normally has green eyes but not my mom. She's also not super skinny, but she's also not fat at all. I know if mom ever decides to date she would not have a problem at all finding someone. I want my mom to be happy again even though it is going to be very, very hard seeing her with a man that is not my dad. But I am not always going to be home. One day I will move out, and get my own home. So yes I want her to have someone that will be there.

Hey sweetie did you order the pizza? Yes I did. I hope you asked for more than just cheese on it this time. I laughed and said yes I asked for pepperoni, ham, and pineapple. Mmmmm that sounds so good my mom says as she walks back towards the bathroom moving the towel over her hair to get more of the water out and wearing a fuzzy white robe. How long until it will be here, I'm starving. In about thirty to thirty five minutes. I was hoping that would be enough time for mom to finish and then I could get into the shower. As soon as mom was done in the bathroom I went in there. I take my hair down and undress. The steam from the shower was already filling the bathroom. after washing my hair and body I rinse completely off. I get out of the shower, dry off, then wrap my hair in a towel. I pick out gray leggings and a long white T-shirt to wear. When I came out of the bathroom I see that the pizza had just arrived. The aroma from the pizza really made my stomach growl. I grab a couple slices then settle on the bed that I am going to sleep on tonight. Mom is on the other bed on her laptop so I grab my iPad and pull up Netflix. I pick out a movie to watch as I eat my pizza. Normally I would go a run after my dinner settles in my stomach but since we don't know the town we are in I decided that probably was not a good idea.

Lauren 🐾

I was getting really tired after driving 16 hours. Haley asked if we were going to stop so we could get some sleep. So As soon as I found a Holiday Inn Express I pull in. Haley stayed in the car as I go to get us a room. as soon as I got the key card to the room I got back in the car and drove it as close to the room as possible. Haley and I each carried our suitcases in so we would have clothes to wear to bed and for the rest of the trip to our new home. Once inside the room I gave Haley my debit card so she could order the pizza while I get in the shower. It feels so good having the hot water running down my body helping me to relax after driving all those hours. After washing my hair and my body I get out and use my extra large towel to dry off. I put on my black leggings and a long t-shirt that belong to my husband. I did keep a few of his shirts so I could wear them at night. That made me feel like he was still here with me when I sleep. When I walk out of the bathroom I ask Haley if she had ordered the food and she said she had so I got my card from her and put it back in my wallet, then I return to the bathroom while running the towel over my hair trying to soak up as much as the dampness as I can, then I brush my hair. Once I was done I went back into the room, I sat on the bed that I am going to sleep on and get my laptop out to see if I have any messages. I also wanted to get some work done. When I sat down I see Haley get up. Are you going to take a shower sweetie? Yeah, is it okay if you answer the door if the food gets here before I am done in the shower? Of course sweetie.

Hailey 🐾

After eating my Pizza I lay on my side to continue watching the movie. The next morning I wake up not realizing I had actually fallen asleep during the movie I had picked out last night. I look over at the bed my mom slept on last night and she was not there. I didn't think much about that because she probably went to the lobby to get a cup of coffee. As I am getting my stuff together mom comes through the door and sure enough she has a cup of coffee from the lobby.

Hi Hailey, are you ready to get going? We can grab a bite to eat on the way. I am ready when you are Mom. For some reason I'm feeling a little excited today about getting to our new house. That is very unusual for me to get excited about something new, well unless it is Christmas but let's face it who doesn't get excited about Christmas unless you are the Grinch. Mom grabbed her suitcase and I grabbed mine. Once we were back on the road mom says only 14 more hours to home. I just smile and look out the window and start watching everything as we pass by.

We pull in the driveway around 10:30 p.m. when we pull in I see a beautiful silver Honda Accord. Mom whose car is that? Mom gets the biggest smile on her face and she looks at me and tells me that it is my car. Mom don't joke with me like that. I wanted so badly for her to be serious, I wanted that car to be mine so bad. Haley I am not joking, the car is yours. It's a gift from your father and I. I was going to wait until you graduate and give it to you then but with everything that has happened lately I thought you needed something to cheer you up. She pulls a keychain out of her purse that has a remote start button a button to lock/unlock the doors, and a trunk opener on it as well as a button for the alarm. There was even a little red ribbon tied to the keychain. I got the biggest smile on my face and I gave my mom the biggest hug. Oh Mom thank you, thank you, thank you. Mom laughs and says you're welcome. I jumped out of the car and run to check out my new car. I was so tired when we got here but now it's like I'm wide awake. This car is so amazing, I cannot wait until in the morning so I can really see everything. I went back to Mom and gave her another hug. Thank you again mom. You're welcome sweetie. I know you will take really good care of the car. Oh yes I will. I grabbed my suitcase and follow mom into the house.

The house itself is breath taking. It's a three-story house. On the outside brownstones make up the walls in the front, sides, and back. On the inside there is four bedrooms upstairs. On the main level a game room, living room, dining room, and kitchen. Downstairs there is a garage, and a finished basement that my mom had the movers to set up as a workout/training room. I went to find my room. The movers had left a note on the front door that they had set up all the furniture. I like that my bed was already set up, not only was I feeling tired again but by them setting up all the furniture that made it easier for me to find my bedroom.

As I was going through my suitcase mom pops in. I hope this room is okay sweetie. Oh yes Mom it is perfect. Also Haley you don't have to rush going back to school. I know Mom but I am starting a new school. I feel like I should go ahead and start on the first day with everyone else. Okay well if you start to feel overwhelmed I want you to come home and get some rest. Okay Mom. After that my mom left my room and I started hanging up my clothes. Once I was done with my clothes I grabbed up the bag that had my bathroom stuff and went into my bathroom to put it all away. I went back into my room grab my PJs then went to take a shower.

That night I think I was asleep before my head hit my pillow. I start dreaming a very weird dream. I was walking through the woods with a boy that was about a year older than me. He is very good looking with strong looking arms, and I could tell through his shirt that he has a muscular chest and a very tight stomach looks like he has a six, or an eight pack. We were holding hands and talking as we walked. His dark brown hair that went to his shoulders made his sea blue eyes really stand out. All of a sudden he pulls me behind him in a protective way. I hear growling, like dogs growling. He tells me to run as fast as I can back the other way. I can feel my heart beating fast and I can feel myself shaking all over from fear. I do as he told me and I am running as fast as I can in the direction we came from. As I am running I look back to make sure I am safe and I see the guy I was walking with run towards what looks like wolves. He jumps in the air and I see him turn into a wolf. I wake up as soon as I see that and I am breathing hard and shaking and I can feel my heart racing. Mom comes running to me. Are you okay Haley? Yes Mom. I said still trying to catch my breath. It was just a bad dream. Do you want to talk about it? No it's okay. I don't really remember it now. I told her that so she wouldn't worry and go back to bed. That dream was so weird. I haven't had a dream like that in around 6 months now. I used to have bad dreams something similar to that for the longest time just before, and after dad had passed away but they were dreams of my dad being attacked by what looks like wolves. It used to scare me so badly and I would wake up screaming and wanting my dad. I would not go to back to sleep after those dreams unless my dad was there to comfort me. Since my dad passed away though it was my mom that had to comfort me and that was not easy for her since I would be screaming for my dad. I laid back down and went back to sleep until my alarm went off.

After I shut my alarm off I got up and went over to my walk in closet. I decided on a mid-thigh skirt, a white button up shirt, a black tank top that goes under my white top, and my flat's. I go downstairs and place my book bag by the front door. As I walk into the kitchen, I see a note on the counter.

Hailey, I had to leave early I forgot that I have an early morning meeting, have a good day at school and I will see you this evening. Love mom P, S, we will probably have to order out.

I made some toast with cream cheese and headed out the door. I really don't care if anyone at this school likes me or not. I had my two really good friends. Nikola moved and even though we Skype almost every day it's still not the same. I'm also still not over Page dying Thirty minutes later pulling into the parking lot at the new school. I take a deep breath and start walking through the parking lot towards the school, but I stop in the middle of the parking lot because I could feel someone watching me. I look around without trying to make it obvious and I freeze right where I am. That's him, that's the boy from my dream. I start walking again towards the school hoping he hadn't noticed. I glance up and he is gone. Once inside the school I start looking for the office. I must have made it obvious that I am the new kid because a boy comes up to me and introduces himself as Dorian.

Dorian

When I saw her walking through the halls looking around I knew she had to be new. No other student here looks around like that, and I pretty much know of everyone that goes to this school. The town isn't that big and everyone pretty much knows everyone. I walk up to her and introduce myself to her.

Hi I'm Dorian, and I'm guessing you are new here. Yes, and I'm Hailey. Damn she is cute I thought to myself. But I know she is not my mate. Everyone has a mate, or they are looking for their mate, or they have already been with their mate and something happened to one of them, or you are just to young. Once you have found your mate it's supposed to be for life. There are those few who reject their mate, but I think that is wrong. So Hailey would you like a guide? That would be great. I need to find the office so I can turn in my paperwork and get my class schedule. Ok follow me. I take Hailey to the office and I wait for her outside the doors. Even though I know she is not my mate she is pretty and I wouldn't mind being seen with her. You know if someone is your mate by if they are within a certain distance from you, you are able to smell the most amazing scent you have ever smelled. Okay, I have my schedule. Good what is your first class? It is English, Mrs. McKay. I will show you to your class. What is your second class? Um it is science. I look over at her schedule and her second and third classes are the same as mine science and history. Great I will meet you after class and walk you to your second class since your second class is with me and I smile at her. Ok I will see you then.

Hailey

I walk into class and see Mrs. McKay sitting at her desk so I walk up to her and let her know who I am and that I am new here. Would you like to introduce yourself to the class? No thank you. Okay then here is your book. Make sure to look it over really good. If there are any torn page's or any other damages make sure to write it down. If there isn't any damage then just sign the slip and return the slip to me at the end of class, but remember if you just skim through the book and don't write down any damage including pen or pencil marks that might be in there you will be responsible for any damages. Yes ma'am. Welcome to your new school. Thank you. I take the book and start to go to the empty seat Mrs. McKay told me to take. There were only two empty seats left in the classroom. They were both in the back of the room. My heart skips a beat because the boy I was with in my dream was setting in the seat right next to mine, and on the other side of him was the other empty seat in the class. Once I was in my seat I opened the book and started going through it looking for damage, but I can feel someone staring right at me. I slowly look hoping I was wrong, but nope there he is sitting next to me and very obviously staring right at me like I am something to eat. It's really creepy.

Jaxson 🐺

As soon as she got out of her car in the parking lot I knew. I could smell the most amazing smell of vanilla, clover, and chocolate. Even when she turned around and saw me looking right at her I didn't care, I could not take my eyes off of her. My mate, my mate is finally here. My pack will finally have their Luna. I wasn't sure if I would see her the rest of the day or not. I go to my first class of the day and I become a little down because I did not see my mate in the classroom. One can be hopeful though. I take my seat and start waiting for the teacher to start the lesson for the day, but then the classroom door opens and she walks in. She is very beautiful and the scent is almost overwhelming. She is looking down and she is talking to Mrs. McKay so she doesn't even realize that I am sitting back here and that there are only two seats left in the class, one on either side of me. I want to reach out, grab her and kiss her as if there is no tomorrow but I don't want to scare her or make her think I'm some sort of freak even though in some ways I just might be a freak. She is finally walking back here. I know when my mate gets close the scent gets stronger. I won't be able to control myself if her scent gets any stronger. She sits down and starts going through her book. Hi, I say to her. She looks over at me and I can feel tingling going through my entire body. I'm Jaxson, Jaxson Carter, but most people just call me Jax. She smiles the most beautiful smile I have ever seen. Hi, I'm Haley. It's nice to meet you Haley. It's nice to meet you too Jaxson. Then she went right back to going through her book. I couldn't help myself, I had to keep talking to her. Are you new here? Yes, it's my first day. I meant are you new to the town, because I am sure I would remember you if I had seen you before especially with this town being as small as it is we would have ran into each other at some point. Oh you think so do you? She said with the most beautiful smile. Yes I do. I said with a smile. Yes my mom and I just got into town last night. And you came to your first day of school on your first real day in town? Well yeah I didn't want to be behind. But from the looks of it I have already done most of this at my old school. Well then you should be able to take it pretty easy then.

Hailey 🐾

My heart really started racing when I sat down and he started talking to me. He told me his name is Jaxson, but everyone calls him Jax. That is a pretty cool name I guess. I would have thought his name would have been Jason, or Ben or something simple. He seems nice enough. I know what happened in my dream was just a dream. People don't turn into wolves, not in real life anyway. That kind of thing only happens on movies, or on TV shows, or in books. I looked through my book and didn't see anything wrong with it, I made sure to look at every page too even though Jaxson kept talking to me. I signed the slip just like Mrs. McKay told me to. That way I would have the slip ready at the end of the class. I like to listen to what the lesson is about, but with Jaxson talking to me it is hard for me to pay attention to what Mrs. McKay is talking about. I'm surprised she hasn't said anything to him about talking during class time. Maybe she thinks that since I am new that he is helping me. I hear Jaxson ask me if I needed someone to show me around. Thank you, but I already have someone that is showing me around a sort of tour guide. I thought I heard him growl which made me gasp. Then he had a whole different tone when he asked me who. He said his name is Dorian. As soon as I said Dorian's name it was like Jaxson got angry. He was the first person I met when I got inside the school. He was nice enough to ask me if I would like for him to show me to the office and after I got my schedule he said he could show me to my classes. Jaxson ask me what my next two classes are, so I told him. Would you like to have lunch with me since we have the same lunch time? I would like to think about that. I can let you know if I see you around lunch time. I'm not so sure he liked that answer, but I really don't care right now. I don't know if it is from not getting enough sleep, or the stress of starting a new school but my stomach didn't feel so good. The bell rings ending the first class of the day. I get up and take the sign slip back to Mrs. McKay. Jackson tries talking to me, but I can see Dorian standing across the hall waiting for me so he can walk me to my next class and I don't want to keep him waiting so I ignore Jaxson and I walked out the door and asked Dorian if he is ready to walk me to the next class.

Dorian 🐾

I couldn't get Hailey off my mind. If I don't find my mate I would like to be with Hailey. But if I do find my mate I hope she is a lot like Hailey. Class couldn't go fast enough for me. All I could think about was the very pretty girl I am going to be walking to class with, actually we will be walking to the next two classes together. Then I realize I should ask Hailey if she would like to sit with me at lunch. I could introduce her to everyone that sits there too. Finally the bell rings ending class. I jump out of my seat at the back of the class and sprint out of the door before anyone else. I don't want to take the chance of missing Hailey. I would feel really bad if she had to wonder around trying to find the next class. I did get to her first class just as the door started to open. I see Haley handing something to her teacher. Then I see Jaxson trying to say something to Hailey but I see her just walk off. I don't know why this makes me happy. I know she is someone else's mate and I should not feel the way I do. I know she is not mine. Hailey smiles as she walks over to me. I can't help but to smile back at her. How was your first class of your first day? It was okay. She sounded like something was on her mind, or something was bothering her. But I don't know her well enough to ask her. So since we have the next two classes together and after the third class of the day is lunch would you like to sit at the table I sit at? I can introduce you to everyone at the table. Sure that sounds like fun.

Hailey 🐺

I was so glad to be out of that first class. So many things was going through my mind already. I felt a very weird sort of connection to Jaxson that I can not explain. Dorian seems really sweet. Like someone I can be comfortable around. Normally I don't like it when school starts on a Friday, but I am glad I started this new school on a Friday. That gives me the weekend to take everything in that happens today. Science and history

15

go by really fast. I walk with Dorian to lunch, he shows me where he and his friends sit. Then he walks with me to the lunch line. That is where I met Abigail, Dorian's sister. When Dorian introduces me to his sister she tells me she likes to be called Abby. She seems really nice. I grab a salad and a coke. Dorian and even Abby grab one of everything there was to eat. Wow you both must be really hungry I laughed. We train really hard. Abby told me. So we eat more since we burn up so many calories. I was told by my mom as we were leaving our old home to come here that I would start training. Abby and Dorian just kind of looked at each other and smiled. Maybe I could train with you two. Sure. Dorian said to me in a weird tone like he wasn't to sure about me training with him and his sister. As we get to the table Dorian introduces me to Tina, Daniel, and Aspen. They all seem to be very nice and they all ate the same amount as Dorian and Abby have on their tray. I have been so used to the girl's back at the school I used to go to eating as little as possible. Are all of you training? They all smiled and nodded. What is everyone training for, some sort of Olympics? They all laughed, Dorian said it's a lifestyle. If you are supposed to be training too you will get used to training everyday especially if you train with us. About that time Jaxson comes into the lunch room with some other guys that look as muscular as he is. Jaxson walks over to the table where I was sitting, puts his hands down on the table, looks straight at me and just says "mine." Dorian shoots a look at Jaxson. If someone could shoot dagger's out of their eye's Jaxson would be dead. All of the sudden I thought I heard Dorian growl. Maybe it's just that sound that people make when they are really pissed here. So Hailey, a lot of us are getting together tomorrow evening and going to just hang out, kind of an official end of summer hangout. Would you like to come and hang out with us? Abby asked. Yeah, I would love to go I just have to run it by my mom first though but I am sure it would not be a problem. Okay well give me your cell phone number and I will text you so that way you have mine and that way you can let me know if you can go. I wrote down my number and handed it over to Abby almost as soon as she saw my number I felt my phone go off in my back pocket. I take it out and see the message from Abby saying "This is my number." I added her to my contacts. I also saw a message from Nikola so I open the message to see what she said. "Hey bff, we haven't Skyped for a few days. I know you have been busy with the move from Indiana to Washington. I need to see you and talk to you it's important." I'm going to have to Skype with her when I get home. It was almost time for the next class. I told everyone I was going to my locker to get what I needed for the rest of the day. Abby said she would see me after school. Dorian asked me if I wanted him to walk me. No, but thank you for offering. I should be able to find my way around now. When I was walking through the hall it felt like someone was following me then all the sudden I feel someone's hands on my waist guiding me over to a set of lockers. I gasp when I see it is Jaxson. I could feel my entire body tingling with excitement. I don't know why my body does that when I am close to Jaxson, but it does.

Jaxson

Ever since our first class let out this morning I cannot stop thinking about her. She's my mate. I'm not going to let anyone or anything take her away from me. That little punk Dorian had better stay away from Hailey. I'm his pack Alpha so he has to respect me and what is mine. After our third class of the day I was going so crazy just thinking about her that I had to find her. I looked into every classroom through the window in the door. She wasn't in any of the rooms. There was only a couple of places I can think of that she could be which would be at the parking lot or the cafeteria. I looked into the cafeteria and sure enough there she was, completely surrounded by Dorian and his cronies. But I don't care at this point. I walk into the cafeteria, put my hands down on their table, looked right at Hailey and said "mine." Dorian gave me a look of death but I don't care. Hailey is my mate. There is nothing anyone can do about that, well except for me. I could reject her then she would be free to be with whoever she chooses. But I don't see myself or my wolf rejecting her. I go and sit at my usual table until I see Hailey leaving alone. I get up and follow her out of the doors. When I get close enough I grab her around the waist and guide her over to some lockers. I wasn't trying to hurt her or scare her. I could also feel Cain my wolf going crazy. You're mine, you are my mate. She looks up at me not with excitement, not with fear, but she looks really mad. I don't care though she is my mate and there's nothing anyone can do about it. I am really hoping she does not know anything about being able to reject your mate. That would kill me if she rejected me. I stay as close to Hailey as possible without smashing her into the lockers. My hands are still on her waist so she can't walk away. The look she is giving me is pure hate. You are mine!! My mate.

Hailey 🐺

I look up at Jaxson with pure hate because of the way he is being. No one is going to force me to be with them. I'm WHAT? I'm your mate. I don't think so!! I don't know who the hell you think you are, but nobody talks like that to me and nobody forces me to be with them. I tried to move his hands off of my waist but he is way too strong. Move your hands off my waist now. I demanded. He just looked at me and smirked. That just pissed me off more so I punched him in the gut. That wasn't too smart on my part because his abs are harder than stone. My hand hurts so bad it brought tears to my eyes. Get away from me NOW Jaxson. I demanded. Finally he moved but I think he moved only because the end of lunch bell rang. My hand hurts really bad from punching Jaxson and it's starting to swell. I wasn't going to go to the nurse but I don't think I have a choice. I have to get some ice for my hand and hope that stops the swelling. I walk into the nurse's office. Hi, can I help you with something. She asked me, and she seems very nice. Could I please get an ice pack? What did you do to your hand dear? I lied when she asked me that. I got some upsetting news from my best friend that lives a long ways away from here during lunch and I punched a tree outside. I know that was not a smart thing to do, but I wasn't thinking at the moment. The nurse just smiled at me and handed me an ice pack. She told me that I would probably need it the rest of the day. I told her thank you and I went to my last three classes. The ice was keeping my hand from swelling anymore but it was throbbing. At the end of the school day, on my way walking out to my car I was hoping that Jaxson wouldn't see me because I swear to God I will go off on him if he comes anywhere near me now. HAILEY. I hear someone yell. But thank God it was a girl's voice. I turn around and see Abby running towards me. When she gets close I see her eyes get great big and her mouth drop. What happened? Abby asked me. I punched Jaxson in the stomach and his stomach was harder than a rock. Do you think you will feel up to hanging out with us tomorrow? Oh yeah, I'm sure I will be fine by tomorrow, I can still move my fingers and my wrist even though it hurts like hell but at least

I know it's not broken. I have just never met anyone with abs that rock hard

Abby

I watched Haley go out of the lunch room doors. Not long after she goes out the doors I see Jaxson go out the doors too and he is moving pretty fast. Just then I hear my brother Dorian growl, he starts to get up and I tell him to sit down. He is our Alpha. Besides, you don't want to get into trouble again and get suspended from school and not get to go to the hangout do you? No. Dorian says with a growl. But I also don't want that S. O. B. Bothering Hailey. I know brother, but if you get suspended from school the only place you will be able to see Hailey is if she happens to come over not to mention that Jaxson is our Alpha in training and we have to respect him, you are his beta and his best friend. Dorian puts his head down and starts whining like a little lost puppy. I know Dorian likes Hailey but I also know she is not his mate. He would have said something to me. I didn't see Hailey in any of my last few classes, so I was hoping to catch her before she goes home after school. Once our last class of the day was over I took off through the doors that led out to the parking lot. HAILEY!! I yell trying to get her attention. She slowly turns around as I am running up to her. OMG, what happened to your hand? I punched Jaxson in the stomach and his stomach is harder than a rock. Do you think you will feel up to hanging out with us tomorrow? Oh yeah I am sure I will be fine by tomorrow. I am so excited that she is still wanting to hang out with us.

Dorian 🐺

That asshole, that S.O.B. he hurt Hailey. How could he hurt her in any possible way. I could tear him apart for treating her that way. I know Jaxson is our Alpha and the pack is supposed to respect our Alpha leader, but I don't know if I can hold back if he does anything to hurt Hailey again, even if I am his Beta and we are supposed to be best friends. No one should treat a nice girl like Hailey like that.

Hailey 🐺

As I was driving home from school I was thinking how grateful I am that the school nurse did not call Mom at work. She would have been all worried and I probably wouldn't be able to go hang out with my new friends tomorrow because mom would want to keep me home and baby me. I get that I am all she has now, but I am not a baby. When I pull into the driveway I see a car I don't know. I'm driving very slow as I approach the car. The driver side opens and out steps Jaxson. If I could growl there would be a very long, very deep growl coming out of me right now. I don't want to see, talk, or be around Jaxson especially right now. As I park my car and get out I see Jaxson walking over to me and I yell at him. Jaxson I don't want to see you, I don't want to talk to you! Hailey I want to say I'm sorry for my behavior at lunch today. That is not how I want things to go now that I have found my mate. You're what? You're mate, what are you talking about? I'm not anyone's mate, and no one can force me to be with them. After telling Jackson that I slid past him. I felt him try to grab my arm, but he just was not quick enough. I unlocked the front door, went in, shut and lock the front door back. Then ran up to my room I watch out the window as he leaves. How in the hell did he know where I live. That was creepy. I hear my phone go off with a text message. The message was from Mom. Hey sweetie, my afternoon meeting is running a little longer than I thought so order some food. I left the credit card on the kitchen countertop. Love Mom I go back downstairs, grab mom's credit card and I will order some food here in a minute. At least the swelling has gone down on my hand I won't have to explain that to Mom and see her freak out. Before I order the food I decide to go put on a pair of yoga pants, and a tank top so I can get a workout in. Mom had asked the movers to set up all the workout equipment in the basement which was a great idea because there is a lot of room down there. After I am dressed in my work out clothes I put my hair up and head down to the basement. I start with some stretches. After about 5 minutes of stretching I go to the treadmill, then the weight bench. 30 minutes really goes by fast when I work out. I better go get that food ordered. I grab my cell phone, look up the number to the closest Chinese place and call to make the delivery order. After I place the order I run back up to my room and grab some leggings and a t-shirt, head off to the shower. By the time I was done showering, drying off and getting dressed it was about time for the food to be here. Once I was back downstairs I hear someone knocks on the door. It was the food being delivered. The delivery guy hands me the slip to sign and I added a $3 tip. I know Mom won't mind me doing that. she would probably be more upset with me if I didn't tip the driver. As the driver was leaving I seen Mom's car pulling in the driveway. How was your day? I asked Mom as she come in. It was good. I noticed mom smiling which makes me very happy, she hasn't smiled since Dad passed away. How was your first day at the new school? It was good I made some new friends at school today. Oh and I wanted to ask you if I could go hang out with some of the kids I met today at school tomorrow. I don't see why not. I do need to talk to you about something Hailey. Is there something wrong? No sweetie. But it does have something more to do with why we moved here. Surely this doesn't have anything to do with a guy, dad hasn't been gone that long. I know Mom is a grown woman but I would think that Mom would wait a little longer.

Lauren

I need to talk to Haley when I get home. I need to let her know the real reason we moved here, I also need to let her know the truth about our family what we are. I can only hope that no one has said anything to her at school. I had really hoped she would have stayed home and waited to start school next Monday. That would have given me the weekend to talk to her and introduce her to the pack and get her started on her training. I know I should have already told her, but she is my baby girl even if she is 16. I wish Hunter was still around. That rogue attack is what took my husband's life, of course Hailey thinks it was a car accident. I really think this transition would be easier for Hailey if Hunter was still alive. I know I can help her train and get her up to speed on everything. I just hope she can understand why I didn't tell her sooner. As I pull into the driveway I see a car leaving. Hailey must have ordered the food. I will talk to her about everything either during or after dinner. I can smell the Chinese food and sweat as soon as I walk in the house. I think Hailey must have done a little workout while waiting for the food. That's one thing about being a werewolf, your sense of smell is more than a normal human's. How was your day? Hailey asked me as I walked in. It was good. I said to her. How was your day at the new school? It was good, I made some new friends at school today. Oh and I wanted to ask you if I can go hang out with some of the people I met at school today. I don't see why not. Well that means that I am really going to have to talk to her now during dinner if she is going to hang out with the kids from here since they are all werewolves. Hailey, I do need to talk to you about something though. Is something wrong? No sweetie nothing is wrong there is just some things I need to tell you. It has to do more with why we moved here. It doesn't have anything to do with a guy does it Mom? I can't believe you just asked me if us moving here has anything to do with a guy. No Hailey us coming here has nothing to do with a guy. Hailey looked at me and said "good." so why did we really move here? She asked me. Well I know you're a very open-minded person and for that I am glad. Now this is going to be beyond anything you could possibly think of and whatever questions you have do not be afraid ask me. I am sorry I have not told you this before, but it does have everything to do with our family history.

Hailey 🐺

I felt like Mom was babbling. It was like she was going on and on for hours and none of what she was saying made any sense to me. Most of what she was saying was getting all jumbled up in my mind anyway. That is until I heard the words were and wolves. WE ARE WHAT!!??!! Mom did you just tell me that we are wolves? That stuff is only on movies, on TV and in fiction books. Yes Hailey I did just tell you that, and it is not just fiction that we exist. please don't be mad at me for not telling you sooner, but you're my baby and it is my natural instinct to protect you. My mouth dropped as mom was explaining this

LOVING MY ALPHA MATE

more. I also want you to know since you have not experienced phasing yet, I want you to know that it does hurt when you phase. Everything in your body moves including your bones. But please don't be afraid to phase just because it does hurt. Some people will say that you never get over the pain which you don't but you get used to it. That is why we all howl the loudest the first time we phase. I really feel like this is a dream, a nightmare. Like the one I just had last night. Mom am I really asleep and dreaming? No sweetie, you are not dreaming. Our families have been werewolves for many, many years. Actually as far back as I know the only reason I have not told you this before now is because I wanted to protect you, you are my only child, my baby, plus I felt that when you were younger you would not have understood all this like you can now. Plus since we moved from here just before you were born because of your father's job, and since you have not phased yet I just didn't see the point before now to interrupt the life you knew. Mom may have been right because this is a lot to take in. Mom can I ask you something since you know so much about all of this. You can ask me anything. When someone calles you his mate, and says a certain person is "mine" what does that mean? Why, did someone say that to you? Well yes. This guy at school named Jaxson. I did my best to not make any facial expressions when Hailey told me this. What's Jaxson's last name? Do you know it? Yes, it's Carter, I was afraid of that, I thought to myself. That means that he is the son of the Alpha. The Carters have always been the head of pack's. Hailey finding her mate was not something that I was ready for, but I know there is nothing that I can do about what the moon goddess has already done. Hunter and I had our own pack, but they all got rehomed when Hunter was transferred for his job. I went on with explaining as much as I could to Hailey, but there is someone that is called the

Moon goddess, from what I have been told she is a real person here on Earth and not just some unknown legend. She is the one that has chosen who you will be with your soulmate. When you find your mate you will be able to smell the most amazing scent you have ever smelled before. But you can also reject your mate, but for it to completely work both you and your mate have to say this together. You have to say: I, then you both state your own names. Such as you would say "I, Hailey Marie Moran reject you Jaxson Carter from being my mate." but there is a downside to this. What is the downside? Hailey asked me. Well your wolf is inside of you and your wolf could start dying off which will make you very weak and it could even kill you. Another thing I want you to know is that there are some perks to being a werewolf. Oh yeah what are they? I hope the perks are better than possibly dying from rejecting your mate. Well say you get a bruise or some sort of cut you can heal faster than a normal human could. I thought to myself well that would explain why my swollen hand healed so fast. After that long conversation mom and I sat down to dinner. She told me about her job and I told her about my new school. I left out the part about what happened between Jaxson and I and that I had hurt my hand punching him in the gut. Thank God the swelling went down pretty fast, but now I do understand why it went down so fast. Werewolf's heal really fast, but just because I found out that I am a wolf doesn't mean I am going to go out and try to get hurt. The pain from getting her is very real. I guess I understand why mom didn't tell me about all of this sooner. I know she felt like I wouldn't have understood and that I would have freaked out more than I already am. I am not sure how I feel about being Jaxson's mate. If he would have approached me differently, or would have been nice to me like he seem to be in class I would have thought differently. When

Mom and I were done with dinner I did the dishes and then I ran up to my room. I could not wait to Skype with Nikola and tell her about everything that is going on. She is going to flip when I tell her everything. I was so happy to see Nikola even though it was just on my laptop screen. As soon as I saw her she told me that I was not going to believe the news that she has to tell me. Let me tell you everything that is going on in Kettle Falls first because you are not going to believe this. We both laugh when I said the name of the town. Well I actually have some really amazing news so let me go first please. Okay, Go ahead and then I will tell you my news. You're not going to believe this. My parents, brother, and I are moving again. My mouth dropped when Nikola says that her and her family are moving again. She says with a big smile on her face. Yes, tell me. I want to know. We are moving to Kettle Falls. I scream with excitement. My mom comes running in when she hears me scream. What's wrong Hailey? Nothing mom. Nikola just gave me some good news, and I got really happy. Hi Nikola. Mom says from my bedroom door. Hi Mrs. Moran. Okay I will leave you girls to chat. So what's your good news? Or just news? Where do I start haha. well first I want to tell you about this really weird dream I had last night and several other times. I was walking through some woods with this guy, we were holding hands and talking. All of the sudden this guy I am with in my dreams pushes me behind him like he was trying to protect me from something. I hear something growl as he is pushing me behind him. Out from between some trees comes these wolves. there was two or three of them. The guy in my dream tells me to run and as I am running. I look back to see if he is okay and I see him jump into the air. While he is in the air he shifts into a wolf and that scared the hell out of me so much I guess I screamed as I was starting to wake up and mom came running into my room. I set up in my bed shaking and my heart racing. OMG girl that is a freaky dream and it would have scared the hell out of me too. Nikola said. Anyway I went to my first day of my new school so I could check it out and get to know where all my classes are before the first full week. In the school parking lot and in my first class I see this boy that is sitting in the back row next to the only two seats that were left. He is the boy that was in my dream. His name is Jaxson. Well long story short I ended up punching him in the gut because he tried to keep me from going outside during lunch so I could text you back and let you know I would Skype you after school by holding me by my waist and had me up against the lockers. Nikola's mouth dropped. His stomach is harder than a rock, I ended up hurting my hand so badly that it started swelling. But I met a girl named Abagail, I call her Abby, I also met a boy named Dorian, he is Abby's brother. They are both very nice. Actually everyone I have met is really nice. Wait. What? I asked her when she told me to wait is your hand okay? I hold my hand up to where she can see it and see it is okay. I am going to hang out with Abby, Dorian, and everyone else tomorrow evening. I also found out some really surprising news from my mom. It's something very life-changing and she said it is one of the reasons we moved here. What is it? It sounds very serious. Nikola said. Well I don't have to ask you to sit down because you are already setting down. Are you ready for this? It's VERY mind blowing. Yes tell me. If you don't want to be my friend after this I guess I will understand. You're not pregnant are you Hailey? NIKOLA!! How could you ask me that? Will the way you said if I wasn't already sitting down, you would ask me to. Also you said if I didn't want to be your friend anymore which by the way girl I would never turn my back on you. Okay well there is no other way to say this but to just say it. I'm a werewolf.

Nikola sat very quiet for a few seconds. Well I have some news for you too. Nikola said. Tell me. I'm also a werewolf. My mom and dad just told my brother and I about a week ago. I didn't know how I was going to tell you that part, but I wanted to tell you. Now we are not only BFF'S but we are WBFF, or BWFF's that's werewolf friends forever. OH MY GOD Nikola, you're a werewolf too? I'm surprised. My mom and dad said that is why we are moving to Kettle Falls because that is where our pack is located. Now we have even more in common. With that we both started laughing. Nikola and I talked for a while longer I was sad when we hung up, but in a week or two she will be here going to school with me and training with me. Oh I can't wait until she gets into town. I know I have my new friends, but Nikola and I have been friends forever. Not just friends but best friends. I went back downstairs to see what mom was up to and to tell her about the call I had with Nikola. Hey Mom what are you up to? She was sitting at the dining room table looking at some paperwork. Just going over some documents. Did you have a nice chat with Nikola? Yes, I miss her so much. We used to have so much fun together. But she had some really good news. Oh yeah is that why you screamed and almost caused me to have a heart attack? I just kind of giggled. Yes, she said her and her family are moving here to kettle falls. Mom took her reading glasses off and looked at me in surprise. Yes I am going to have my best friend back. There was something else Nikola told me. What else did she say? I know just knowing that she will be living here in the same town as us is big news. I smiled. Yes it is. She told me that her parents told her and Chad about a week ago that they were werewolves too. No wonder Nikola and I are so close. Mom and I talked for a while. I started getting very tired. I think I'm going to go and take a shower then go to bed. Good night sweetie. Good night mom. I ran upstairs, for some reason I decided to check my phone before taking a shower. I never do that, but what the heck everything is changing. I click the home screen and there is a message from Jaxson. Hailey, I am truly sorry for my behavior today. I am also sorry about your hand. I hope your hand starts feeling better soon. I don't know why but something about you drives me crazy. I could not control my actions today but I promise I will control how I act when you are around. Please let me take you to dinner tomorrow to make up for the way I was at school. I just put my phone down and went to take my shower. Once I was done I got dried off, put my pjs on and blow dried my hair. I don't like going to sleep with my hair wet. I fell asleep pretty easy. Probably because of being exhausted from my first day of school. I dream the same dream as a first night in the new home. At least now I know his name. Jaxson and I are walking through some woods hand in hand. He pulls me behind him, I hear the wolves growling. Jaxson tells me to run as fast as I can back the other way. Again I can feel my heart beating fast, and I can feel myself shaking all over from fear. I don't understand though, if I am a wolf, actually if we are both wolves then why is Jaxson making me run from them. Why are the other wolves growling at us. I woke up from the dream breathing fast and sweating, but I didn't scream this time. I look over at my clock and it is 3:00 in the morning. I lay back down and go right back to sleep. I don't know if I dream the rest of the night or not. If I did I don't remember.

The sun shining through wakes me up at 9:15. I get up smelling food being made. I go over to my desk and take my phone off the charger. I noticed there is a text message from Jaxson again. I'm still wondering how he got my cell phone number. I don't really think Abby would give him my number, at least I don't think she would without at least asking me first. I open the text. Why didn't you message me back? Please Hailey let me take you to dinner. I texted him back and told him that I am hanging out with friends and these plans were made in advance. I set my phone down and went downstairs to see what mom made for breakfast. I was amazed when I seen all the food mom was making. There was bacon, sausage links, sausage patties, pancakes, eggs fried, scrambled eggs, over easy eggs, hash browns…..etc. Mom are we having company for breakfast? There's so much food. She laughed and told me that since we are werewolves and we have to train we need to eat a lot cuz we burn up a lot of calories. I grabbed a plate and put a little of everything on it. I didn't think I would eat all of what I put on my plate, but I also didn't want to disappoint mom. To my surprise I was hungrier than I thought. I ate everything that was on my plate and I didn't feel overly full. When I was done I took my plate over to the sink and rinsed it off and placed it on the counter. Thank you Mom for the amazing breakfast. You're welcome sweetie. I hate to eat and run, but I have to finish getting ready. I decide on my light blue ripped jeans, and a v-neck tee, I was finishing up when my phone rings. God, that better not be Jaxson I thought. I looked at the screen and seen it is Abby so I answered it. Hey I am out front waiting for you so get your butt out here. Okay I'm on my way. I hang up, slide my phone in my jacket pocket. Bye Mom I say on my way out the door. I see a nice white Lexus sitting in the driveway. As I get in Abby is driving. She has Aspen in the front passenger seat, and Dorian is in the back right behind Aspen, so I get in the back behind Abby. They have classic rock playing which is cool with me. I actually like classic rock. Dorian looks over at me and says hi with such an amazing smile. I say hi back. He is so cute, I could actually see myself with him.

Lauren 🐺

Hailey took the news better than I had expected which I am so glad. I am happy that she has made friends at school too. After Nikola moved away and Page passed away Hailey kind of went into a shell of herself and didn't make any new friends until we moved here. I was a little surprised to hear that Nikola's family is moving here, especially with her father being in the military. I wonder why they would have him move here unless he isn't in the military anymore for some reason then him and the rest of his family moving back here would make sense because he is a member of the Golden Sun pack. That will be good for Hailey. I guess this would be a good time for me to mind link Kaden and see what he is doing. I feel so bad about lying to Hailey about Kaden, I want to be completely honest with her and I know when the time is right I can explain to her how Hunter and I chose someone for us to be with in the event that something happened to him or I. I know she will understand, but she has been through so much already and she has had to find out so much I am sure she is overloaded.

Jaxson 🐺

I have felt really bad ever since Hailey punched me. It didn't hurt me at all, but I could see the pain in her face and the tears in her eyes. When she yelled at me to get away now, that made me snap out of it. I let go of her and she walked away. I couldn't concentrate in my last few classes. I have never looked so forward to the end of the day but I needed to see my Luna. I needed to check on her, to make sure she is okay. As soon as the last class let out I ran outside to see if I could see her anywhere, no such luck. So I get into my car and drive to her home. She's not home yet. I sit in my car and wait for her to come home. Soon I see her silver Honda pull into the driveway and she is driving very slowly. As she pulls in and stops her car I start getting out of my car and walk over to her side of her car. Hailey get's out of her car. She doesn't seem very happy to see me. I don't want to see you, or talk to you Jaxson. There is no reason for you to be here! I just want to say I am very sorry for my behavior, that isn't how I want things to go now that I have you, my mate. I think I messed up by saying my mate again, because Hailey got even madder. Your what, your mate? What are you talking about? I'm not with anyone, I'm not anyone's mate and no one can force me to be with them. After that Hailey went running into her home. God I am so stupid!! If she finds out that she can reject me I think she will. I would be so crushed if she was to reject me. I try another approach and I send her a text then I drive home as I wait for her to reply. Hours go by and it's getting late. I end up falling asleep just waiting for her to reply. When I wake up I see it is almost 6:00 in the morning. I checked my phone to see if Hailey texted me back, but no such luck. I sent her another text. Why have you not texted me back? I would like to take you out to dinner, out for a real date if you will let me so I can apologize for my behavior. I lay my phone back down and plug it in so it doesn't die. I guess I fell back to sleep because I start dreaming that Hailey and I are walking in the woods towards the clearing. There is a small cabin with a fireplace and some furniture that each one of us in the pack, well each one of us high school kids brought up there. I take Hailey to the cabin so we can be alone. When I open the door there are rouge's in there and the furniture is all torn up. I hear them growl at us I tell Hailey to run, run away from here. As she is running I jump towards one of the rogue wolves. Just then I wake up with a loud growl. I'm breathing hard and I'm all sweaty. I looked down on my phone. There is a text from Hailey. I already have plans with friends that was made in advance. I can hear Cane growl. What, We cannot do anything about it. She already has plans. I sent her another text. Can I please take you to dinner tomorrow then? I send it. Not too long after I get a text back. Yes, what time? I feel a smile creep across my face.

Dorian

When Hailey got into the car with Abby, Aspen, and me I could smell her body wash and shampoo. She smells so amazing. I keep having to tell myself that she is not my mate. But geez she looks so good as she always looks, very good. Hi Hailey, you look very nice. Thank you Dorian, you look very nice too. She says to me with that bright beautiful smile.

Abby

Dorian and I have to go pick up Aspen and Hailey so they can go to the clearing with us. I put on my blue skinny jeans, my forest green shirt and my running shoes. I leave my dark curly hair down as there is never anything I can do with my hair anyway. I apply some mascara and eyeliner that really makes my green eyes stand out I yell at Dorian. Hey brother of mine, hurry up we need to get going. Once Dorian and I are in the car I look over at my brother. You know when we get to Aspen's you have to get in the backseat so she can sit up here with me, right? He growls but my growl at him is more intimidating. After we have picked up Aspen who only lives one road over from our home we head over to Hailey's. On our way there I mind link Dorian. Remember Hailey is someone else's mate. I don't want any trouble started. I know sis, you don't have to keep reminding me. I am just looking out for you dear brother. I disconnected the mind link. When we got to Hailey's I call her, it takes about three rings before she picks up. Once she answers I tell her to hurry her butt up and get out here. I'm on my way out the door. Hailey tells me. I hang up my phone. I hope she likes classic rock because that is what we listen to.

CHAPTER 2

THE CABIN

Hailey 🦊

Once we get to the edge of the woods Abby Parks her car as far over towards the trees as she can in what seems to be a makeshift parking area. Everyone gets out, Abby and Aspen walk ahead of Dorian and I. The woods are like the one in my dream, but I know I am safe right now because I am with Dorian, Abby, and Aspen not with Jaxson. I don't have to worry about wolves jumping out and attacking us. We walk for what seems like forever, then we reach a clearing that has no trees in the middle, a nice grassy area that would be great for picnics. There is a cabin off to the back behind the clearing which is where we go to. Inside of the cabin there is some furniture. It's not the best furniture, it's probably stuff that their parents were going to get rid of so they brought the furniture here so they could have stuff to set on when they come to hang out. There is a couch, love seat, recliner chair, a couple of end tables with lamps on them, and a coffee table. I can tell there are rooms upstairs too. Abby tells me that is where all the teenage high school kids come to hang out, and sometimes we will have parties here and there have been couples who have gotten married and had their honeymoon here instead of going away somewhere.

Abby 🦊

I don't know if Hailey knows it or not that she is one of us. I would be able to smell her if she was just a human so I figured that she may already know what we all are. So Hailey this is where we come to hang out sometimes. We have parties here too and there have been couples that have gotten married and have their honeymoon here. Now being your friends we do want to welcome you to our group. You can sit wherever you would like. There is a fully stocked kitchen here, and people ready to cook anything we like or that you like. I wait for Hailey to sit down and get comfortable before I go into everything. I don't know if you know this already or not but I don't want to freak you out, or for you to be afraid of us but as our new good friend I want you to know something about us. That is when Hailey spoke up. Are you talking about being werewolves? I am so glad you know. I said laughing. I was laughing at the way she just blurted it out like that. Yeah that is exactly what I am talking about. I am curious about one thing though. Hailey said to me. What is it that you are curious about? When I said something at school when we were at lunch about me training with you and Dorian you both gave me a strange look like you didn't want me to train with you. Oh no Hailey that was not it at all. I think we looked at you like that because we were not really sure if you knew what we are or you are for that matter. We have been werewolves for as long as any of us know. One little piece of advice though. You don't want to go around just blurting it out like that. All though we are werewolves there are a few that are not werewolves in this town and would freak out. We are a pack and we have a pack leader that you have already met. I don't know how you are going to feel about this person. His name is Jaxson Carter. Most of us call him Jax for short, or just plain Alpha. But he is our Alpha in training. If we need help with anything he is here to help and we all respect him. Also we all have our duties/ chores that we do at the pack house, or as guard's around the boarder. If you have any questions you can ask Jax. He is normally pretty busy with Alpha duties though. But his number one job is to be here for any member of the pack that might need him. Right now he is just acting Alpha while his parents and his brother Jace are away. Also you need to know about mate's too. I think that is why Jax came to our lunch table and said "mine." You must be his mate, which is a great honor to be a Luna of the pack. We have the upmost respect for you if you are Jax's mate. Also if you are our Luna you won't be doing any of the chores. We will be doing everything to make sure our Alpha and Luna are happy. I also want to tell you that I am so sorry about your dad and the way he died. Our pack got most of the rouges that killed him and I promise we will get the rest. As soon as I said this Hailey gives me a very weird look. My mom told me that my dad died in a car accident. I am going to have to talk to her when I get back home. I am so sorry Hailey I had no idea, I don't want to cause any problems between you and your mom. No it is okay, I need to know the truth about everything. My mom likes to be very protective of me. I am all she has now. When will we be going back home? Hailey asked me. Well we will probably be going back tomorrow since the end of the summer hang out normally last all night or at least until late at night, plus we also do some training things while we are up here. Oh yeah speaking of training you said something at lunch about training with us. We do training as a pack, and we train up here most of the time.

Hailey 🐺

After I tell Abby that I am all my mom has I got a very weird vibe and a feeling like more information was being kept for me. I will find out everything though when I get back home. Wow, taking all of that in is a lot. I just found out that I could possibly be what is called a Luna because I might be the mate of the Alpha, well the acting Alpha. It's kind of nice to know that, but Jaxson, really. He is really good looking, but his attitude is what makes me not want to be with him. Why can't I be the mate of Dorian. He is so much nicer than Jaxson. But I guess I cannot choose who I am with. It's almost like pre-arranged marriages. I tell everyone about Nikola. Nikola has been my best friend for as long as I can remember. She has had to move around a lot because her father has been in the military, but he has retired now and they are moving here to Kettle Falls. Nikola's parents recently told her and her brother Chad that they are werewolves. So she and her brother will be joining the pack as well. I see Dorian perk up. Who knows since Nikola is also a werewolf the way Dorian perked up it's very possible that she could be his mate. I will know when she gets here and meets everyone. Just then the door opens and Jaxson comes in. Everyone except Abby and Dorian get up and moves out of the way. Jaxson comes over and sits down next to me on the couch. I know why he drives me crazy when he is around. It is his scent and it has been the entire time. I look over at him and he has the most amazing sea blue eyes, he also has the most kissable looking lips. I need to stop looking at him but I can't. Hello Jaxson. I say to him with a smile that I was trying to hide but couldn't for some reason. Hi Hailey. I hope everyone has been good to you. Yeah they have and very informational too. Hailey can I talk to you outside?

Jaxson 🐾

I don't think Hailey realizes she can mind link because I have heard everything she has been thinking. I don't like that I have made her think the things she has been thinking, but hopefully I can fix that by controlling how I am around her and with her. Now that she knows she is my mate, and that she knows she is a wolf like the rest of us it will be a lot easier. Once we are outside away from everyone else I grab Hailey and kiss her. I have been waiting to do that since she got out of her car yesterday morning at school. So now you know that you are my mate. Well I know I could possibly be your mate. I understand why you have been acting the way you have towards me, why you cannot control yourself. I'm not sure what all you have been told. You said that everyone has been very informational. Well I know that I am a werewolf just like you and everyone else here, I know that I could possibly be your mate and Luna of the pack. I don't really know what it means to be a Luna of a pack though. Well Hailey there is another thing you should know. What else. She says with her arms crossed in front of her looking up at me. Are you ready for more Hailey? I want everyone to be completely honest with me. If everyone isn't honest with me then how am I supposed to trust anyone? Good point. Well there is something you need to know. Tell me. When you turn 17 you will be moving in with me at the pack house. WAIT!!!! WHAT? When I turned 17 I am supposed to move in with you? I have so much to think about. My mom has told me a lot, Abby has told me a lot, and now this. I am going to need some time to process all of this. What do you mean you are going to need time. I don't even really know you Jax and now you're telling me that I am supposed to move in with you at the pack House of all places. Do you mean that you will need like a few hours, or a few days? I don't know Jaxson the only thing I do know is it will most likely be more than a few hours. When Hailey said that it would be more than a few hours I felt mine and Canes's heart dropped to our stomach. My mate just started to actually talk to me and now that she has been told everything that everyone has told her she wants time to think about all of it. I cannot handle the thought of not being around her all the time. I need to go text my mom and let her know that it may be tomorrow before I come back home that way she won't worry about me. Hailey finally said to me. Okay babe. I will hang out here while you do that. When Hailey walked back inside I mind link all of the guys. Hey I need to talk to all of you tomorrow it is important so don't forget. Okay Alpha, I hear all of them say to me. When I do walk back in the cabin I see everyone sitting at different tables playing some board games, or they are setting at different places around the front room just talking to each other. I walk over to the couch where Hailey is sitting and I sat next to her. Is everything okay? Yeah I just wanted to make sure my mom knows what I am doing because if I don't let her know then she freaks out. I kind of laugh. Well she sounds like a very good mom. I smile at Hailey.

Hailey 🐺

I cannot believe my mom kept the information from me about how my dad really died. I know she wants to protect me, but if she keeps lying to me she is going to lose me. She raised me to be an honest person and I am finding out all of these things I should have known growing up. I really feel it is not fair that she has kept all this from me. I pulled my phone out of my pocket and text my mom. Hey mom, I am going to stay the night at a cabin with my friends tonight. I will text you in the morning. Love Hailey. Jaxson and I stay on the couch and just talked. So tell me about being an Alpha, what is it like, how did you become an Alpha. I want to know how all of this is supposed to be. Well, I was of course born a werewolf. I'm not really an Alpha yet though I'm what is called an Alpha in training. There will be a ceremony to make it official soon. But everyone is already calling you Alpha. It is because they respect me as an Alpha already. I am over this pack right now because my dad, mom and brother are away visiting other packs and helping out where help is needed but they will be back soon and since I now have found my mate there will be a celebration, and my dad will officially hand over the title of Alpha. But I am going to do all the duties now while they are away, and I have been trained for this all my life. it has a lot of perks being Alpha, but it is very hard to. So you get to boss everyone around? Hahahaha kind of, but not like it sounds. I make sure everyone does as they should. That they train, that they follow the rules of being in a pack and if they don't then it is my job to send them away and they become rogue. What does being rogue mean? Hailey Asked me. Well they are on their own without a pack, they end up aging really bad, they don't live by any rules. Unfortunately you might have a chance to see some rogues, or at least one. But I am going to protect you as much as I can. Hailey you are my everything. Now that you are here, now that I have met you I cannot live without you. Oh another thing that comes to mind that you might want to know about is when wolves mates are together they mark each other, but that is something we can talk about another time. I don't want to overwhelm you with more information. Tonight is about kicking back, relaxing, and having a great time. Thank you Jaxson for telling me everything you have told me. I have learned so much in such a short time. I hope you understand why I need time to process everything. I do understand, do I like that it's time we will be apart, no I don't like that, but I want to give you everything you want and need. I don't think you heard me tell everyone else that my best friend in the whole world is coming to Kettle Falls to live. She is a wolf too and she will be joining the pack. Yes, I got their transfer papers, and she has a brother, right? Jaxson ask me. Yes, his name is Chad. I will welcome them into our pack and I look forward to meeting them. It was getting to be around dinner time. Everyone in the cabin was heading towards the kitchen. Are you hungry? Jax ask me. Yes I am a little hungry. I didn't realize until just then that I had not ate since breakfast with my mom. Jax takes my hand and leads me into the kitchen. The kitchen to my surprise is really big for being in a cabin that a bunch of teenagers hang out in. There was so much food. burgers, pork chops, steaks, lasagna, spaghetti, pizzas, French fries, every veggie you could think of, garlic bread. The cooks here are amazing at fixing all the food. It all smells so good. Once we were all seated at the table the cooks started serving everyone. I had a salad, lasagna, and garlic bread. It's my favorite by the time I was done I was so stuffed. It started getting late and I started getting tired. Jaxson and I laid down on the couch and talked. Feeling Jax's arms around me feel so good. I could get used to laying in his arms like this and feeling his lips on my cheek, and moving to my neck. Then I hear him whisper "I never want to be without you Hailey." I close my eyes and drift off to sleep. I start dreaming that same dream. Jax and I are walking through the woods smiling and talking while walking hand in hand. I feel him pull me behind him protecting me as I hear wolves growling. Run Hailey. Jax says and I run back the way we had came. I still do not understand why he is making me run, that is until I look down. I see that I am pregnant. It is like all the pieces of the puzzle are coming together.

Lauren 🐺

As soon as I get a text from Hailey saying she is staying she is staying the night with her friends I mind link Kaden. Hey sweetie I just got a text from Hailey saying she is staying the night with some friends tonight, so if you would like some company............... Hey babe, you know that I would love for you to come and be with me. Ok it will take me a little while since I have to drive instead of shifting and running through the woods. Take your time love and be safe. I look forward to you being here. After Kaden said that I disconnected the mind link and grabbed my keys. It would be so much faster to shift and run through the woods, but I would be by myself and the risk of a rouge or several rouges being out there is to much of a risk to take.

Kaden 🐺

I can not wait for Lauren to get here. I have waited for this night since she moved here. Now I have to make sure everything is ready and that I set the mood. Walking over to the fireplace I light the logs, then I grab the bag if rose petals and sprinkle them over the white bear rug. I put the rest of the petals in the freezer. Then I go back into the living room and grab the box that has the bikini that I bought for my sweet Lauren. I walk through the kitchen to get to the back door. Once out back I sit the box on the chair that sits against the outside wall. I turn on the whirlpool/ hot tub. I want, no I need tonight to be perfect. It has been so long since I have held Lauren in my arms and now I am going to be able to not only be able to hold her in my arms, but so much more. I walk back into the house through the kitchen back into the living room just in time to see headlights shine through the living room window. I wait until I hear a knock on the door. Hi my beautiful Lauren. I say with a smile after I open the door and see her standing there. Hi my love, it has been so long. Yes I agree. Would you like to lay by the fire first, or would you like to go outback and get into the hot tub? Oh the hot tub would be amazing right now. That would help me relax after the long drive from Indiana to here and all the unpacking I have had to do. Ok I will lead the way. But I did not bring anything to wear. It's ok, look over there on the chair. I said to her as we got outside. She smiles and then picks up the box and opens it. Oh Kaden you didn't have to go out and buy me a bikini. I do love it but you really didn't have to. I wanted to. I will go put it on, and then I will be right back.

Lauren

When I got to Kaden's house I noticed he had the fireplace lit, and rose petals on the big white bear rug in front of the fireplace. Then when he takes me out back he has a box for me sitting in the chair outside. When I open the box there is a beautiful white bikini. I go and put it on then go back outside. Kaden is already sitting in the hot tub. I climb in and he pulls me in front of him. I sit facing away from him and he wraps his arms around me. This is so amazing. I could get used to this Kaden whisper's in my ear. Have you told Hailey about us yet? No. I turn to Kaden and see the look of disappointment. Sweetie I promise I will tell her soon. I don't like keeping things away from her. She has been through so much already I am afraid telling her to much all at once will be to much for her to handle. I know, but I want to always be with you Lauren. I want to always be with you too babe. We just have to wait for the right time. Shall we go inside now? Kaden asked me. Yes let's go. He grabs my hand and leads me out of the hot tub and back through the house to the dinning room. There was a candle burning on the table, and beautiful white china plates. The food smells so amazing. I have not eaten since I had breakfast this morning with Hailey. Lauren sweetheart you need to take better care of yourself. I know, but sometimes I just don't think about eating. We will soon be together everyday and I will be able to take care of you and I will be able to make sure you are eating like you should. I smile up at Kaden as he pushes my chair in for me. What are we having it smells amazing. We my dear are having roasted lamb, green beans, and baked potatoes. I could get used to this. I hope you do, because I promise to take very good care of you Lauren. After we ate I took the dishes to the sink and rinsed them off. Then Kaden takes me by the hand and leads me over to the bear rug. Before we lay down I feel Kaden undo the strings on my bikini top, then I feel him slide my bikini bottoms off of me. You have such an amazing body sweetheart. I smile and wrap my arms around his neck when he stands back up. He gently lays me down on the bear rug. I feel his lips on mine, and he starts kissing me so passionately, I feel his tongue enter my mouth and my tongue playfully teases his. Then he moves to my neck. It drives me crazy the way he moves his tongue over my neck and his lips softly kissing and sucking on my neck. Kaden moves his hands gently over my body. I feel his hand over one of my nipples and his lips on my other nipple as he brings himself between my legs. He looks at me with a smile and then kisses me deeply as I feel him enter me slowly. With each passionate kiss he moves faster in me then out, then back in. It has been a long time and it does not take me long to reach my climax. I feel it building then I can not hold back any longer. I grab his ass cheek's as I moan out in pleasure and I feel him explode in me. Afterwards we lay in each other's arms. Kaden caresses me and I start falling asleep. The next morning the sun comes shinning through the window waking me and I feel Kaden kiss me. Good morning beautiful. Good morning sweetheart. Are you hungry? He asked me. I am starving. Kaden gets up and I see him going into the kitchen. I reach for my phone and I see that I have a text from Hailey. Hi mom, I just woke up. I am going to have breakfast here at the cabin with my friends. I will text you when I am on my way home. Love you xoxox I put my phone on the charger and I get my clothes on then I go to see what Kaden is doing.

Hailey 🐺

As I am slowly waking up I realize I had fallen asleep in Jaxson's arms. Even though I have been trying to avoid Jaxson, and he has been a real jerk as far as I am concerned, it is so nice to have him here and holding me as I sleep. I can get used to this. I realize what I was just thinking and the fact that I fell asleep in Jaxson's arms. I can not believe that I did that after the way he treated me at school. But here at the cabin when he walked in my heart felt like it was going to jump out of my chest and he smells so amazing that I want to be near him. Plus the fact that he is treating me better now than he did at school. God what is happening to me I was never like this before. I hear others waking up as we all smell the food being cooked. Good morning beautiful. I look at Jax and he is smiling as he is waking up. Good morning. Did you sleep well? I asked him. I slept better than I have in a very long time. He almost knocks me off the couch as he stretches. JAXSON!! I yell at him and he just laughs. I start to get up to go brush my teeth to get rid of my morning breath, but Jax scoops me up in his arms and carries me to the breakfast table. There is so much food being made. Muffins, omelets, bacon, sausage patties, sausage links, fried eggs, scrambled eggs, eggs over easy, pancakes, biscuits and gravy. But there are a lot of people that stayed the night here last night. Everyone that cooked the breakfast brought the food to the table on serving trays. Believe me there was nothing left once everyone filled their plates and wolves eat a lot everyday.

What do you have planned today? Jax ask me. Well I was going to go home and take a shower and talk with my mom about some things. I see him acting like a little lost puppy. Oh what's wrong? Well I have to be the head of the training since I am acting Alpha, but after training I was going to see if you would like to go on a real date with me. Well I don't know Mr. Carter I may have to check my calendar. I laugh, but I don't think Jax thought that was too funny since I heard a low growl come out of him. Oh lighten up Jax I was just joking, of course I would love to go on a real date with you. But I am supposed to be training too. I have just been doing my workouts at home in the basement that Mom has set up as a workout room. Well working out and training are really two different things. You will be very worn out after either one though. Jax said to me. But if you really need to go home to talk to your mom, I understand. Then he put his head down and started whining like a little puppy again I have all day that I can go home and talk to my mom but I have nothing to wear to train in. Oh I am sure one of the girls here has something you can wear for today. Okay, but I need to text my mom again and let her know I am staying to train with everyone here. I told Jax well then I will go and talk to some of the guys while you do that.

Jaxson 🐻

I am so happy that Hailey decided to stay and train with all of us that means I get more time with her today. When she takes her phone out to text her mom I get up to get ready to go outside so I can talk to some of the guys about the plan of building a house for Hailey and I to live in once she turns 17 next month. I know with all the help I have here we can get it done within a month. There is still so much she needs to know about being a wolf though. I will tell her all of it after training is done for the day. As I get up to go outside Dorian comes running yelling something. I stop him. What is going on? Rouge's, the rogues are attacking down at the border. Go tell the rest of the group and make sure someone stays here with Hailey she is not strong enough yet to fight. I run out and shift into Cane as I run towards the border. I jump over some already dead rogue wolves as I get close to the border. My guards are really good at handling these situations, but as acting Alpha I have to be there too so I can make sure my pack handles it. I ripped the throat out of some of the rouges as my pack takes out more that come out of the woods. Once things start to calm down I find some clothes to put on for when I shift back to my human form. As I go behind a bush Allison mind links me. Jax HURRY!! Rouge's are trying to get into the cabin. I am trying to hold the door closed. My heart sinks to my stomach. HAILEY, Cain howl's as I think of Hailey being in the cabin with rogues trying to get in. I dropped the clothes and take off towards the cabin. When I get there I can see that they have broken down the door. I start to run faster and when I get inside the cabin I see Allison on top of one of the rouges tearing it's throat out. I go towards the kitchen where I see a table knocked over and a rogue wolf on top of Hailey. I jump and knocked the rogue off of her. I rip its throat out and send it flying back towards the front door. Hailey is laying on the floor. Her eyes are closed. I go to her and feel that her heart is still beating but her breathing is very shallow. Allison we have to get her to the pack hospital NOW. I see Abby coming in just then. Abby help Allison get Hailey into one of the cars to take her to the pack hospital. We can't go to a regular hospital because we are not regular humans. They would not know how to treat us medically. I can see cuts and scratches on Hailey, they do not look bad, but I don't know if there is damage on the inside. I WILL KILL those damn rogues if anything happens to my mate.

Lauren 🐾

When I walk into the kitchen I go and wrap my arms around Kaden as he is cooking us breakfast. It smells so good. Are you hungry? Kaden ask me. Starving. I told him. I go over to the table and sit down as he serves the toast, eggs, and bacon. Thank you sweetie. You are very welcome my love. As we are eating I hear my phone go off with a text. Kaden looks at me. Do you want me to get your phone for you? No it is probably just Hailey. I will check it after we are done eating. I am so glad you are not rushing off to go home. I want as much time with you as possible. Sweetie I am going to tell Hailey about us when I see her today. Kaden smiles when I tell him this. I know you wanted to wait until everything else was taken care of, but I want us to start our lives together. Besides Hailey will be 17 next month and since she has found her mate she will be moving out. I know, it's just that she is my baby, my only child. I wanted to hang on to her as long as possible. Lauren we can have another child, you are still young enough to have another pup. I cannot replace Hailey by having another child. I know and that is not what I was saying. I was saying it would be nice if we had a pup of our own. I smile at Kaden. That is something to think about. As soon as I was done eating I finished my coffee and then I get up to get ready to go home. Kaden pulls me into his arms. I love you Lauren. I love you too Kaden. Please be safe on your way home and mind link me to let me know you made it safe. Oh that reminds me. I grab my phone and check the text. OH MY GOD!! I have to go now. Lauren what's wrong? It's Hailey she is at the pack hospital. What? What happened? I don't know, I just know I have to get there now. Let me drive you. Kaden and I both go running out the door and get into his jeep. When we get to the hospital I found out what room Hailey is in and I go running to her room. When I walk in she is sleeping and Jaxson is there by her side. Alpha Jaxson, what happened I asked him and my heart went to my stomach when he told me it was a rogue attack. I had a flashback of when Hunter died from a rogue attack. I wish I would have been there today. I know she is growing up, but I still want to protect her.

Hailey 🐺

When everyone except Allison and I left I was worried about Jaxson even though I knew he would be okay. Allison and I sat at the table and just talked, I think she was trying to keep my mind off the rogue attacking the land here. I am sorry but I overheard you say that you have a lot to process. Allison said to me. Yes, I did not grow up knowing that I am a wolf or that wolves were even real. I thought it was just a myth. Allison kind of laughed when I said that. What all have you been told about being a wolf? Well I have been told that next month when I turn 17 I will be moving into the pack house with Jax. Most kid's my age or even at seventeen do not move in with their boyfriend. That doesn't happen until way later on. Just then I thought I heard someone coming through the front door. I wonder if that is Jaxson. I said to Alison. We get up, and then we hear a growl. I see a wolf coming into the kitchen. Alison and I scream because we both know the wolf is not from our pack. The next thing I knew I was being knocked to the ground and everything went dark. When I start waking up I did not know where I was everything looks so different. As I open my eyes everything is blurry and my head hurts really bad. I start to grab my head and my sight slowly starts to clear up. I see Jax. Hey, how do you feel? He ask me. My head hurts really bad. I feel his arms going around me. It will stop hurting soon. Hailey? I hear my mom say. Mom, how did you know where I was? Alpha Jaxson sent me a text telling me that you were at the pack hospital. I hear mom ask Jax what happened and he told her. What happened to the wolves? I asked Jax. They are all dead. No one or nothing is going to hurt you again. He said. When can I leave here? I asked Jax. The doctor said you can leave as soon as you feel up to it. Jax told me. I want to leave now. I don't like hospitals. I will go find the doctor. Jax said and he walked out the room. Hailey I am so sorry I was not there to protect you. Mom it is ok, I am fine as you can see I just want to get out of here and go take a shower. The doctor and Jax come into the room. How do you feel? The doctor asked me as he looked into my eyes with that pen light, then he listens to my heart, then my lungs. I feel ok except for this headache. That is to be expected since we are pretty sure you hit your head in the attack. When can I go home? I will get your discharge paperwork and write you a prescription for pain killers to help with your headache and then the nurse will come in and get you on your way. Do you want to come back to the pack house, of course you don't need to train today after what you have been through. You can .... Just then mom cut Jax off. She will be coming home with me. I kind of laugh. What is so funny? You could have died Hailey. My mom says. I look over Jax and tell him that my mom is overly protective. I hear mom sigh. It's ok. Jax says. I still have to go and make sure everyone train's I can come by later and see how you are doing. Then he leans down and kisses me. When Jax leaves I look over at my mom. Mom we need to talk when we get home. I want you to take it easy Hailey. You have been through a very traumatic experience today. I know, but we still need to talk. There is still so much I still don't know about and I want you to explain to me. Ok sweetie when we get home and you get settled in bed we can talk.

Jaxson 🐺

I leave the hospital after Hailey's mom comes in and Hailey wakes up. I made sure she was okay before I left though. I could tell her mom was not going to let Hailey come back to the pack house with me which I can understand. Hailey's dad was killed in a rogue attack. He was one of our best warriors too. It was two on him though. My dad and I went to help Hunter, it was too late. Once back at the pack house everyone was there and started asking how their Luna was. I told them that she will be fine and going home with her mom for the day to rest. We need to get training so we stay ready in case the rogues decide to attack again. So everyone I need you to get ready and meet me at the training area in your human form to start with. Everyone starts getting up to go change into their training clothes and I head outside to go to the training area. I see everyone coming up the hill. Okay we are going to start with some stretches, ready? I have them to sit down and reach out for their feet and hold, then back up. We do that five times then up on your feet. 50 jumping jacks. Once we were done with that, I told them that I want them to do 50 lunges and then 50 laps around the border. I wait until the last person runs by me and then I join in making sure no one falls behind. I let everyone rest for about 5 minutes before I tell them that we are going to break up into partners and do some sparring. Once everyone was coupled up I told them on my signal they could start. Allison said she wants to spar with me. She knows I show no mercy on anyone and I think that is why she picks me when we do the sparring activity.

She is one of my strongest and that is why I wanted her to stay at the cabin with Hailey. I know that she didn't expect any of the rogues to make it to the cabin, that is the only reason they were able to get as close as they did. Once the group was done with sparring, I told them that tomorrow we would do run attacks. That is where they will be running and our warriors will try to catch them before they get to the finish line. I go back to the pack house to take a shower before going to see Hailey. After my shower I put on my jeans that have a hole in each knee and a gray v-neck tee. I grab my keys and head over to Hailey's.

Hailey 🐺

My mom got me home she helped me up to my room. Mom I can make it up the stairs by myself. No Hailey I am going to help you. I am not going to take any chances of you passing out and falling. I want to get you settled in your bed, then I will go down and make you something to eat. I knew there is no point in arguing with her. She has been very protective my entire life and when my dad died she became even more protective even though I didn't think you could become more protective than she already was. I decided to get my iPad out and put a movie on since I know Mom won't let me get out of bed today. I decided to watch some comedy to get my mind off what happened today. Normally when I am bored out of my mind like I am now I will watch some action, but that would only make me keep thinking about what happened today. Hey sweetie, Mom says as she comes back in. I have a sandwich and some soup for you. I also brought you some juice too. Thank you mom. You're welcome sweetie. Would you like to talk about what happened today? No I just want to watch a movie and relax I think. Have you heard anything from Jaxson since we have been back here? I asked just in case he got a hold of my mom thinking I might be sleeping. No I haven't. Mom I do need to talk to you about some things, but it has nothing to do with the attack today. Okay sweetie, what would you like to talk about? Well first I would like to know how Dad died. My mom looked at me funny. Then she put her head down. Hailey I am so sorry I didn't tell you myself and I was going to. I was hoping I would be able to tell you before anyone else. But so much has happened so quick. So how did he really die mom? We were at the pack house and there was a rogue attack. Your dad was a border guard and an amazing warrior, as was Jaxson's dad. Well Corbin is a guard and an Alpha. Your dad was attacked by two rouges and he was doing good at holding his own with them. He was an amazing warrior. But of course they got him down. Jaxson And his dad seen this happen and when they killed the rogues they were fighting they went to help your father, but they were too late. The rogues didn't tear his throat out like what normally happens, there was a vampire named Alaric that was there too and went over to your dad. He had a gold knife that was covered in wolf bane which is very poison to us. By the time Jaxson and Corbin got over to where your father was Alaric had already jabbed the knife into your father's chest. I heard your father scream and I ran over to him. I held his head on my lap. Oh mom, you were there when daddy died. Yes, it was the hardest thing I have ever been through. The pain in my heart was so bad. Everyone thought for sure I would end up dying from a broken heart, which can happen when a wolf loses their mate. But there is something that only your father and I knew that kept my heart going. What was it that you and Daddy knew that no one else knew. I want to know everything mom, no more surprises. I see mom taking a deep breath. Well your father and I made each other a promise. Since we had you and would always need to go on for you we chose someone for the other to be with in the event that one of us was to die. I felt my heart drop when my mom told me the details of my dad being killed and I could see the tears in mom's eyes as she continued. What do you mean you and Dad chose someone for the other? Well I chose Selena and your father chose Kaden for me to be with in the event of his death. We chose these people for each other because the moon goddess does not choose someone to be your mate in the event of your mate's death, that is on us to do if we choose to do so.

Lauren

I hate the idea that my baby girl got hurt in a rogue attack. I feel like such a horrible mom because I was not there when it happened. I could have protected my baby girl. Now she wants to know everything and I know I should have told her everything a long time ago. Okay, first of all I need to tell you that since you now know you are a wolf you can mind link which is much better and easier than texting or calling because it is faster and you don't have to worry about finding your phone. Hailey and I both laugh at that because she is always asking me to call her phone so she can find it. I explained the mind link to her. Now about Jaxson saying you are moving in the pack house when you are 17. That can be done by choice, only if you want to be with Jaxson and only if you want to move into the pack house. You can reject Jaxson. Even though your father and I were together, we were not always together even after we found out we were mates. Hailey's eyes got big when I told her that her father rejected me the morning after we mated. Yes it is true Hailey, your father said Lauren Elaine Crimpton I Hunter Daniel Moran reject you as my mate. I was so hurt. I am so sorry that happened mom. Hailey said to me. It's okay sweetie, it all worked out. I did not reject him because I was in love with him. In order for mates to not be mates anymore both mates have to reject each other. What happened after that? Hailey asked me. Well after a couple weeks I found out I was pregnant with you and I told your father. He came back to me and made up for rejecting me everyday after that. We were both very young of course just like you and Jaxson are. Your father was a bit of a player back then. But he and I had you and we had a beautiful life together.

Hailey

If I had known that I could have rejected Jaxson I probably would have done that when I first met him and found out we were mates. He was such an asshole. I told my mom. Just then my phone goes off. I look and see that it is Jax. Hey babe, I am right outside your front door. If you are awake and feel up to it can I come in and see you? I told Mom that Jax was at the front door and wants to come and see me. Mom went downstairs to let him in. When he came into my room he came straight over to me, bent down and kissed me. Hi babe, how are you feeling? Well I still have somewhat of a headache. I said. But mom made me a sandwich and some soup. I ate most of it and I am feeling better. That's good. Did you get the training done, or did you skip it? I asked Jax. I made sure everyone got training done today and we are training again tomorrow. I want to make sure everyone is ready in case another rogue attack happens again. I couldn't wait to be with you, to be by your side. I hate to be away from you for a minute Hailey. I smiled at Jax. I am a little tired. Well I will lay here by your side and we will take a nap, okay? I said as I started to close my eyes. The next morning I was feeling like my old self again. I had that dream again. The one where Jax and I are walking through the woods and the rogues came out and Jax tells me to run. I run the way we had come from, I look back to see if Jax is okay and I see him jump to attack the rogues and he shifts in mid-air. I run all the way to the car. I am out of breath and shaking. I looked down and I have my hands on my pregnant belly. You are okay my sweet baby. Your mommy and daddy are always going to take very good care of you. As I see Jax walking towards me in my dream I knew he was okay and that is when I wake up. Jax went back to the pack house after we woke up from our nap yesterday. I got up and go take a shower. After washing my hair and body I rinse off and I get out and dry off. I decide to wear my black jeans and white crop top with my dark blue over shirt, and my high top shoes. I told Mom I am meeting Abby and Aspen at the cabin to hang out and that I didn't know what time I would be home. Okay sweetie, please just be careful and if you need me for anything and I do mean anything mind link me and I will be right there. I went over and gave my mom a big hug. Don't worry mom, everything will be fine. I drive to the cabin I can see that Jax is there with Dorian, Michael, Jace, Aspen, Abby, Allison, Beckah, Jaden, and a few others. I got out of my car and go in. I find everyone setting in the living room. I go over and sit next to Jax how are you feeling babe. Jax asked me. I am feeling great. Are you going to let me train with everyone else today? Well I don't think I have a choice do I. I laugh, no you really don't. You know I would be right out there with all of you no matter what you say. Jax just sigh's and rolls his eyes at me. We all get up and go outside. I have on my Nike running pants and my matching sports bra which I know drives Jax crazy. He hates it when I wear such little clothing, but I know that I am going to be hot and sweaty so I want to be as comfortable as possible while training. I hear Jax start to tell everyone what we will be doing.

Jaxson 🐾

Okay everyone, like I said yesterday you all will be running to the finish line, or should I say you all will try to Run to the finish line. Our guards will be attempting to catch you so you all better run fast. Let's get started. I head over to where we will be starting from with Abby and Aspen. We hear one of the guards. Get ready, get set, go. He yells and we all take off running. Not long into the run I can hear people getting knocked to the ground by the guards as they catch them. I am determined to not get caught and I start running faster. I hear my wolf Casey tell me that we got this. I know she is very fast, but we have to do this exercise in our human form. I can see the finish line and no one has been able to cross it yet. As I get almost there my heart is really racing, and Casey is telling me we can do this, we got this when I feel myself going to the ground. I am turned over and I see it is Jax that caught me. How is that possible, you had to have cheated in order to even catch up to me let alone knock me to the ground. He just laughed at me. I roll him over to the ground and straddle him as I sat on top of him and laugh. How does that feel having me roll you? Once that exercise was over we all went back to the pack house and I go to take a shower before lunch. Once I was done getting all the sweat and dirt off my body and my hair I shut the shower off and get out, dry off and get dressed. I go downstairs and join everyone else at the table to eat. We were all setting and talking when I hear the front door open. Jax looks over at me like I am expecting someone. I have no idea who is coming in and I really hope it is not another rogue trying to come into attack. Jax and

I get up along with a few of the guards. We all walk into the front room where I scream when I see it is Nikola and Chad. OH MY GOD!! I I run over and hug her almost knocking both of us to the ground. When did you get into town? We got in late last night. I wanted to surprise you so I got the directions here from your mom and here I am. Well come on in we are all sitting down to eat lunch. I can introduce you to everyone. I take Nikola into the dining room and point around the table as I tell her who everyone is. I know it is a lot of people to remember all of their names, but you will learn who everyone is in time. Everyone this is my very best friend for as long as I can remember Nikola. I see Dorian perk up the same way he did when I first mentioned her.

CHAPTER 3

TRAINING

Dorian 🐺

I hate the exercise of chasing down everyone, but we have to do that because we could be chasing rogues when they decide to attack again. When we got back Hailey went into the master bedroom to shower so I went out back and used the hose to rinse off. Once I was dried off I went into the dining room to wait until the food is done. Even though I hate that exercise I am still always very hungry when we get done with it. Once everyone was setting and the cooks served the food I ate a lot of everything. We all hear the front door open then close. I get in defense mode. I follow Jax and Hailey into the living room and even though I am right there I just about jumped out of my skin when Hailey screams. Who the hell is she jumping on. I knew I smelt a very amazing smell, but I thought it had something to do with what the cooks were cooking. But when we go into the living room I realize it is Hailey's friend. I realize my mate is here. She smells so amazing, clover and honeysuckle and I am very happy that my mate is Hailey's friend. I think Nikola knows she is a werewolf too because I see her looking over at me and smiling like she can smell my scent.

Nikola 🐺

My family and I get into Kettle Falls so late and I was very tired, but I was also excited about the idea of being in the same town as my BFF and I cannot wait to see her in person. We have not been around each other in 2 years. Even though we Skype almost every day it is just not the same. My parents has the movers to set up everything at our new house and I am glad they did that because I am very tired. I think I was asleep before my head hit the pillow. The sun woke me up the next morning because I have not hung my curtains yet, but that is okay. The earlier I get up the earlier I get to see my best friend. I know my mom and dad will want me to have my room all put away before they will allow me to go anywhere. That is the way most parents are and my dad being ex-military he is even worse about that. I am just glad that I don't keep a lot of junk. It won't take me long to get my room done. I go take a shower and after I am done I get right to putting everything away in my room. I was right I got it all done before my mom called Chad and I down to breakfast. There is always so much food, but between the four of us nothing goes to waste. Dad is it okay if Chad and I go to see Hailey today? Well I know you have waited a really long time for this so I don't see why you couldn't. Don't forget your training and you will have to meet the new pack. Mom said to my brother Chad and I. Yes mom. Chad and I both say at the same time. After we all were done eating Chad and I got ready to go see Hailey. We stop at her house. Her mom comes to the door and tells us that she is not home, but she gives us the directions to the pack house so we go there. When we get there we walk in. Everyone is at the dining room table. Hailey and a couple of guys come in the living room and Hailey almost knocks me over running up to me and hugging me. We are so excited to see each other. when I walked in I smelled the most amazing smell ever. I knew it was my mate. Dad explained about being a werewolf and that each werewolf has a mate. I know it bothers dad to think about me finding my mate. I am sure he is hoping I won't find my mate until I'm around 30. But Mom was the one that told me I would know when I have found my mate because I would smell the most amazing scent I have ever smelled before. I cannot believe my mate is here in Kettle falls. I am very happy. Hailey introduces me to Jax, and then to Dorian. She tells me Jax is acting Alpha of the pack, and that Dorian is Jax's Beta. Then she takes me and Chad into the dining room and introduces Chad and I to everyone else. When she introduces me to Dorian I knew that was him. My mate and he is so cute with his jet black hair and his deep blue eyes.

I can't believe you are here. When did you get in town? Hailey ask me as we sit down at the dinning room table. Well we got in town last night, but it was so late and I was so tired but excited at the same time. What do you think of Kettle Falls so far? Dorian asked me. I haven't seen much of it yet. Dorian is a great tour guide. Hailey tells me. I hear a low growl coming from someone at the table. Oh calm down. I hear Hailey say to Jax. What is that about? I ask Hailey. Oh Jax is still a little upset because Dorian showed me around school my first day of school. But what he needs to realize is that I am with him and not anyone else. She smiles at Jax. They are so cute together.

Jaxson

Can I have everyone's attention please? We need to welcome the newest members of our pack, Chad and Nikola. I want to let you both know that we do train every day rain or shine and we don't go easy so I hope you both are ready. Our dad is military. Chad says. Well ex-military, but it is still part of his life. Well then you both should be used to hard work then. Both Chad and Nikola nod their heads. When everyone was done with breakfast most of us go into the living room. I whisper to Hailey, do you still want to leave to go talk to your mom? She smiles up at me and says no, I have already talked to Mom about everything I think. I know a lot more than I did, and I told her that I don't want any more surprises besides I have my two favorite people here now I am in no hurry to leave. Oh so Chad and Nikola are your two favorite people. I say joking around and Hailey playfully slap's me on the arm.

Hailey 🐺

I am so happy that Nikola is here. It looks like she has found her mate too and that makes me very happy. At least now I know I won't lose my best friend to a move again. I am happy for Dorian too. He is such a great guy and deserves to be happy and he looks really happy now. I can't wait to show Nikola around school too. I hope we have classes together.

Hey Nikola, Yeah. Are you starting school tomorrow? You know how my parents are, it is straight to work for them so it is straight to school for Chad and I. I see Dorian telling Nikola not to worry he will show her around school. I spoke up then. She is MY best friend, I will show her around school thank you very much. Jax laughs when I say that to Dorian. You want a spar and see who wins. Dorian asked me. I would bet on Hailey. Jax says. Thank you babe. I say to Jax. I know you can take him in a heartbeat. Everyone laughs when Jax says that and I can see Dorian's face turn red and I hear a low growl come from him but I see Nikola kiss Dorian which calms him really quick. I also noticed Chad and Abby hanging together. It would be so cool if Chad and Abby are mates. I tell Jax. Well babe, I think they just might be. Does that happen? I ask Jax. Brother and sister being mates with another brother and sister? It's not uncommon. Well I hope Dorian can let Nikola go long enough for her and I to hang out. I have not seen her other than on Skype in 2 years. Well what makes you think I'm going to let you go long enough to hang out with her. Jax says with a smile on his face.

Chad

I have no idea if I will ever find my mate or not, but that is not one of my top priorities. I am hoping to be a guard at the new pack. I have always wanted to be a guard, maybe then my dad will be happier with me. I have always felt like I have been a disappointment to my father. No matter that I study my ass off and make all good grades in whatever School Nikola and I have went to, or that I get perfect attendance at school as well when the other wolves have to miss days for different reasons. I know Dad wants me to join the military like he did, and I think that is why he is disappointed in me because I don't want to join the military. I have been in the ROTC program and I seen how happy Dad was when I joined the ROTC and I think that is when he really thought I would go into the army, air force, or at least the national guards. Just before my 18th birthday dad asked me to come into his office at our house. I went in there and he had flyers on his desk about different branches of the military. I told Dad then that I was not so sure that I wanted to go into the military. I could see the look of disappointment on his face. I just want to see what it is like to actually be a kid now that you are out of the military dad. We have moved from base to base. Nikola nor I have ever been able to make real friends. I know I still have to be careful of what I do even if my dad hasn't been in the military. He was brought up by strict parents so I know Dad would be strict on us even without being military. So that is one reason I know I always had to stay out of trouble, plus the idea of getting into legal troubles just didn't sound like a life I wanted to live. I have known of people who have been in and out of legal trouble and that is not what I want to do with my life. Besides if I was to get into legal trouble I wouldn't be here to help my sis. When Nikola and I get to the pack house not only does everyone here seem really cool, but I smell the most amazing smell I have ever smelled in my life. I look in where everyone is sitting at the dining room table and there she sits. Beautiful black hair, brown eyes, and the most beautiful smile I have ever seen. Once we were introduced to everyone some start coming into the living room including the one that I smelled. Her name is Abby. I cannot wait to get to know her.

Hailey

We all hung around the cabin for a while just talking and letting everyone get to know Nikola and Chad, and for Chad and Nikola to get to know everyone in the pack. It was so much fun. I know I could not be happier than I am right now. I have my BFF and my mate, as well as Nikola has her mate that I will beat up if he does not let me show Nikola around school tomorrow. Abby and Chad are mates. It is so perfect. It's been almost a month since Mom and I moved here. I really didn't think I could be this happy in a town called Kettle Falls. What time do you have to be home by Nikola? Oh you know my dad, since it is a school night we have to be home by 11:00. I hear Dorian whimper like a puppy. Nikola moves her hand very comforting over Dorian's head and face. Oh Dorian get over that crap. I yell at him. She is going to be here forever now. That brought a smile to not only Dorian's face, but also on Nikola's face, Chad's face, and Abby's face. The rest of the time at the cabin went by so fast. I see Dorian walking Nikola out to the car her and Chad drove. Jax is taking me home. I will see you in the morning at school Nikola. I yell over to her as I am getting in the car. Nikola comes running over to the car. I am so happy to be here, to be reunited with my bff. I give her a big hug. Then I get into the car. It was so hard for me to sleep that night just thinking about everything that has happened so fast. I have met my mate even though I could not stand him at first, Nikola my BFF gets to live in the same town that I am living in and she has met her mate which tells me she is not moving anymore and tomorrow we will all be going to the same school. The last time I looked to see what time it is I seen that it is 2:00 in the morning. I think I finally went to sleep then, but it didn't feel like I slept very long before I heard my alarm go off. You would think with me not getting much sleep that I would be sluggish. Nope I am wide awake and ready for the day. I decide to wear my dark blue skinny jeans that have a rip in each knee, my long sleeve white shirt that has four buttons from the middle of my stomach area to my cleavage. I find a note on the dining room table. Hi sweetie, sorry but I forgot I have an early morning meeting at work. I will see you after I get done at the office today. Have a good day, please tell Nikola hi for me. I love you always xoxoxo – mom Just then I hear a horn honk outside. I didn't plan on a ride today so I look outside and see Jax in his car in the driveway so I grabbed my backpack, and my jacket. When I go out the door I lock the front door and walk over to his car with a smile.

Dorian

I cannot wait to get to school today. Wait did I just say that out loud? I have never thought I would say that about school, but now that I know my beautiful Nikola is going to be at school today I cannot wait to get there. I hope Hailey doesn't have too big of a problem with me being right there as she and I together show Nikola around. I wish I could go pick Nikola up, but she told me last night that her dad wants to take her and Chad today to make sure they get there safely. After I get dressed I go downstairs. The cooks in the pack house have breakfast done and as always it smells so good. Dorian. I hear Jax say. Yeah? Let's not forget that after school today there is training. I know, it's the same everyday. Well I just wanted to make sure you didn't forget considering your mate is here now. Of course Alpha. I couldn't get through breakfast fast enough, I want to get to school and see Nikola. I see Jax leaving before I finish my breakfast. Screw it, I take off out the door. Once I pull up in the school parking lot I get out of my car and run inside to the office. I see Nikola, Chad, and their parents in the office so I wait outside just like I did for Hailey on her first day. Just before Nikola, Chad and their parents come out Hailey and Jax walk in the school.

Hailey 🐾

When Jax and I pull up at the school I see Dorian's car is already in the parking lot. I'm going to kick his ass. I say to Jax. who's? Dorian's. Why? Because he really thinks that he is going to beat me to school so he can show Nikola around. I hear Jax laugh. It's not funny. I have known her longer and she is my best friend. Oh I thought I was your best friend now. I give him a sideways look. You know what I mean. Jax and I get out of the car and walk into the school right by the office. Real cute Dorian. What are you talking about? You know what I'm talking about, you thought you would beat me to the school so you could show Nikola around. I am going to kick your butt. I hear Dorian laugh. We can show her around together Hailey. Just then Nikola walks out of the office. What classes do you have? I asked her. She hands me her schedule and I get really excited. You have all the same classes that I do. I look over at Dorian as I start laughing. You two. Nikola says while shaking her head. Jax and Dorian walk me and Nikola to our classes. Oh poor Dorian you don't have the first class with us hahahahaha. We wave by to Dorian as Nikola, Jax, and I all walk into the first class of the day together. We have the next two classes with Dorian and Abby then after that we have lunch and then you and I will have the last couple of classes together without the guys.

Nikola

It is so funny that my BFF and my mate are in competition with each other over who is going to show me around school. I am not choosing one over the other. They can both show me around, sometimes I feel like there needs to be two of me and this is one of those times. I am glad that Jax tells Chad that he would see where he could use him in the pack. I know Chad wants to be a border guard so badly. I really hope he gets it. Mom and dad didn't even tell us that we are werewolves until shortly before we move so Chad was upset about not being in the ROTC program for very long at our last school. I honestly cannot wait to see Dorian again, I hope our first class goes by fast. I didn't think I would miss him this much, but I didn't get to spend that much time with him before class. When Mrs. McKay asked if I wanted to introduce myself to the class I told her I would rather not. She seemed to be okay with me not wanting to.

Dorian 🐺

I hated letting go of Nikola so she could go to her first class with Hailey and Jaxson. It sucks that I am not in the same first class they are. I cannot stand being away from Nikola at all. But I will be with Nikola the next two classes and then at lunch too. The time seems to be going very slow this morning. I cannot help but to think about her and her scent is so intoxicating. As soon as the end of class bell rings I jump out of my seat the same way I did when it was Hailey's first day. I need to be with my mate. I never realized how much of a connection mates have and what it is like to be away from your mate even for 30 minutes for a class at school. I'm glad she likes me and didn't reject me. That would have hurt me so bad if Nikola would have rejected me. But my life is complete now.

Jaxson 🐺

It has been month now since I seen my beautiful Hailey getting out of her car in the school parking lot. So many changes have taken place, besides me finding my mate Hailey. We have Chad, and Nikola added to the pack. Chad has become one of the guards to patrol the borders. He is very fast and has taken out a lot of rogues before anyone else could get to them when they have tried to attack the last couple of times. Dorian and Nikola are mates, Chad and Abby are mates, and that has made Hailey very happy. But we do so much more couple things now which doesn't leave much alone time for Hailey and I. But her 17th birthday is tomorrow and the house I had built for her and I is finished so we will be moving into that house instead of the pack house. We will get plenty of alone time then. She will be going into heat tomorrow as well. It is going to be very hard for me to keep my hands off of her during her birthday party. I am supposed to keep Hailey out of the house all day tomorrow so her mom, Abby, Aspen, Nikola, and a few others can decorate. Hailey thanks that her mom, her and I are just going out to dinner for her 17th birthday party. She has no idea her mom is throwing a birthday party for her.

Lauren

Hailey, yeah mom. Can you come down here for a minute. Sure. What's up? Hailey says as she comes downstairs. There was a package delivered for you. Really? I didn't order anything. I just smile at her. There has been an outfit she has been wanting for some time. I told Kaden it would be something he could order for her for her birthday since he said he didn't know what to get her. When Hailey open the box she gets the biggest smile on her face. Oh mom, thank you. Don't think me I didn't get it for you. She looks at me with a confused look on her face. It was Kaden. Kaden ordered this for me? Yes he did. Well I cannot wait to see him so I can thank him. He will be coming by later this evening you can thank him then. Do you think it would be okay if I wear this outfit to dinner tonight? Yes of course. It is your outfit now and I don't think Kaden would mind as long as he gets to see you in it when he stops by later. Hailey takes off upstairs. I guess she is going to get ready for the party which she thinks we are just going out to eat. I cannot believe I am actually pulling this one off. When I have tried to surprise her in the past she has figured it out before I have everything planned out. As soon as she was upstairs I mind linked Kaden. She LOVES the outfit you got for her. She is upstairs now getting ready for "dinner". So you haven't given it away this year? Kaden ask me in the mind link. I laugh, no I haven't and I know I am surprised too that she hasn't figured it out. When should I come over there? I have to mind link the girls as soon as Hailey leaves with Jaxson. When will that be? I miss you so much already, and I was hoping you and I could have a little alone time together before the girls get there to help you decorate. Awe babe, I know but we are going to have plenty of time for that soon. I am sure now that Nikola is in town Hailey is going to be gone a lot hanging out with her. I hear Kaden sigh. Okay my love just let me know when you want me to be there. I will. I close the mind link just in time because Hailey is coming back downstairs. How do I look mom? When I look at her my mouth drops and my eyes get great big. Oh baby, you look so grown up. Well I am 17 now.

Hailey 🦊

When Mom told me that she had been seeing Kaden I couldn't believe my ears. I mean it was nice of him to order my outfit that I have wanted for months and to get it here the day of my birthday. I never would have thought of my mom being with him. Don't get me wrong, Kaden is a very good looking man for his age. I guess I just never thought about my mom being with anyone at all after my dad even though I didn't want my mom to be alone when I move out. Now I don't have to worry about her she has Kaden. Can I go try on my new outfit now Mom? Jax will be here soon to pick me up. Are you sure it is okay for me to go out with him for the day? Yes sweetie, it is your birthday. I want you to have a good time. Just don't forget to be back here in time for us to go out to dinner. I won't. Is Kaden coming to dinner with us? yes he is. Okay. I run up to my bathroom to take a shower. I wash my hair twice, I want my hair to be extra shiny today then I wash my body. Once I was done and have everything rinsed off I get out and dry off. I wrap my hair in a towel while I try my new outfit on. It fits perfectly. I can't help but to smile as I look at myself in the mirror. Oh my god, I love this outfit. It is the newest black ripped jeans and a dark gray three quarter sleeve shirt, and new high tops. I go back in the bathroom to put my makeup on. I apply some foundation, powder, eyeliner, and eyeshadow in a smokey eye. Just as I'm about to do my hair I hear my phone go off with a text. I go to see who it is. Hey beautiful, happy birthday. I hope you are about ready. I will be there shortly. I have some things planned for us I really hope you like. I love you and I will see you soon. I smile as I put my phone back on the charger. I go back into the bathroom to dry my hair. once my hair is dry enough I put it up in a messy bun, then I go back downstairs. What do you think mom? My mom turns around and as soon as she looks at me her mouth drops and her eyes get big. You look so grown up. Talk about perfect timing. As soon as I was done showing mom how I look in my new outfit the doorbell rings. Mom opens the door and it is Jax. Jax comes in carrying some flowers in his hand. You look very beautiful Hailey. He says as he hands me the flowers. Thank you, that is very sweet of you. Are you ready to go now? He asked me. Yes I am. Mom will you put these in water for me. Yes of course. Have a good time you two. We will. Jax says to my mom. He opens the door to his Jeep for me, and I get in. Once I was in Jax closes the door and gets in on the driver's side. Where are we going? I asked him.

Jaxson

When Hailey ask me where we were going I just smile and shake my head. I told you it is a surprise. Since I won't tell her where we are going she turns on the radio and starts singing with the song that is playing. She does have a beautiful voice and I am not just thinking that just because she is my mate. I turned down a long driveway. It takes every bit of 5 minutes to drive the driveway. When we got to the house, I get out and go around to open the door for Hailey. Who lives here? Hailey ask me as she gets out of the jeep. I just take her by the hand and we walk up to the house. Jax. Hailey say's. Yes babe. Who lives here? When she asked a second time I pulled the keys out of my pocket. Well babe, we live here. Her mouth drops open. What do you mean we live here? I thought we were supposed to be living at the pack house. Well I didn't think you would want to live with anyone else. I figured we could have our privacy so the guys and I built this house for you and I. It's kind of a birthday/wedding gift. I said as I was getting down on one knee. What? Hailey asked. JAX what are you doing? Hailey Lean Moran, I have been in love with you since the moment I saw you get out of your car at the school parking lot. You make me happier than I have ever been and I never want to be without you. You are everything I have ever wanted in a mate, in a wife. Will you make me the happiest man/wolf by marrying me? I see tears falling down her face as she says yes. I stand back up and put the ring on your finger then I pick her up and we spin around as I kiss her. Would you like to go in and take a look around. That is if you would like to live here with me. Oh Jax of course I want us to live here.

Lauren 🐺

As soon as Hailey leaves with Jaxson I mind link all of the girls and let them know it is safe to come over so we can get the house decorated. As I am pouring another cup of coffee someone rings the doorbell. That was fast I thought. I go to the door and to my surprise it was Kaden standing there. Hi. I say when I see him. Hi beautiful. I thought you might want some help decorating for the party. Well I have the girls coming to help decorate the house, but I am so glad you are here. I have missed you. I say as I put my arms around him. After I kiss Kaden I ask him if he would like some coffee. Yes, and thank you. Kaden and I sit and have our coffee as we wait for the girls to show up. Is the birthday girl with Jaxson? Yes she is. I can't wait for you to see her in the outfit you got for her, she looks so grown up. I did have to mind link the girl's to get them over here to help with getting the house decorated for the party, I don't know what is taking them so long. If I don't I know you and I will end up making love, not that I would mind but think about it we will have all night to do that after the party is over because I am pretty sure they are all going to an after-party at the cabin. Well I am looking forward to our after party. Kaden says as he grabs my ass and pulls me into him. I could feel he is really excited. Just then the door bell rings again. I go to see who is at the door this time. Hi girls. I said as I opened the door and see they are all here. Where would you like for us to start? Abby asked me. Well I thought since the party will mostly be downstairs you girls could grab these decorations and decorate down there. They grab the decorations and headed off to the workout room in the basement. I stayed upstairs with Kaden and we decorated the front door and the stairway just inside the front door.

Hailey 🐺

I never expected Jax to ask me to marry him. I know we are mates and I thought maybe we would not go through the traditional marriage, but he obviously wants the traditional stuff. After I said yes Jax swoops me up and carries me bridal style inside of the house. Jax you don't have to carry me like that yet. He just laughs. I wanted to carry you like that. Once he sets me down I start looking around the inside of the house. It is all made of wood inside and out. It is so beautiful. Who decorated? I asked Jax. I got Abby, and Aspen to pick out the furniture and everything else. Do you like what they picked out? If you don't we can get something different. Oh no they did an amazing job, I love what they got. The house is a three-story house. The main level has a living room, dining room, kitchen, and an office. The upstairs has four bedrooms, one is the master bedroom that has two walking closets, and a full bathroom. The bathroom is huge. There is a shower that is separate from the whirlpool bathtub. When I walk into one of the other bedrooms it is decorated as a nursery for a girl. I smile. Jax why is this bedroom decorate as a nursery for a girl? Are you trying to tell me something? What would I be trying to tell you? He says with a big smile on his face. Are you saying you want to have a baby? Well I think it will be impossible for me to have a baby. I laugh and playfully nudge him with my elbow. You know what I mean. Yes I know what you mean. He says as he is laughing. And yes I would love for us to have not just one child, but as many as possible. I go to the next room and open the door. It is another nursery, but this one is decorated for a boy. After seeing the rooms upstairs which the last one is made up as a guest room we go all the way down to the bottom level of the house. Yes the basement. It is a finished basement that is set up as a workout room with all of the workout equipment you can imagine. There is even a big flat screen TV down there and a stereo system with bluetooth. Well babe, what do you think? Do we keep the house, or do we sell it and move into the pack house? I turned to Jax and smile. Oh Jax I love this house. It is perfect. Okay then we will put it on the market to sell. I lost my smile. What do you mean, I just said it is perfect. Yes you said it is perfect but you didn't say you would like to live here. Oh Jax you know I want to live here. I love the house. Good so do I and I cannot wait to move in here with you. He comes over, picks me up and kisses me so passionately. Now all we have to do is set a date. Jax says to me. But for now we need to get out of here because you are in heat and it is driving me crazy. Well we are alone here. I say to him with a big smile. He gives me a devilish smile and sweeps me up. Jax carries me all the way to the master bedroom. Once in the bedroom he tosses me to the bed which by the way I feel like I am going to sink all the way into because of how soft the bed is. As he is taking his shirt off he comes and lays on top of me and starts kissing me like he cannot get enough of me. I feel my shirt being torn off of me. Sweetheart be careful with this outfit. I tell him that Kaden just got this entire outfit for me for my birthday. If we go back to pick up Mom and my outfit is all torn up she is going to know what we did or she will freak out thinking I was attacked by another rogue. I hear Jax growl, or maybe it was his wolf I hear coming out of him. Okay then maybe you should take all of it off because if I do then it will be shredded. He laughs. I start taking my clothes off slowly teasing Jax more. I hear him growling again and I just smile at him. As soon as I have everything off I was pulled down on the bed.

Jaxson 🐾

She is driving me crazy. I knew she would be in heat today. It is her 17th birthday and her first heat. But I want her to see the house the guys and I built. Once we walked through the entire house I joked around with her by asking if she like the house and would want to live here. She said it is perfect so I told her we could put it on the market and sell it then move back into the pack house. It was all I could do not to laugh as I was saying that to her. I could see that irritated her. I told her that I asked if she would want to live here but she didn't say that. So she said she loves the house and that yes she wants to live here. I was about to lose all control. Babe I think we need to get going so we can go pick up your mom and go to dinner. I am not supposed to tell Hailey that her mom is getting her house all ready for Hailey's seventeenth birthday party. She's surprises me by saying that we are here alone and she smile. That was it, I swoop her up and take her to the master bedroom. I want so much to rip her clothes off of her, but she tells me that I can't because Kaden bought them for her as a birthday gift and she has a point. If I rip her clothes off of her then she would have nothing to wear when we have to leave here. Too bad I hadn't already had the girls go get Hailey a whole new wardrobe of clothes that I planned on having them to get her, then I wouldn't have stopped and her new outfit would have been in shreds on the floor. But since there wasn't any new clothes for her yet and there isn't another outfit here just like the one she has on I decided it would not be a good idea to shred her outfit. You better be the one to take your clothes off then because I am afraid I will shred them if I take them off of you. Hailey starts teasing me as she slowly takes her clothes off and does a sexy little dance move as she takes each piece of clothing off. I feel like I am going to burst before we even do anything. GOD she is beautiful. Once she has her clothes off I grab and pull her down on the bed. We kiss like we can't get enough of each other. I kiss her neck trying to be careful not to mark her just yet. But I just can not help myself my mark is now on her with the crescent moon in the middle of the mark that symbolizes our pack. I moved down to her nipples. I can hear her breathing and it is getting very heavy. Her scent is getting more intense and driving me crazy. I cannot take it anymore. I slide myself between her legs. I want to be gentle with you babe since it is our first time. I know this is not the proper time to say this. Hailey says as she looks me in the eyes so loving and caring. I know this is not your first time. I look at her in surprise what do you mean? Jax I could smell another girl on you that time you backed me up against the lockers at school. I put my head down on her. You're right babe and I am sorry. I had no idea I would meet you and have my mate this soon. I really thought it would be a few more years before I met you. I know that is no kind of excuse, I should have just waited for you. It's okay babe, we're together now. Hailey said to me. With that I very gently entered her. I can feel her breath on my neck which drive's me even crazier. With every movement of me moving in and out of her I can hear her moan.

Hailey 🐾

I gasp as Jax enters me. It hurt so much, but at the same time it feels so good. I know how he was feeling before we started making love. It was driving me crazy wanting him as much as I did, or as much as I do. But at the same time it is very weird for me because I have always been so shy when it comes to anyone seeing my body. At school when I was in gym class and we would have to dress in our sweat's I would always go into a bathroom stall because I didn't want anyone at all seeing me without clothes on. I have also never talked sexy in front of anyone. But with Jax it is so much different. I dig my claws into him as he moves in and out of me slowly. He is driving me crazy. My body starts to trimmer as I get close to my climax. I know he can feel me as I start to shake because he is moving so much faster. With my legs wrapped around him and my claws into his flesh I moan out loud as I release and I cum. I hear Jax moan and I feel him explode inside of me. I am so out of breath. Jax collapse's on me. I love you Hailey. I love you too Jax, that was so amazing and I don't mean to rush us but we are going to have to shower and get going. I know everyone will be able to smell what we have done here. Are you ashamed? Jax says with a smile. Of course not. We are each other's mate. I just don't want everyone to smell what we have done. Okay. He takes me by the hand and leads me to the shower. It was a quick shower though. We get out, dry off. Jax, why is my neck down by my shoulder bleeding? I marked you. What do you mean you marked me? It is what wolves do to their mate. Remember I told you about that when we were at the cabin that first night. If you are not marked then the unmated male wolves will think you do not have a mate and they will think you're for the taking. If you look at it you will see that it has a crescent moon in the middle. What about you? What do you mean, what about me? Well you marked me, don't I get to mark you? Yes of course you get to mark me. I walk over to him and act like I am going to mark him, but I only kiss his neck. He looks at me with a confused look. Tonight my love. I say with a smile. He flick's me the towel he is using to dry off with. OUCH JAX!!!! That hurt. He just laughs. Ohhhh you are in for it later.

Lauren

Well what do you think babe? Kaden ask me about the way everything is decorated. It all looks so good. The D.J. will be here any minute now. I hope he gets here before Hailey gets here. Mrs. Moran? I hear Nikola say. Yes dear. Will you come downstairs and see what you think of everything down there. Ok, I am on my way. I walk downstairs and I am in awe. It all looks amazing. The stars are hanging from the ceiling, the rest of the decorations are hung just the way I imagined them. I hear a knock on the outside door that comes into the basement. I go to see who it is. Hi, I greet the D.J. You can set up over here. I lead him to the part of the room I want him to set up in, then I start to go back upstairs. Girls would you all like to come back up with me while the D.J. sets up? They all follow me. Now all of you hid your cars well, right? Yes, Mrs. Moran. They all say. Just as the D.J. mind links me to let me know he is all set up I hear a car pull in. I look out the window and see it is Hailey and Jaxson. Ok everyone here they come. Places. The girls and Kaden all hide as Hailey and Jaxson walk in. Hailey ask if I am ready to go out to dinner. On cue everyone comes out and yell's SURPRISE. I see Hailey almost jump out of her skin?

CHAPTER 4

SURPRISE PARTY

Hailey 🐻

Jax is really quiet on the way back to my mom's. What are you thinking about? I ask. Everything really. The first time I saw you, how I thought it was going to be a struggle to get you to be with me. Awe sweetie, it was a bit of a struggle and I didn't think you and I would be together but you wouldn't give up. No way, I knew you were my mate and I don't let what is mine get away. WATCH OUT!! I yell at Jax as I see a deer run out in front of us. He jerk's the steering wheel and we almost hit the rock wall on the side of the highway. We stop just Inches of it. Are you ok babe? Jax ask me. Yes I am ok, that was just a little scary. Jax leans over and hugs me. It was hard to get the Jeep to start again, but Jax got it to start and we head back out onto the highway. It takes about thirty minutes to get from mine and Jax's new house to my mom's. Once we pull in I ask Jax if he wants to just wait while I go get my mom. No, I think I will walk in with you I don't want to be away from you for a second. I smile at him. It seems silly for both of us to go in to get her when we will be coming right back out. Well if she isn't completely ready then it will take a couple of minutes. That is true. I said. Plus if she sees your ring I want to be right there with you. Okay, come on then. I think he would give me any reason just to come with me. So it would be pointless to argue with him when I might as well just let him come in with me. When we walk in Abby, Aspen, Nikola, Dorian, Jason, Daniel, Robert, Josh, and some others jump out and yell SURPRISE!!!! Which scared the hell out of me, but made me happy at the same time. They all started laughing because of seeing me jump. I look at my mom and Jax. You both. I say shaking my head. How did you do all of this? I asked. I had Jaxson to take you to see the house he had built for you and him and while you were out of the house as soon as you left I mind link all of the girls and told them it was safe to come help decorate, and the guys came in just before you and Jaxson pulled in. Mom said. This isn't all of it though. Go down to the workout room. I look at Mom and then at Jax before heading down to the workout room and just smile and shake my head. OMG this looks amazing. Thank you mom. You're welcome sweetie. But I thought we were going to dinner. Would you have rather went out to dinner or had this amazing party with all of us? Nikola asked me. You know I love spending my birthday with everyone I love. Just then Aspen says OMG!!!! What is that on your finger? Everyone looks over at me. Oh yeah, Jax and I have an announcement to make. I grab Jax's hand and pull him next to me. So Jax asked me to marry him today and I said yes. Everyone started clapping. I could see tears going down my mom's face but Kaden pulled her over to him and held her. Just then the DJ started playing the song "what if" by Kane Brown and Jax started lip singing it as he pulled me to him and we started to dance. This song is for the birthday girl from Jax. The rest of the party went great. We all had a blast. While we were all dancing, partying and having a great time Jax had some of the other guards and some of the other wolves come to collect my stuff and take it all to the new house. So when is the wedding? Nikola asked me. I look at Jax and he shrugged. Hey mom. Yes sweetie. How about a June wedding for Jax and I? Would that be okay for you? That way we can graduate from school first. That sounds very good to me. I know it is tradition for the family of the Bride to pay for the wedding. Nikola walks over to Jax and I. Can I take her away for just a couple of minutes? She asked Jax. Hmmm I don't know, I have a very hard time being away from her for even a second. He says as he is looking down and smiling at me. Oh I will bring her right back. It's just some BWFF stuff. BWFF? Jax said. Best

Werewolf Friends Forever. Nikola and I said at the same time. Oh okay I guess, but remember I can smell her scent so I know where you two are at and I will come find her. Jax said smiling. Oh sweetie I will be right back. Then I whisper, if you behave you will have me all night. He quickly let go of my hand.

Nikola

Once we got moved to Kettle falls, and I went to see Hailey at the pack house I also found my mate. My mom and dad had told Chad and I all about finding your mate, about being a wolf and everything we need to know. When Chad and I got to the pack house the day after we had moved here I smelled that amazing smell. It was Dorian, he is my mate. I spent the next month getting to know him and he got to know me. Now I cannot live my life without him. Well the day before Hailey's birthday party Dorian took me out to a really nice dinner. Halfway through our dinner Dorian got down on one knee and asked me to marry him. It was so sweet and so romantic, it was better than I could have ever imagined my mate asking me to marry him. I have something to tell you and to show you. I said to Hailey. I lift up my left hand. OMG!!!! You are engaged to? Yes, Dorian asked me yesterday. OMG Nikola I am so happy for you. Hailey gives me a big hug. Why didn't you say something earlier? I didn't want to take away your thunder on your day. That is not all. I told her. What else is going on. BWFF promise me you won't say anything to anyone. I Hailey BWFF of you Nikola promise I will take the secret you are about to tell me to my grave. We both laugh. That has been what we have said for as long as I could remember when we promise the biggest promise to each other. I am pregnant. OMG I scream. Hailey shhhh everyone will hear you. I am sorry, I am just so happy for you. Thank you. We go back to the dance floor. See Jaxson I told you I would return her to you. Dorian was standing there next to Jaxson waiting for me to return to him after I talked with Hailey.

Kaden

After helping Lauren with the decorations we set and just talked. Now I am really glad you told Hailey about us. She will be moving into the house Jaxson built for her and him. We won't have to sneak around. Yes, I am glad I got that out in the open about you and I as well, I really hate keeping anything from Hailey. There is only one question remaining. What is that? Lauren ask me. Which house shall we live in? You have this big house and I have mine. Well your house has the hot tub in it, mine has the workout room. There is a solution to all of this. Oh yeah, what is that? She asked me. We could keep both houses and we can live here that way you are closer to Hailey. I know that would make you happy my love, and we can keep my house as a get away home. I see Lauren's eyes light up with her smile. Really Kaden, you would do that for me so I can be close to my daughter. Our daughter, that is if you will marry me. With that question Lauren came over and sat on my lap. Of course I will marry you Kaden. I gave her a very passionate kiss. She has been through so much with losing Hunter, having to finish raising Hailey on her own, and then moving back here. I sat with Lauren and watch the kids dance and then Lauren stand's up.

Lauren 🐺

Hey everyone, I think it is time for the birthday girl to blow out her candles on her cake and open her gifts. Everyone was in agreement with me on that. Hailey and Jaxson head over to the gift table that was piled up with gifts for Hailey.

Hailey 🐺

Jax and I go over to the gift table that mom had set up. It was piled with gifts not only from everyone that was here, but also from friends and family that could not make it to my birthday party. Omg, it is going to take me all night just to open everything. Everyone laughs when I said that. I end up getting everything I could possibly want and need. Mom I will have to have Jax come back with a truck to pick all of this up later if that is okay with you. Of course. My mom said. I want to thank all of you for coming and helping me to celebrate my birthday. It has been a bittersweet day and night. There is someone that there is no way he could have been here, but I know he is here in spirit and in mine and my mom's heart. I hope you are not offended by that Kaden. But it is my father that could not be here, but I know he is watching from where he is at and I know he is very happy. I see tears going down my mom's face as I feel tears going down my face at the thought of my dad watching over us. I also want everyone to know that my car was supposed to be a graduation gift, but my mom thought since I had already been through losing my father, and having to move from the only home I have ever known and come here that she would give me the car early, but she said that it was a gift from her and my dad. It is a gift that I will treasure always. One of the other gifts that I got today there is no way it could be brought here. Jax and some of the guys that are here and some of the ones that could not be here built a house for Jax and I. It is a beautiful home and I cannot wait for all of you to come over and see it. But for now, I think me and my husband to be are going to go to our new home because I have had a very big day and I am very tired. I squeeze Jax's hand as I say that I am ready to go home. We tell everyone good night. I gave my mom a big hug and thanked her for the amazing party. Thank you so much for everything mom, you're welcome Hailey. Nikola came up to me and gave me a hug. Will I see you tomorrow at school? Yes of course you will. Just because Jax and I have our own place now does not mean that I don't have to go to school anymore I have to graduate still. I hug Nikola back and I see Jaxson talking to Dorian. Whatever they were talking about looked very serious. When we were finally able to get through all the people that wanted to say good night to Jax and I we finally got to leave my mom's house. It is so weird to me that is not my home anymore. It is also weird that I will no longer be living with my mom. Yes but you and I get to start out our lives. Jax's says to me with a smile. I know, it's just going to be an adjustment. What were you and Dorian talking about? It looked pretty serious. It was just alpha and beta stuff Jax said to me. I have so much to do when we get to our new home, but all I really want to do is take a hot shower and go to sleep. As I am getting ready to get into the shower Jax comes in the bathroom. Do you mind if I take a shower with you? He smiles as he asked me. I couldn't say no to him. As long as you promise to wash my back. You got a deal. Needless to say the shower didn't last too long. Jax picks me up, throws me over his shoulder and carries me to our bed where he playfully tosses me down. We are both naked and he climbs on top of me and looks me in the eyes. I love you Hailey.

I love you too. I have loved you since that first day of school, but your attitude is what kept me from really wanting to be with you. I know and for that I am sorry, I will spend the rest of my life trying to make it up to you. Jax you don't have to do that. As soon as I said that he doesn't have to do that Jax covers my mouth with his hand. Shhhh I do have to do that. I want to make sure that each and every day you know how much I love you. You are everything to me Hailey

Jaxson 🐾

After Hailey's birthday party she and I went to our new home. She went straight to the shower so I follow her in there and asked her if she was okay with me showering with her. I of course had to wash her back at her request. Once we were done in the shower I pick Hailey up, throw her over my shoulder and carry her to our bed. I toss her down on the bed playfully. My heart races every time I look at her and here she is completely naked. The chills that go up my arm, my heart also races, I cannot believe I have this beautiful woman here. That she is my mate. I laid down on top of Hailey. I love you Hailey. She tells me that she loves me too. I don't know if she realizes how much I love her. I move myself between her legs.

Hailey 🐾

Jax moves himself between my legs I can feel his hands slide down between my legs and two of his fingers playfully feeling around, then I feel him enter me. I arched my back and moan out as it feels so good. He moves slowly at first and with each movement he goes a little faster each time until he has me losing all control and at that point I flip us to where I am on top of him. I arched my back as I move my hips grinding myself on him. I feel his hands moving up my body. His fingers reaching for my nipples. This drives me crazy. I cannot help but to moan out loud as I start to climax. Then I drop down and lay on top of Jax. We are both completely out of breath and sweating. I think we may need another shower. I say to him and we both just kind of laugh. Jax rolls me off of him to where I am laying next to him and he looks me in the eyes. I want everyday with you to be like now. So do I. I said as I raise my head up to kiss him. Just then there is a pounding on our bedroom door and we both jump. WHAT!! Jax growl's. There are rouge's and vampires attacking at the border. Jayden, one of the guards tells us. Okay we will be right out there. We here Jayden leaving, running down the steps. Why are we being attacked so much? I asked Jax. I don't know but we are going to kill these rogues and vampires. I don't understand why the vampires are attacking though we have a treedy with them. Jax also says.

Jaxson 🐾

I don't really want Hailey going out to fight the rouges and the vampires. I want to protect my mate in every way I can, but I know how stubborn she can be and I know I won't be able to stop her from going out there. What makes me even more irritated about this rogue attack is it will be Hailey's first phase. I wanted her and I to phase together and then her and I to be able to run through the forest and enjoy the freedom of running and feeling free. As I was getting close to the border I can see a couple of our wolves injured. I mind link Dorian. Is the pack doctor on his way? Has anyone mind linked him to let him know we need him? Yes and yes, he is on his way. Good when he gets here I am sending Hailey in with him that will be the only way I can get her away from the fight. Once I get to the border I see Alaric and my heart starts racing. He is one of the strongest vampires to fight and very hard to take down. Why is he here? I asked Dorian. I have no idea, but he has been very hard to get off of the other wolves. I run straight for Alaric and jump on top of him knocking him off of one of my best warriors. I pin him to the ground, his eyes are so dark I almost cannot see any white of his eyes. Why are you here? Why are you helping the rogues attack us? We have an agreement. He smiles and says but she wants you back and she said that if we kill your mate then we would have more access to the land because she would talk to you into giving us more access. Who are you talking about? I am with my mate, I love her and no one is going to take her away from me. Lena, she said that she should be your mate and not the one you are with now. She told us she would make sure that we are treated better and she signed an agreement with us to ensure she was not lying to us. Lena will NEVER be my mate, she is a rogue now and she will never be allowed back here. Just then a rogue caught me off guard and knocked me off of Alaric? Alaric gained control and was on top of me about to stab me with a knife that has wolf bane all over it. Just as he was about to plunge the knife in me I see a wolf knock Alaric off of me. I get up and see that it is Hailey's wolf Casey. She is such a beautiful, very rare wolf and I know it is Hailey's wolf because none of the wolves in our pack look like that. She is all white, you hardly ever see an all white wolf. She is on top of Alaric, I run to help her but another vampire jumps on me and I lose sight of Hailey and Alaric. I can't help but to worry about my mate.

Hailey 🐾

Alaric is a very strong vampire, but I am a very strong wolf. I have him down when another vampire knocks me off of him. It takes me no time to rip the head off the vampire that knocked me off of Alaric. When I get up I can see that all of the rouges are going back into the woods since there is only about five rogue wolves left after the rest was killed. Even Alaric and what was left of his vampires ran back into the woods. Jax and I go to the creek to wash all the mud and blood off of us before we change back into our human form. I look into the water of the creek and see Cane and Casey standing there side by side. Our wolves are so beautiful together. Once we were done we went back up on the hill just above the creek where we kept extra clothes for changing from wolf to human, we stand there side by side for a couple of minutes on the edge of the cliff. The night Moon is high in the sky but so full and big that it looks very close to us. Once we were changed back to human and in our clothes Jax and I walk back to the house. I wonder what that was all about. I say too Jax. He looks at me and says that he knows. What do you mean you know. Well when I attacked Alaric he said that one of the rogues that used to be in our pack and had a thing for me sign an agreement with the vampires that if they were to kill you that she would be with me and get them more access to the land where they would be able to hunt more. My heart sank to my stomach when Jax told me that. Then Jax walks over to me and put his arm around me. Don't worry babe I am never going to let anyone hurt you, take you away from me, or come between you and I. Oh I'm not worried, but why would this girl think you would ever have anything to do with her. Jax put his head down again. When I was around thirteen I dated Lena and she I guess was in love with me, she got so overly possessive so I ended things. She didn't take me breaking up with her very well. She yelled things at me and one of the things she yelled was that I would never be happy, that I would never have a love, or a mate because she would see to it that even if I did find my mate she would make sure to take my mate away. She went so crazy and started doing everything against the rules so she was turned away and became rogue. I thought all wolves had their own mate. Did she not find her mate? I asked Jax. Her mate was killed in an attack. That is another reason I think she went so crazy. When you have been with your mate and then you lose your mate your wolf starts to die unless you find someone that you can love and that loves you back. Since I did not and do not love Lena I think is going crazy because her wolf is dying.

Jaxson

I could see that Hailey was very upset when I told her about Lena. Babe, I promise you that nothing or no one will ever take you away from me, and that Lena nor anyone else will ever harm you in any way. I will ALWAYS protect you. Then Hailey starts laughing. Do you really think I am afraid of some rogue that thinks you belong to her? No Jax I am upset because you didn't tell me about her. Hailey that was years ago and I didn't think anything of it. We were so young. Oh Jax you have so much to learn about females. I guess I do, but still I am not ever going to let that dumb bitch do anything to you or anything she sends to attack us. We are going on with our plans. Oh I know we are. Hailey says to me as she comes up to me and kisses me a long, deep, passionate kiss. Please don't ever underestimate me Jaxson. Hailey said to me. I will not let her take me away from you. I can handle that rouge. I pick Hailey up and carry her bridal style again to the bedroom where we mad love almost all night long.

Lena 🐾

I found out that my Jaxson found his mate and when I found out everything went flying into the walls of the cave I have been reduced to living in since I was turned away from my pack. I should be the Luna of the pack. Alaric!! Get in here NOW. YES MY LUNA. GRRRR I growl at Alaric. I am not your Luna!! Get that right. I belong to you Jaxson and no one else. But Luna, he has found his mate. When Alaric said that to me I threw the glass I had in my hand at his head. I am sorry Luna. You know how much that upsets me that, that bitch is with the man I am supposed to be with. He is my everything and I will stop at nothing to get my wolf back. Everyone knows Jaxson and I are supposed to be together and he would have come to his senses by now if that bitch had not moved here, but that is okay we are going to get rid of her. We need to attack now and get rid of her. I don't want my Jaxson to end up getting her pregnant. If he gets her pregnant not only will I have to get rid of her, but I will have to get rid of that mutt too. You know that will cause a big war. Alaric says. I am aware, but we can handle it. Now go and I will mind link the others.

Dorian 🐾

I did not want Nikola having to fight in the rogue attack especially since she hasn't been in town all that long and also because we have not been together all that long. But I did say that I wanted my mate to be like Hailey hahahahahaha and that is what I got. A very stubborn mate, just like Hailey. I now know what Jax is going through but I would not trade Nikola for the world. We will be having a pup soon, but we have not told anyone yet, well except for Hailey. I know that Nikola told Hailey at Hailey's birthday party. That is another reason I didn't want Nikola out there fighting those rogues. She won't listen to me when I tell her I don't want her fighting especially since she is pregnant.

Alaric

I want to break those mutts in two with my own two hands. I want to hear and feel their bones break. Who are they to say where me and my crew can hunt? How much of the land we can hunt on? This little bitch Lena, I can't stand her, but she is the one that can get us close to the other land. If there is ever a problem though that little bitch will be mine. She will dangle from my hands as I walk across that land and take what I want.

Hailey

The next morning I woke up to two things. The first being Jax kissing my cheek. I smile at him as I wake up. The other was the food being made. I swear from the stories I have heard about living at the pack house I feel like that is where I am even though I know we are in our own home. But with the smell of the food I ask Jax who is here. It's just the ones that are supposed to be here to cook for us. But Jax I want to be the one who cooks our meals here. We don't need to take anyone from cooking at the pack house. There are so many more people there than there is here. Babe you don't need to cook when you can be doing what you need to do for the Luna duties. Oh and what does that involve? I ask Jax. Well you will be in charge of some of the training, and there are other tasks that Luna's take care of. He says as he smiles at me. Oh you are so funny Jax. Those tasks I would take care of anyway. I said back to him with a smile. Hahahahahaha Hailey that is not what I am talking about. You can help me with paperwork, emails, meetings, transfers, you help the women of the pack and when needed, you will help out with the little children.......etc. well for now I am STARVING. I said as I was getting up and beating Jax to the dining room table. There was so much food which is a good thing because since I have been having to change into my wolf and fighting off those rogues, and training everyday I have been so much more hungrier than normal. I filled my plate completely full plus more. There was pancakes, biscuits and gravy, different kinds of sausages, waffles, eggs made in any way you can think of, fruit and so much more. As I was eating, I might link Nikola and ask her if she would like to help me in the task of leading the training session. She was so excited that I asked her to help. You know I will help with anything you need Hailey, but why are you asking me for help? You are our Luna and I know you are strong enough to handle it. I just want my BWFF helping me. Also after training, and school I was wondering if you will be free. Free for what? Nikola asked me. Well with graduation coming up I think we need to go shopping for a dress for graduation and for our senior prom. Oh yeah shopping. Nikola and I both laugh when she says shopping. So I will see you soon. Yes Dorian and I are on our way. I hope that it is okay that it will be me and Dorian. Of course silly, Dorian is Jax's Beta he has to come over here. Okay see you soon Luna. Don't call me Luna that just sounds too weird. Okay Luna Hailey. We both laugh and then I ended the mind link. Once we were done with breakfast Jax and I went into the office part of our home to check emails and messages. So far my Luna duties are going pretty easy, but I have not started being head of the training process and I'm a little nervous about everyone listening to me. I tell Jax about me being worried that maybe some will not listen to me. They have not worked with me yet and I know they are all supposed to respect me as their Luna. They will all listen to you. They know what will happen if they do not listen to you, if they show any disrespect towards you at all they know what will happen because it is the same as disrespecting me. I don't know if Rita likes me. I keep getting a very weird vibe from her. Babe, if ANYONE and I mean ANYONE does not listen, or does not show you the same respect that they show me they will be sent away, or put in a cell in the dungeon. I don't know of any of the members of the pack that wants to be turned away and be a rogue. After that Jax hugged me and said it will be okay, you will do great. I have complete faith in you. Well I did ask Nikola to help me in leading the training practice. Oh and you didn't want me to help with that? Jax said then laughed. I playfully smack him. You know I would love to have you out there by my side leading your pack in training. Ummm it's our pack. Jax reminded me. Well that is something I'm going to have to get used to saying, our pack. Well I better go get ready for training. I gave Jax a kiss and headed up to the bedroom to change. I heard the doorbell as I went into the bedroom, then I heard Jax talking to Dorian. I am so happy that Nikola is here to help me. She always has a way to calm my anxieties about new things.

Nikola 🐺

Once Hailey ended the mind link Dorian grabs me and tries carrying me back to the bedroom. DORIAN!! What my love? He says as he smiles. We have to go to Hailey and Jaxson's. I know but I thought we would have some time to play around. No babe we can't Hailey is very nervous about leading the training practice and she wants me there to help her out. But you are not Luna, or Alpha. I know that, but I am her best friend and I can help calm her anxiety. Besides she said that she has something very important to tell me when we get there that she couldn't tell me through the mind link. Is everything okay with Hailey? Yes, don't worry. Is everything okay with her and Jax? I know they got off to a pretty rocky start in their relationship. Yes, there is nothing to worry about, your real true love is just fine. I said to him in a joking tone and that is when he tossed me to the bed and jumped into a wolf's stance on top of me. We both start laughing because Hailey being Dorian's real love is just something that Dorian and I joke about because he told me that when he first met Hailey that he liked her but he knew she was not his mate but that he had hoped his mate would be something like Hailey and then he met me. But of course he would have been very happy with me even if Hailey and I had not been best friends. Come on babe we better go. Jax doesn't like to be kept waiting. Dorian said with a disappointed look on his face. I will promise you something my love. What's that? Dorian perks up and asked. When we are all done with what we have to do over at Hailey and Jaxson's we can come back home and do whatever you had in mind just now. That put a VERY big smile on Dorian's face. But we have to go to school after training is over, I don't want your dad coming down on me thinking you are not going to school because of me. He might make you move back home. Well then after school then I smile at Dorian. After we got ready we got into my car. Dorian drove us over to Hailey and Jaxson's house. When we got there Jaxson answered the door. Where is Hailey? I asked. She is upstairs getting ready for training practice.

ℒauren

It has been a while since Hailey moved out into that very nice house that Jaxson had built for him and Hailey. So why don't we figure out what we are going to do as far as our living arrangements. I said to Kaden. Well actually isn't there a training practice today that Hailey is leading? Oh that is right, I am glad you reminded me. Hailey would be so pissed at me being her mother and not showing up for her first time leading the training practice. This is something her father would be so proud of. Kaden could see that I was getting upset thinking about Hunter not being here to see our daughter leading her first training practice. He came over to me and put his arms around me to comfort me. It is okay sweetheart. I know I am not Hailey's real father, but I think of her as my daughter and I am going to be so proud seeing her leading the training today. I just hope she doesn't work us to hard, I don't want to be to worn out by the time we are done. Kaden smiled up at me when he said that. Oh you are so bad. I said while laughing because I know what he meant. We better get out of here before we end up in the bedroom, or the living room, or any room of the house for that matter and miss the whole thing. Okay let's go. Kaden leads me out of the house, he took my keys and locked the door. We got in his car to drive over to the pack house where the training is held. There were so many already there when we got there. Oh I hope we are not very late. I said to Kaden when we pulled up. Babe, it is still pretty early. I would say that if anything we are right on time.

Hailey 🐺

Hi everyone, I want to welcome you all here today. I am Hailey Moran your Luna and your instructor for today, well I am the instructor for most of you today. We will be splitting up into groups. Some of you will be going with Alpha Jaxson? If you think just because you might be partnered with someone as in your mate that you will be training with your mate you are very wrong. I laughed as I said that out to everyone. It looks like there was over 150 people standing there listening to me, and they're probably is that many if not more since it is my mom's old pack that her and my dad had when he was alive and living here, and the pack Jax is over until his mom, dad, and brother come back home. I just hope they all can hear me. Okay so the ones who have mates, the girls will all go with Alpha Jaxson and the guys will come with me. Anyone that is 16 through 18 will go with Nikola. Nikola waves at everyone so they knew who she was. The ones that are 10 through 16 will go with Dorian, and just because she is not standing up here I hope she does not think she is going to get out of helping me with this. My mom, Lauren Moran, will be taking the ones that are 5 through 10 years old. Now everyone break up into your groups and make sure you listen to your instructor and if you don't listen and do what you are told to do you will deal with me and Alpha Jaxson. Once I was with my group I got them all quiet down. Okay, we are going to start with a warm up. I want 50 jumping jacks and go. It didn't take everyone very long to complete the 50 jumping jacks. Okay, Now 50 squats. I noticed that several were having a little trouble completing the squats, but that is okay they will get used to it. Okay now we are going to do lunges, and sit ups, then 50 laps around the pond and yes it will be 50 laps. I heard some moan and complain. If you want to complain I can find something a little harder for you all to do. When I said that everyone shut up and started doing the lunges. Once they were done with the warm ups they went right into the run around the pond. You would think that a bunch of guys would not complain especially when they have a girl instructor, but it is what it is I guess. When we got done with the laps around the pond I could see that they were all out of breath. Okay everyone take a few minutes to rest and then we will spar. When Jax, Nikola, Dorian, and mom's groups got back over here with mine we started sparring. You all can pick your partner for the sparring exercise. I could tell who was our best warriors during the sparring training, and I could tell who would have a lot of possibilities of being a guard for the borders. Okay everyone, we will all meet here again on Monday morning. Have a good weekend. I said to all of them as we ended the training for the day. So when do you want to go shopping for dresses for graduation and prom? I know we didn't have a lot of time to talk when Dorian and I got here this morning. Well we could go shopping after school today or over the weekend. When do you think Dorian will let go of you long enough to go shopping? We both kind of laugh. I can go at any time you are ready. Nikola said. I can not believe school is almost over. I agree with you Nikola, it's almost scary to know that part of our lives is over. I agree with you Nikola, it is very scary but we are starting a new chapter in our lives and with two very amazing guys.

Jaxson 🐾

During this training we will be running two miles so that is four times around the pond. Then we will sparse so when we get back we will go over to your Luna's group to spar. Okay let's go. I drop in behind all of them in case someone decides to fall back. I always run at the end of the line. I was wondering the whole time how Hailey was doing with her group. I hate being away from her like this, but we have to keep our pack in good shape in case of another attack. It's not easy being Alpha. I have a lot of work to do, I have to make sure I get all the emails taken care of, return phone calls, look over the transfer request from other packs, make sure my mate is well protected and help her with the planning of our wedding. Yeah it is going to be very challenging, but I wouldn't be acting alpha, and about to be Alpha if anyone thought I could not do the job. Once we were all done with the training for the day and Hailey told everyone when to be back here Hailey, her mom, Kaden, Dorian, Nikola, Chad, Todd, Lily, and I all went back into the pack house where Hailey, Nikola, Dorian, and I got ready for school. Hailey tells me and Dorian that her and Nikola want to go shopping for prom dresses and graduation dresses after school today Well Dorian and I need to go get fitted for our taxes too maybe we could all go at the same time. Babe as much as I love being with you all of the time and I cannot stand to be away from you as much as you can't stand to be away from me, but you and Dorian cannot see the dresses that we get until the prom. I didn't know that that was a thing, I thought it was the wedding dress that a bride wears on her wedding day that the groom is not supposed to see until the bride is walking down the aisle. Well babe now you know you cannot see the prom dress until the night of the prom as well. Hailey and Nikola laugh. Okay babe you get your way. I can give you the credit card.

Todd

I could have done a better training practice than these kids did. The military training is so much harder. These kids have no idea what they are doing, but Jaxson's dad did leave him as acting Alpha while he was gone with his wife and their other son. I hope this Dorian kid realizes I could rip his head off with my bare hands. The military trained me in special forces and I know how to take a life just with my hands it isn't just a figure of speech when I say that. Todd you need to calm down, Nikola Love's Dorian and that is her mate you know there is nothing we can do about the person the moon goddess chose for our daughter to be with as her mate. I think Dorian is a sweet boy and I can see that he loves our daughter very much. Lily said. Well picked by the moon goddess or not I am going to keep an eye on that boy. He better do right by Nikola or he will have to deal with me. Todd you cannot control everything.

Kaden

I can see that all of this is affecting Lauren in a very emotional way. She has had to raise Hailey pretty much all on her own. Hunter died when Hailey was so young. But I am going to be here for Lauren, it is the time of our lives where we need to do whatever we want to do as far as being together, traveling, or whatever comes to mind that we want to do. The kids are planning a shopping trip for prom and graduation. Hailey and Jaxson are engaged to get married. Lauren did Hailey ever say what day in June her and Jaxson want to get married or what kind of wedding they want to have. No babe they have not talked to me about any of that. Why are you asking? Well since it is supposed to be the responsibility of the bride's parents to pay for the wedding I want to help with that. Oh sweetheart that is so nice of you to want to do that but you don't have to, I can pay for the wedding. Lauren will you please let me help you. I know you have had to be independent for so long, but we are a couple now and soon we will be getting married. I already told you that I think of Hailey as my daughter. Okay, okay babe. I am sorry, I am so used to doing everything myself when it comes to you Hailey. I do need to learn to let go and let you help me.

Katie

Lena, LENA!!!! What, what is t Katie? I have some news. Well tell me. Lena said in her usual hateful tone. Hailey and her best friend Nikola are both going shopping for their prom dresses and their graduation dresses. I can see that Lena is getting really mad. Luna please don't get mad at me. You said that you wanted me to report whatever they are doing. Oh don't worry I am not mad at. OMG THAT BITCH!!!! That WHORE!! Lena started screaming. He should have had me as Luna of that stupid pack, I am the one that should be with Jaxson. But since I was turned away, thrown out like trash I will get even with them. Katie I do not want you to get caught sneaking over here to tell me things. If Jaxson or anyone from that pack catches you coming out here you will be banned forever from the pack and I need you to keep being my spy. So sneak back to where you were and thank you for letting me know. You're welcome Lena, I thought that maybe you could catch her out there shopping and do whatever you had planned. God I hate Lena so much, but she would be my way back to Dorian. That is the only reason I agreed to spy on what is going on with the pack, with Jaxson and Hailey is because Lena agreed to help me get Dorian back.

Hailey

It is so nice having my BWFF here at school with. Not only did Dorian get his way about showing Nikola around school, but so did I. It was me, Jax, Dorian, and Nikola walking through the halls at school after Nikola and Chad got their schedules from the office. I was even more excited when I seen on her schedule that she has all classes with me. I stuck my tongue out at Dorian when he started whining like a puppy that he only has two classes with Nikola. Oh Dorian, stop whining like that you have the rest of your life to spend with her. Besides whining is not attractive. I start laughing at the look Dorian gave me when I told him that whining is not attractive. He smiles at all of us and says I know. The school days are flying by now that I have my BWFF here with me, and of course my mate too. I have started feeling much better over the last few weeks. Are you and Dorian coming for dinner tonight? I asked Nikola. Oh you can count on it. Well then that is it, breakfast and dinner at my house every day and night and then once we are done with school you can be at my house for lunch too. I feel Jax lean down and he whisper's in my ear. Now when will we have time for us to be alone and have some fun together? Don't you have fun when Dorian and Nikola are over? I laugh when I say that because I know what Jax is actually talking about.

It feels so good to see the entire family sitting around the table at mine and Jax's house in our dinning room. The only ones that are missing is Jax's mom, dad, and little brother Jace. They will be back from their vacation soon. Jax and I can not wait to tell them the good news together. But for now I am enjoying this time. I feel so good about everything and I could not be happier. Hailey have you thought about setting up appointments with wedding coordinators? My mom asked me and brought me out of my thoughts. No I haven't yet, I have been looking at reviews for some of the coordinators but I didn't know if it would be to much to try and have a coordinator. The cooks tonight made so much food I felt like I ate way to much. They had made my favorite lasagna, salad, and garlic bread. It was so amazing but after we all ate, and talked it was getting late and everyone was getting ready to leave to go to their own homes. First Nikola and Dorian. Good night Hailey and Jax. I gave Nikola a big hug. Thank you for coming tonight. Well I know I would not have heard the end of it from Alpha. We all laughed. As Nikola and Dorian walked out the door we also said good night to Lily and Todd who followed Nikola and Dorian out the door. Then my mom and Kaden. Good night mom. I gave her a big hug and then I give Kaden a hug and I said to him, make sure you take good care of my mom. Oh don't you worry she will be very well taken care of. I'm going to hold you to that. Good night mom. I heard Jax say to my mom which made me feel really good that he is comfortable enough to call her mom. After everyone was finally gone, not that I didn't enjoy them all being here I told Jax that I am so tired. I feel Jax rubbing my back and my shoulders which feels very good. Babe, you know it won't be long until we will be planning our family. Jax says to me. How long is a female wolf pregnant? I ask Jax. I am not sure, but I think it's around fifteen to twenty week's. Wow that is not long at all. We still have a lot to do before I get pregnant. What do you mean we have a lot to do? I made sure we have a nursery for a boy and a girl. I thought you liked them both. I do like both of them, but a baby is going to need clothes and diapers. I can buy neutral color clothing. Not to mention that we still need to plan our wedding. I reminded him. Also there is still all the things you have to do as Alpha, and the things I have to do as Luna. Babe I want you to relax and not worry about so much stuff. I know stress cannot be good for you, if we are going to have a baby. I love that you are so caring, but I am not stressing about everything that needs to be done I just don't want us to fall behind in our duties especially to our pack. I have an idea that might help you to relax. Jax said to me. Oh you do, do you? He grabs my hand, but I was really confused at first when he takes me outside in the yard. What are we doing out here babe? I asked him. I thought we could go for a run. That is something I have wanted us to do together ever since your first phase. Jax and I walk towards the edge of the woods and strip down to almost nothing. Once we phased we take off running through the woods with not a care in the world. It was the most awesome feeling of being free that I have ever felt. Once we came back to the house we didn't worry about finding clothes to put on, we just phased back into our human form went inside and upstairs to the shower. After our shower I really was so tired that when my head hit the pillow I was out like a light.

Lauren 🐾

On the drive home I just kept smiling as I looked out the windshield as Kaden drove us back to my house. What are you thinking about over there with that smile on your face? I jumped because Kaden startled me out of my thoughts. It's going to be so different that Hailey is graduating, and going to be getting married. I cannot believe that my baby is starting not just a life but a real adult life of being married and I am sure she will be having a baby probably not long after she gets married if she is like me. It is such an amazing feeling. I can still remember when I found out I was pregnant with Hailey. I could not wait until I had her. I know you are going to be a very good grandma when the time comes. I looked at Kaden when he said that to me. You are going to be a very good grandpa. Well that is if Hailey is willing to let me be a grandpa to the baby. Oh Kaden, I know Hailey is going to be very happy to have you as the baby's grandpa. I wonder if she is going to have anyone to walk her down the aisle. Kaden said. I know what he is getting at. Well sweetheart I am hoping by the time she is planning her wedding she will realize that her father trusted you to be with me then she will ask you to walk her.

Jaxson

I scoop Hailey up in my arms and carry her to our bed. As I walk upstairs I cannot help but to keep looking at my beautiful mate. I could not be happier. I want to make sure she has everything she could ever want or need. I cannot believe I almost messed all this up in the beginning when I first saw her at school. But then again I knew she was mine and I was not going to let anyone or anything get in the way of my mate and I being together. Now that we are together nothing or no one will ever come between us. I love you Jax. Hailey said in her very sleepy voice. I love you more than you will ever know, but I am going to spend each and every day showing you just how much I love you. Hailey and I take a quick shower before going to bed. Once we were done in the shower I carry Hailey over and lay her down in the bed. I walk over to the window and look out. I can see Laine running towards the house. I run downstairs. I don't want anyone waking Hailey up. He reaches the door as I am opening it. Alpha. He says all out of breath. What is it Laine? I got news about your mom, dad, and brother. What do you mean? They are on vacation. They were taken by Alaric's vampires and some rogues. They were on their way back home. That is all I know, I don't know where they were taken to. I could feel Cain trying to come out, I was instantly mad. Get the rest of the pack together we are going to find my parents and my brother. I will kill that vamp. I don't want Hailey, or Nikola going though. Hailey is very tired and Nikola is pregnant. Yes alpha. Damnit!!!! I yelled not thinking. I start to go upstairs to kiss Hailey before going to instruct the pack on what is going on and come up with a plan to rescue my family when I saw Hailey starting to come down.

Hailey 🐺

As I start to go downstairs I see Jax coming up. What is going on babe? I was just coming up to give you a kiss. I have to go get the pack together. Why? I asked him. Laine just came and told me that Alaric kidnapped my mom, dad, and brother. Oh my god, let me go get ready. NO!!!! Hailey I don't want you going. Why not? You're very tired and I want you to get some rest, I don't want to take any chances that something might happen to you. But you can ask Nikola to come over here since I will be having Dorian to go with us. I told Laine not to let Nikola go either. I told him to tell Dorian that I want Nikola to stay home or she can come over here and be with you, but you two are not going. Jax I am fine I can. He cut me off. I said you're not going and that's that. But they are my family too. Hailey please, there is no time to argue. I want you to stay home. Call Nikola or mind link her and have her to come stay with you. FINE!!!! I said as I stomp off back up to our room. Jax followed me. I am sorry babe, but I have to protect you. I almost lost you once I am not taking any chances now. Okay, but please be careful and let me know what is going on. I will, I promise. Now you can call Nikola. I have to get going.

Dorian 🐺

As soon as I got the news about Jaxson's parents and brother I got right up. I have known them my entire life and they are like my second family. I will rip that asshole's throat out when we find them. What's going on? I hear Nikola ask. Jaxson's mom, dad, and brother were taken by Alaric, and some other vamps, and some rouge's I have to go help find them. I'm coming too. No Nikola I need you to stay here. I see Nikola get really still and quiet. I'm sorry babe, but I don't want you to get hurt. Hailey just mind linked me and asked me to come over to her house while you and Jaxson are gone. Okay you can go over with me. I want to make sure you get there safely. As Nikola is getting ready I mind link Jaxson. I will be there soon, I am bringing Nikola to hang out with Hailey. Good I want them both to be safe. So do I. With that I closed the mind link. Nikola and I headed out the door and off to Jax and Hailey's.

Alaric 🐺

Take these prisoner's to the dungeon and lock them in separate cages. I know that mutt Jaxson and his clan of mutts will be coming for them. I will wipe them out. Yes master. Wadjet say's as she makes Corbin, Jace, and Vondra walk to the dungeon in front of her by force with her mind. I will have my submissive vampires and rouge's waiting for those mutts and when they come we will destroy all of them.

Lena 🐺

I heard you have Jaxson's parents and brother here. I said to Alaric. Yes I do and when those mutts show up to try and save those worthless wolves I will destroy all of them and the land shall belong to me. NO!!!! Alaric looks over at me when I yell at him. I do not want Jaxson hurt at all. Oh silly child, I plan to destroy all of them. I SAID I DON'T WANT MY JAXSON HURT!! Do you have a hearing problem? Alaric hisses at me but I don't care. I am not afraid of some vampire. If you are not on my side I will have my spy to let Jaxson know just where to find you and that you have your little cronies waiting. Do you understand me? Oh I understand you. Alaric says. I don't trust a nasty vampire so I mind link Jessie and tell her to stand by incase I need her in a hurry to give a message of importance to Jaxson. Okay Lena I will be waiting to hear from you.

Jaxson 🐺

Once my pack was here and everyone was quite I started telling them what is going on. Okay everyone, Laine has informed me that my parents, and brother have been taken by Alaric. I don't know where he has taken them so we have to be really careful. Watch out for each other. We are going to rescue my parents and brother and I want you all to make sure and rip the heads off all the vamps that try to get in your way, and to rip the throats out of any rouge's that try to get in your way too. When we find my family and once they are safe we burn down whatever place that blood sucker is holding them in. YES ALPHA. I hear everyone yell. Let's go. I tell them all. Everyone shifts into their wolf and we are all off to find my parents and my brother. I mind link Hailey. We are taking off now babe. I love you. I love you too babe, and please be careful. Come back to me safely. I will. I turn off the mind link so I can have all my focus on finding my family. Damn you blood sucker. I wanted tonight to be about spending time with my mate. But because he wants to be an asshole and take my family.

Jace 🐺

I just got a message from Jax. What did he say? My dad ask. He has the pack and the Midnight Moon Pack ready and they are coming for us. How can he find us? We don't even know where we are at to let him know. My mom says. I am sure he will find our scent mom don't worry. I still have the mind link open to Jax. Be careful brother he has rouge's and blood sucker's waiting for you count on that. I know brother. Jaxson say's back to me. Do you know where you are at? No he had us under some kind of black out spell that he had that witch put on us. Well as long as he didn't cover anything with a potion and wolf bane I should be able to find your scent. He didn't use any wolf bane on any of us. Do you know where he got you at? I think we were just fifteen miles north of the pack land when a tire blew out on the car. When dad and I got out to fix the tire that is when we were attacked. Oh don't worry we are all coming and we won't stop until we find you. Okay Jax, try to hurry. I will. I close the mind link.

Jaxson 🐺

I had Lauren to bring her pack, Midnight Moon Pack. They had not been together until Lauren and Hailey came to town, but once Lauren was back she got her pack back together. Kaden was always the best warrior of that pack and I know he has stayed in shape. He showed that when we were all training. I am also glad to have Nikola and Chad's dad Todd. With Todd and Kaden I know we will not lose this fight. I mind link the group I have with me. You all will have to find my parents and brothers scent. I was mind linking with Jace and he has no idea where they are at. He told me that him and my parents were put under a blackout spell. If any of you pick up on their scent before me, let me know. Yes Alpha. I heard Kaden say. I hate not being with Hailey right now. This should be a time that she and I are together all the time. We just moved into our new house and we have all these plans that we need to make. All the more reason I am going to rip the heads off of any blood sucker I find. Just then I hear hissing in the woods. I can smell their stinch. We have blood sucker's up a head I yell out in mind link to my pack and the Midnight Moon Pack. I see some of both packs attacking the vamps. I can see vampire head's flying through the air as their head's are being torn off the bodies. I smell my mom and dad's scent's, but I don't understand why I don't smell Jace's scent. They better not have done anything to my brother. I will make Alaric wish he had never been born. Just then I run into something so hard it knocks me backwards.

Alaric 🐺

I see Jaxson's wolf running, but I don't think he see's me standing right in front of him. His body hits me hard enough to where he is knocked backwards and land's hard on the ground. Hello Jaxson. He just stairs up at me. I am going to rip your head off of that stinking body of yours, but before I do you are going to know what it feels like to be tortured. Hahahahahahaha my evil laugh comes out. Oh Jaxson you have no power over me. You are nothing but a whinny little worthless mutt that I will very much enjoy destroying. As Jaxson gets up and comes running after me I grab him and toss him against a tree. I could hear a thud as his body crashes into a tree. I walk over, I kick him in the ribs. He howl's as he rolls away. I walk slowly over to where he landed, as I lift my hand with the knife in it I feel a hard hit from my back that knocks me to the ground. I look up and see a white wolf coming towards me. I hear someone say Lauren.

Lauren 🐾

When I saw that blood sucker Alaric knock Jaxson down it went right through me. That blood sucker is the reason my husband is no longer here. It was the attack of his vampires and the rouges that followed him that attacked our pack and killed Hunter. I will not let him hurt Jaxson. Hailey needs him. When I saw Alaric lift his hand I saw the knife, and that brought all the memories flooding back from the attack where he killed Hunter. I run over and knock Alaric off of Jaxson. You will not hurt him!!!! I think and I howl as I knock him off of Jaxson. Alaric hisses at me and starts towards me with his fangs out. Just as he is about to pounce on me I see Cain jump on him. They both roll. All of what was left of the rouges and vampires are running back into the woods. So I run in the direction of Jaxson and Alaric. By the time I get to where they are all I see is black smoke?

Jaxson 🐾

You really think you are going to get the best of me you blood sucker? I say to Alaric as I am running towards him.

It hurts to move from hitting that tree and then from Alaric kicking me when I was trying to get back up, but I am not going to let that stop me. DIE YOU SON OF A BITCH!! I yell as I run up to him and jump up on him knocking us both to the ground. I feel someone knock me off of Alaric. I look up once I was on the ground and see Dark, which is Todd's wolf. Dark and Alaric go rolling on the ground. I hear a hiss like I have never heard before. Right after the hiss I see a ball of smoke rise up from where Dark and Alaric are at. Once the smoke clears enough where I could see there was a shape walking towards where Lauren and I are at. It is Dark, he was walking up to us and he had Alaric's head dangling from his mouth. Dark had torn Alaric's head off after he had kicked that blood sucker off of me. I groan as I try to get back up. Now to find my parents and my brother. As I start to try and pick up their scent I get a mind link from Laine. I think I found your parents and brother Alpha. Where are they? I ask. Not far from where you are, just keep heading north and you will find their scent getting stronger. Laine was right as I was running north I picked up their scent more and more. It looked like a regular house only dark as only a blood sucker would want it. When we went in I could smell the stench of vampires all around. I hear a hiss and I grabbed the vampire by his leg and sink my teeth in. Where is my family? I don't have to tell you anything. He says to me. I squeeze his leg even harder with my teeth. His eyes look like they were going to pop out of his head. Okay, okay, they are in the dungeon. Show me. I said as I let loose of his leg, but not letting go all the way. I walk behind the vamp. As we go down into the darkness of the dungeon I could smell other people down there. I yell out for my mom, my dad, and my brother. I can hear them yelling back. When I got to the cage's that they were being held in I realize it is pure silver. Open it vamp.

NO!! He hissed. OPEN IT NOW!! I yell at him. Just then I see Lauren poke something almost all the way through the vamp's side. He hissed but he moves over to the cage's and open's each one. Once my family was free I knock the vamp against the wall hard and I tell everyone else to run out. Once we were all outside I set the house on fire. You could hear all the screaming and hissing from the vampires for miles.

Hailey 🐾

I was getting worried because I have not heard anything from Jax since he said he was leaving with the pack. Nikola said she has not heard from Dorian either. Maybe I should mind link Jax. I said to Nikola. If he responds ask him about Dorian. I will. I open the mind link. Babe are you okay? Yes babe, we are headed home now. I'm sorry if I worried you. Did you find your parents and your brother? Yes we did, and Alaric is dead thanks to Todd. We burned down the house and dungeon where he was keeping my parents and Jace. Is Dorian okay? Nikola is very worried. Yes he is fine, he is right next to me. Okay babe, please be safe and come home. I will be there very soon my love. I closed the mind link. Jax says that they are on their way back here now. Oh thank god. Nikola said. Did you ask about Dorian. Yes, Jax said Dorian is fine and right next to him. About that time the door crashes open. Where are you? I heard a female's voice. Nikola and I both jumped up and went racing into the front room and seen Lena standing there. What are you doing crashing down my door and coming into my house? You bitch, if it wasn't for you I would have my Jaxson. She lunges for me as soon as she said that. I put up my fist as she runs for me. She runs right into it. She tries to grab my throat but by that time Nikola was behind her grabbing her by her hair and dragging her back away from me. What the hell Lena, this is my house and I am with Jax, you will NEVER get my mate. You know how pissed off Jax would be if you were to hurt me. I should be with Jax not you, you are nothing you don't know him like I do. As she says that she gets away from Nikola for a short moment and tries to come at me again but I was ready. I knock her to the ground. As I get on top of her and start punching her in the face Nikola is kicking her in the side. She doesn't stand a chance. LENA!! I stopped punching her and Nikola stops kicking her when we hear Jaxson yell her name. I got up off of Lena as and I went over to stand next to him. Why is she here? He asked me. She knocked our door in and came in at me and Nikola. Jax walks over to Lena grabs her by her hair, pulls her up from the ground, walks her over to the door tosses her out of the door and yells DON'T COME BACK TO MY LAND OR MY HOUSE AGAIN!!!! I run up to Jax and put my arms around him. I am so glad you are okay. I was so worried. I told you I was okay. Jax said as he wrapped his arms around me and leans down to kiss me. I feel him kind of stiffen his body and I back away. Babe what is wrong? Nothing, I am just kind of sore after fighting. Do I need to get the doctor here? No I will be okay.

Lena 🐾

I let out a howl as I run back to the cave I've been living in. That BITCH!! She poisoned Jaxson's mind. That's okay though. I will get my love back. All I need is a potion from Wadjet. A potion that will make Jaxson sleep until I can get him here. I know he still loves me. If he does not come back to me I will kill his bitch. Then he will have nothing just like what he left me with when he turned me away, threw me out just like some trash. James. Lena call's out. Yes Lena. I need you to go find Wadjet and bring her to me. Yes Lena. James say's as he bow's to me then turns to run out of the cave to go find the witch. James used to be in mine and Jaxson's pack too, but when Jaxson got rid of me he got rid of James too. I don't know what James did to get kicked out of the pack but he will return to the pack when I am Luna again.

Corbin 🐺

Jaxson I am so proud of you, the way you have looked over the pack and came to rescue your mother, Jace, and me. Dad I would have stopped at nothing to find you all. Now that you are home though Hailey and I have some news to tell you. Oh yeah son, what do you have to tell me. Well it is something we want to tell you, mom, and Jace. I hope everything is okay. Yes everything is better than okay. Jaxson says with a big smile on his face.

Jaxson 🐺

I am so happy that I was able to rescue my family and bring them home safely. Dad, Hailey and I have some news to tell you. What do you have to tell me? Dad asked me. Well it is something that Hailey and I want to tell you, mom, and Jace all at the same time. I hope everything is okay. Oh things are more than okay. I look at Hailey who is standing next to me with a smile as big as the one I have on my face. She walks over and gives my mom and dad a hug. Well do you want to tell them babe? I asked Hailey. Yes. She says. While you all were gone, Jax asked me to marry him. But I don't see a future for us at all with his attitude. Hailey says with a smirk on her face. My mom, dad, and brother all just look over at me. Son! My dad says. I'm just joking Mr. Carter. Call me Corbin, or dad. When you say Mr. Carter I feel like my dad is here. My dad says to Hailey. Jax did ask me to marry him and I said yes. My mom gets all excited. Omg!! I hear my mom scream. Then she comes over to Hailey and I and hugs us both. Now that is news worth coming home too. My dad says. Congrats bro. Jace say's. Thank you Jace. Now that you've heard the good news. Oh no I hear my mom say. Yes there is something else going on. As you may have seen I threw Lena out the door when we got back. Yes what was she doing here? My dad asked. She attacked Hailey. OMG... my mom says. I see Jace's eyes change two black. Calm down little brother. I sent her away, but she might be a problem so I mind linked the border guards and told them there is a high alert, to be on the lookout for her. Just then Hailey collapses to the ground, my Dad tried to catch her and got her before she hit her head. What's going on? Why did she collapse? My mom asked in shock. I don't know mom. I mind link the pack doctor. I need you here now, Hailey just collapsed. I'm on my way. It will be okay Hailey, the doctor is on his way. I won't let anything happen to you. I could feel my mom and dad around me. She's going to be fine son. But I did not take my attention off of her. I swear to God if this has anything to do with Lena attacking I will KILL THAT BITCH myself. No one or nothing is going to hurt Hailey. When the pack doctor got here Jace let him in. I carried Hailey up to our room so the doctor could examine her. Jaxson I need you to wait outside. You can either wait outside the door, or you can go downstairs with your parents and brother. I am not leaving Hailey. Jaxson, I know you and I know if you think I am doing anything that might hurt Hailey you will not be able to control yourself and

I don't need you interrupting anything I do. You're right doc. I will go wait downstairs.

Jace 🐻

I follow Jax into his office after he comes back downstairs. She is going to be okay Jax. I hope you are right bro. Just then Mom and Dad came in. Jaxson you impressed us tonight. I knew you had it in you to take over the pack while we were gone, but you have done so much more. Dad says. He's very worried about Hailey right now dad. Jace say's. I know he is. Listen Jaxson if there is anything I can do you just name it and I am there for you. I really appreciate what you all are doing, but really you all should go home and get some rest. You all have been through enough. I can take you both home and then I can come back here and help Jax with whatever he needs. I am not going anywhere until I know that Hailey is okay. Mom says. I agree with your mother. Jaxson and Hailey need us here. Our dad says. Now that I am back I can make sure that the guards and warriors are up to speed on everything and I can help with training as well. Yes brother your old job is still here and waiting. I am going to need you to be doing that for sure. Even if nothing is wrong with Hailey I am not leaving her again at least until I know she is okay. I could see in Jaxson's eyes that he is very worried. Are you worried about Lena? No it is not Lena I am worried about. It is Hailey. I know she is a strong wolf, but I want her safe. I almost lost her in a rogue attack, the first one we had after Hailey and I moved into this house. I know that did have you very worried, but maybe it is her stubbornness that helped her heal. Just then the doctor walks in.

Pack Doctor 🐺

Jaxson I need Hailey to be brought into the hospital. She looks to be okay on the outside, but I cannot see what is going on the inside with out having her at the hospital so I can run some tests on her. Okay doc I will bring her right in.

Hailey 🐺

It was almost like a dream. I could hear everyone around me but I could not open my eyes. Then I see a white light. Not like what you would see on TV when someone is close to death but it was lights that led me from the reality of everything to dreaming. I'm in a field with Jax, and I can see that I am very much pregnant. Jax and I are very happy. I have on a red and white spaghetti strap sundress. Jax has on jeans and a pale blue t-shirt. We are just walking through a field hand in hand, smiling and talking. We walk up on a blanket laying in the field, and a picnic basket filled with fruits, cheeses, and bread. There was even a bottle that look like wine, but it was grape juice. We lay down on the blanket and Jax starts feeding me the strawberries as I lay with my head on his lap. We are talking and having a great time. Just then a wolf approaches us. It is a dark gray wolf and it is not from our pack. Jax jumped up and is looking straight at the wolf. I could tell from the look the wolf has it is not there to make friends with us. It was already showing teeth. Of course we are in the middle of nowhere. Then I hear Jax start talking to the wolf. Lena, you don't want to do this. You need to leave Hailey and I alone. Hailey has not done anything to you. You and I were through long before she even came around so you can not blame her for me not being with you, you were turned away from the pack before Hailey came around as well so you cannot blame her for that. You need to just turn around and go back to where you came from and leave us alone. I see Jax reach for me so I raise my hand and grab his, he pulls me up and has me to stand behind him. Lena it is in your best interest for you to just walk away now. I could tell that the wolf was not going to listen. I see the wolf coming towards us and it was moving very fast. Jax tells me to back away fast. As I back away I see Jax moving towards the wolf. Jax shifts into his beautiful wolf. Jax in his wolf form Cain takes off running towards Lena's wolf. They meet in the air and when they land Lena is on top of Cain. I see Lena going down to bite Cain, but that is when I realize I am starting to wake up. I have no idea where I am when I wake up.

Jaxson

Doc I will not be able to control myself if anything happens to her. I know Jaxson and I am going to do everything I can to make sure she is okay. I am sure there is nothing serious, but I want to be positive. Thank you doc.

As I walk back into Hailey's room I see that she is waking up. Babe are you okay? Where am I? What happened? You are in the hospital, you collapsed while we were talking to my mom and dad, and Jace about us getting married. Do you remember that? Yes I do, but why am I in the hospital? I want to make sure there isn't anything seriously wrong with you. I am going to take very good care of you. It scared the hell out of me when you collapse. I'm sorry Jax, I didn't mean to scare you. Just then she reached her hand out to me. I walk over to her and set on the side of her bed holding her hand. How are you feeling? I have a headache. Well you did hit your head on the floor when you fell. I tried to catch you so you wouldn't hit your head, but that was the one thing I was not quick enough at. It's okay babe, all that matters is that you are here with me. How long do I have to be here? Just until we know that you are okay. What about the pack? Who is there to take care of everything? Dorian and Nikola stayed to watch over everything. Mom, dad, and Jace is here waiting to see how you are doing. Where is my mom? Did anyone call her? I haven't yet because I didn't want to worry her I wanted to wait until we knew what is going on. That is probably a good idea since she would freak out. We need to make sure you are better Hailey, we still have graduation to go through. Hailey got a smile on her face. Yes and after graduation we can get married. Yes we can, so see you have to get to feeling better because we have a lot to do.

Pack Doctor 🐺

I see you are awake Hailey? How are you feeling? Well I have a little bit of a headache. That is to be expected with a head trauma. But I have not seen any injury serious or not but I still want to keep you overnight for observations. If all goes well you can go home tomorrow, but I want you to take it easy when you do go home for at least a few days. Yes doc. Hailey said.

Hailey 🐺

The doctor kept his word. The next morning I was released and my headache was gone. Of course Jax would not allow me to do anything on my own, not even walking out to the car. He had a nurse to get a wheelchair and push me out to the car. As soon as the nurse brought me up to the car Jax got out and help me into the front passenger seat, he even put my seatbelt on for me. Jax come on you're going a bit overboard don't you think. Nope, the doctor said to take it easy. Yes he said take it easy not be a vegetable. Hailey you are going to be waited on hand and foot. I have a feeling I would not win this one even if I try to argue with you. Hahahahaha you are right you wouldn't win. You are my mate and it is my job to make sure you are okay.

I was actually happy to be back home and in my own bed. I hate hospitals. Of course Jax had to carry me up to our room and lay me in the bed. I just wonder if he is going to carry me around in town when Nikola and I go shopping for our graduation dresses, and if he is going to carry me through the shop and try the dresses on me. I just laugh at the thought. Babe I have to go down to my office to go over some paperwork. If you need anything you can text me. Will you hand me my phone please Jax. Yes of course. Do you need anything else before I go down to the office? No I think I will be okay. I'm going to call Nikola and make the arrangements for her and I to go shopping in a couple of days for our graduation dress is and our prom dresses. Okay babe, but make sure you get some rest too. I will. I love you Hailey. I love you too Jax.

Jaxson 🐾

Jace, Dorian, I need you both in my office now. They both followed me into the office. I want Lena found. I'm going to kill that bitch myself. She could have caused serious harm to Hailey. I am not taking any chances. If we were to take her to the elders for them to decide what to do with her she would get a death sentences anyway. We all know that causing harm to a Alpha or a Luna is a sentence of death. She was warned when I broke up with her not to mess with me. She didn't listen so she shall die by my hands. Yes Alpha. Both Jace and Dorian said. The pack member that brings her to me will be greatly rewarded. Yes Alpha. Dorian said.

Hailey

By the time the weekend was over I was back to my normal self and Jax was letting me up a little. Nikola and I went shopping for our prom and graduation dresses. I can not believe we are graduating high school tomorrow. I know. I am so excited too. Nikola said. It's almost a relief to me. I feel like I will have more freedom from my dad. Your already living with Dorian, how much more freedom do you need from your dad? I asked Nikola with a little chuckle. Well you know he said that he told me that if I start missing school that he would make me go back home. Now he won't have that hanging over my head. That is true. We have so much coming up we are going to be so busy.

Corbin

I could tell that there is something going on with Jaxson. I know my boys very well, I have been able to read them since they were born. I'm pretty sure what ever it is will be relieved once I tell him that I am stepping down as Alpha and handing it all over to him. We will have to do a coronation ceremony, but with graduation coming up I know Vondra will want to have a celebration for Jaxson, Hailey, Dorian, and Nikola. I know my mate well enough to know she has to celebrate everything that can be celebrated which is fine by me. It is all part of the Alpha duties to make sure everyone is happy.

Hailey 🐾

I'm finally out of the hospital. I was only there overnight, but that is overnight to long for me, I can not stand hospitals. Ever since my dad died it just creeps me out to be in one. But at least I have graduation to take my mind off of being in the hospital. Jax, I think I will mind link Nikola and see if she wants to go dress shopping. Okay babe, I can give you some money to get whatever you want. Actually just take the credit card that way you will for sure have enough money. You don't have to give me the credit card babe, just a little cash will be fine. Jax gave me a look that tells me he is not going to give in. I want you to have whatever dresses you want for graduation and prom. Jax we don't have to go to prom. Hailey I am not going let you miss one of the most important nights of your life. Okay, okay I know not to argue with you when your mind is made up. It's a good thing because you know I would take you myself and we would not leave the store until you have picked out a dress for each event. I know. I said with a pouty face. After Jax gave me the credit card and then went into the office I opened the mind link to Nikola. Hey can you go shopping with the? Jax gave me the credit card to buy the dresses with. Yes I can go, I was about to mind link you anyway to ask when you would like to go. I guess Dorian has to go over to your place to do some work with Jaxson. Okay so I will see you when you two get here, then you and I can leave from here. Sounds good to me. We will be there in a few. I closed the mind link and started getting ready to go shopping with my bwff.

Nikola

Babe we need to get going, Hailey is waiting on me and I know Jaxson doesn't like for you to be late. Okay I am as ready as I am going to be. Alright then let's go. I start running out to the car, racing Dorian out there and of course I always win. You know babe, if you let Jaxson see me beating you every time racing to the car or anywhere for that matter he just might make me Beta. Dorian just gives me a look and I laugh as I get into the front passenger seat of our car. We don't live very far from Hailey and Jaxson's so it only takes us about ten minutes for us to get there. I am so excited to get to ride in the new car that Jaxson got for Hailey. The car is so awesome. It is all black with some chrome wheels, dark tinted windows all around. Everyone that sees the car is just in awe of it because it is brand new and very few of that car was made and so expensive that not many people can even afford this car. But having the money that Jaxson has he could afford anything for Hailey. I'm just so glad that she is happy and that she has her mate. Dorian didn't try to race me inside of Hailey and Jaxson's house. I know he didn't want Alpha to see him get beat by a girl. I laughed at the thought. What's so funny babe? Dorian asked me. Nothing my love, just a thought that popped into my head. Have fun doing all that work with Alpha. Oh I am sure you and Hailey will have more fun than I will. I just smile at him and I give him a kiss before he goes to Jaxson's office and I go to see if Hailey is ready. HAILEY WHERE ARE YOU! I yelled through the house. That is what Hailey and I used to do to each other when we were younger and I would go to her house or she would come to mine. We drove our parents nuts by doing that too, but we still did it. I know when we have children of our own we will have to chill out on doing that. I'm up in my room Nikola. Come on up. I thought you would be ready by now. I am almost ready, just putting on some lip gloss and some eyeliner and then I will be ready. Did someone get up late? I asked Hailey with a smirk on my face. Hey Nikola. Hailey said back to me as she laughed. You know how it is, or at least you should know by now. Hailey says with a smile.

Hailey 🐾

I tried getting up early enough so that I would be completely ready by the time Nikola got here this morning so she and I could go shopping, but Jax kept pulling me back down on the bed and kissing my face all over. Don't take this the wrong way because I do love him with all my heart, but sometimes he can be such a pain especially when I need to get ready for the day. So of course when Nikola got here I was finishing up getting ready. I hear her yell through the house for me the way she and I have always done when we would go to each other's homes when we were younger. Our parents hated it that we would come in yelling for the other but they never tried to stop us. I'm up in my room finishing getting ready Nikola, come on up I'm almost done. I know Nikola is very excited about going to town in the new car Jax bought me as a graduation gift. Since I have been driving the car people that see me in it always stop's everything they are doing just to stare at me and the car. I think they are mostly looking at the car but it's only because my car is brand new just out on the market and very expensive. There are so many people that want this car but not many can afford it. When Jax gave me this car I told him that people are going to think that I am just trying to show off because my mate has more money than he knows what to do with. Of course Jax reply was that he didn't care what other people think he just wants to make me happy. So I accepted the car with a smile. So what do you think Nikola should we go to the regular department store, or should we check out the new dress shop that just opened last week. OMG Hailey I honestly don't know if I can afford that dress shop it looks really expensive. Nikola and I both just laugh when she said that because Dorian may not have exactly as much money as Jaxson and his family but he is pretty close. Okay so the new dress shop it is. Of course driving through town everyone turns their heads to look as we drive by then. It's always a pain in the ass to find a place to park. You would think with this town not being that big parking would not be that hard, but it is. The mayor of this town wanted to put up a sign in certain parking spots that made the spot only for the Alpha. But that was turned down real fast. Jax's family from the early days to today refuses any special treatment such as a special parking spot at every block of the town.

Jaxson

Now that the girls have left I want to talk to you about something very important Dorian. Anything you need Alpha. I'm glad you said that because I want you to stand up with me at the wedding when I marry Hailey. Don't you think Jace might be hurt by that? I'm asking you to be my groomsmen. Of course Jace is going to be my best man but if something happens to where he cannot be there then that would automatically make you my best man. I would be honored. Good, that was easy enough. Now on to business. We have some transfers to look over, and oh no! What is it alpha? It's the New York pack. Is there a problem there Alpha? Yes there seems to be. Hailey and I are going to have to go there after graduation. It seems that they have a couple of pack members that are starting to be very disrespectful to their Alpha and Beta. The Alpha of the New York pack is asking for me to come with my Luna and see if we can get them in line so they don't have to be turned away and made rogue. I know how much every pack hates having to do that to a member let alone two members. Don't worry Alpha, whenever you have to go you know I am here to take over. Nikola and I can handle the pack and you will not be disappointed. I know and thank you Dorian. You're very welcome Alpha, but thank you for trusting in me enough to choose me as your Beta. Well you know that you are my best friend and I would not trust anyone else. I guess I should let Hailey know tonight that we will have to leave right after the graduation party. I will let Nikola know as well but I will also wait until after the party. I want everyone to have a good time. That is a very good idea Dorian. See it is things like this that make me know I chose wisely making you my Beta. You are so quick thinking.

CHAPTER 5

GRADUATION

Lauren 🐺

I cannot believe that my baby is graduating high school tomorrow. Time goes by so fast. I know it does my love. You know it is not too late we can still have a child that is yours and mine together. Kaden say's. I know, but then again wouldn't that be a bit selfish if we did have a child? How so my love? Well we both have a child or in your case Kaden you have a couple of children that are already grown plus I am not so young anymore. But sweetheart you are still in great shape. You're very sweet Kaden. It is something to think about. But I want you to think about all the things we can still do not being tied down to a baby. I say too Kaden as I give him a very passionate kiss. You keep kissing me like that Lauren and we just might do some baby making practice. I just start laughing when he said that to me. You know how much I love teasing you my love. Yes I know. I said to him with a smile.

Nikola 🐺

Tomorrow is graduation. It is going to be so different not being in school anymore and to be the girlfriend of a Beta. But I am glad that even if my mom and dad have to leave again for whatever reason I will be able to stay here with Dorian and my BWFF Hailey. I hated being away from Hailey. We grew up together and just like her I am not that good at making new friends so I was pretty much alone at the school I went to when my dad was transferred. I was so depressed, but the sadness went away once my dad and mom told me and Chad that we were moving to Kettle Falls. I already knew that Hailey was living here because we Skype every day and when her mom told her that they were moving here Hailey told me. It worked out so perfectly for both Hailey and I. Now we are both starting this amazing life with our amazing guys.

We have to be at the auditorium at 8:00 in the morning for rehearsal, and then the commencement starts at 10:00. I just cannot wait to get it all over with and behind me. I know babe. Dorian said. It was only Dorian that I confided to about everything that happened to me the last time my father was transferred because of the military. He knows how I was beat, and that I was raped by some of my father's military friends but my father and mother would not let me do anything about it because of how harsh the military is on people who commit crimes while in the military. Had I have been able to phase into my wolf back then I would have ripped those guys to shreds that raped me. But now I am here in Kettle Falls with my best friend and my amazing mate who I love with all my heart.

Commencement Day

Hailey 🐾

Babe are we driving? Or are we riding with Nikola and Dorian? Well I have a surprise for you babe. Jax says. Oh yeah, what is it? Look out in the driveway. I go to look out the bedroom window into the driveway and I see a limo out there. OMG babe, you rented a limo for graduation? Yes I did. We will be picking up Dorian and Nikola in it. Well I am almost ready. You better hurry up because we are all going to be late. Jax says to me. Oh pfft, you know I always have to make sure I look just right, and if you think I am bad about being late you don't know Nikola and very well. I always tell her she was probably late for her own birth. Jax and I both laugh when I said that. Okay babe I am ready, what do you think? I asked Jax as I walk out of the bathroom. OHHHHH babe you look so amazing. I think you have really outdone yourself this time. Thanks babe, you are just so sweet. No I really mean it Hailey I think so you look amazing. Well we only graduate high school once, right? Yes you are right and I cannot wait to get you back home and take that dress off of you tonight. I started laughing when he said that. Babe we have the graduation party to attend after the ceremony. Oh I know, but after the party you are mine. Jax walks up to me and puts his arms around me then he bends down and kisses me. Mmmmmm I could stay right here with you all day and night. Jax get a big smile on his face when I said that. But everyone would be wondering why their Alpha and Luna was not at graduation if we did not show up. Well we better get going if we are going to be there in time to get our seats.

Dorian 🦊

Wow Alpha, you really went all out. I said as I climb into the limo right behind Nikola. Well as Luna said, we only graduate high school once. That is very true. You look very beautiful Hailey. Nikola said. Thank you Nikola, you look very beautiful too. The girls just kind of laughed when they told each other how good they looked. Are you we ready to party after the graduation? YES WE ARE!! We all said at the same time. When we got to the school Jax pulls me aside as the girls walk on in. I don't even think they realize we were no longer walking with them. Dorian I need you to be sure you can handle everything while Hailey and I are in New York. I am ready to take over for you Alpha while you and Luna are away and I am more than positive that I can handle the pack. After the graduation party

Hailey and I are going to have to go to New York to help the Alpha of the New York pack with a couple of pack members that are acting up and they want to see if Hailey and I can get them into shape so they don't have to be sent out to become rogue. Alpha you know I will help you with anything. Well I just wanted to ask anyway, and I also wanted to say happy graduation Beta. Happy graduation to you too Alpha. After that we walked in and found our seats. I really don't like the idea of setting through long speeches, and this is just the practice run I wish they would just do the actual graduation and give our diplomas and skip the speeches.

Hailey 🐺

Once they got through all the boring speeches of course it seemed like forever until they finally got through the practice run and to the actual graduation then to my name to come up and get my diploma. Of course my mom, her soon-to-be husband, and everyone they invited was standing and cheering for me I was just ready to get it all done and over with, just get my diploma and then to the fun of the party. I think this will be the first time that Jax will be able to relax since before his parents and his brother was taken by that vampire. Once I got outside of course mom was coming up to me for pictures. I had to go find Nikola, Dorian, and Jax because Mom would not let up on wanting graduation pictures of all of us. But once we got to the after graduation party we all just let loose and was having a really good time. Babe I need to talk to you for a minute. Jax said as he walked up to me. Is everything okay babe? Yes everything is okay, I just need to talk to you about something important. What is it? Let's go over here. We walked away from everyone and Jax turn to me. We are going to have to go to New

York tomorrow. My mouth dropped and my eyes got big. New York, why? Well because they have a couple of members that are not doing what they're supposed to be doing so instead of turning them out and having them become rogues they are trying to give them a chance and have us come there and try to see if we can get them back to the way they should be. I am willing to go with you Jax, but why can't their own Alpha take care of them? He has his hands full with the rest of the pack and he says that these two need more of one-on-one lessons. I think he knows how I am and I think that is why he has asked us to come out there. You know I will go with you babe. Let's have some fun though tonight before we have to leave tomorrow. I said too Jax.

Jaxson

The party seemed like a blur to me, all I could think about was having to go to New York and what all it was going to involve by being there. Even though Hailey and I were having a good time at the party we had to leave a little early because we had to book the tickets for the plane and we had to be up early to leave for the airport. When we got to New York we were met by the Beta of the pack and he drove us to the pack house. Hailey and I were in the office with the Alpha of the New York pack for most of the afternoon going over what is going on with the two pack members and mine and Hailey's plans to straighten them out. Once we were done we were shown to our room so we could unpack and freshen up. Once we were done, then we went down to the dining room for dinner. It was like a feast for Hailey and I. The Alpha here said that he had a special dinner arranged for us and I can see that he did. We were introduced to the entire pack at dinner as well. Once dinner was done Hailey and I were shown around the grounds. We seen the training area, and it was a larger area than the one we have at home so there is a lot of room for Hailey and I to train the two members that are causing trouble and we won't even be near the rest of the pack here as they train. Well Hailey are you ready for this? You know I am. She said with a smile. I really feel kind of sorry for the one you train Hailey. We just both laughed because whatever Hailey puts Devon through he deserves and I know that Hailey will put him through a training that will either break him or he will be out. If it doesn't break him then he is a lot stronger than any other pack member I have ever seen because I have seen Hailey put our strongest pack members in pain. Hailey and I decide to have a small chat with the entire pack real quick.

I just want you all to know that my mate and I will be here until the job that required us to be here for is done. But besides working with the ones we are here for if any of you have any questions feel free to ask them. All we ask is that we are not bother during training as that should not be a problem I don't think since everyone should be very busy with training during training time. Also on behalf of my mate and I thank you for having us here.

Hailey 🐺

As always Jax is up before the sun. I know he is thinking about having to be here. Him nor any other Alpha likes to be called away from their own pack due to some unruly pack members. Those two are very lucky that they are given a second chance at all. Anyway, as soon as I wake up I can smell bacon, eggs, pancakes, waffles, muffins, everything you could think of being made. So when those smells hit my nose I was up and putting on my robe so I could go down for breakfast. I knew I was going to have to power up for this first training session. I have seen the two that Jax and I are going to have to be working with and I can see it will take a lot of work to get these two where they need to be so they will be allowed to stay in their pack.

Once breakfast was over the kitchen help stayed behind to clean up and start the prep for the next meals. Jax and I took Devon, and Alex to the training field to start our discipline training with them. We took them to the far end of the training field so that we are completely away from all the others to where these two cannot even see their pack because we don't want any distractions. We want them to keep complete attention on what we are having them to do. Jax starts by telling Devon and Alex that Alex is going with me and Devon is training with Jax. I took Alex far enough away from Jax and Devon that we would not be distracted. I started Alex out with basic jumping jacks 50 of them, then it was 50 push-ups, then it was 50 laps around the pond and I went with him to make sure he did all 50 and did not slack on the laps. He not only has to do the laps around the pond but he had to carry a log on his shoulders the entire time. Then it was time to see how well he could fight. I could tell by the look on his face that he really thought he was going to be able to kick my ass, but what he didn't realize is that I am not a weak Luna. He went flying into a tree a couple of times. He landed on his back with me over him several times. You have to watch your opponents every move Alex. I have told you that over and over. You're not listening to your Alpha is why my mate and I were called out here to work with you and Devon. Do you want to be pushed out and forced to become rogue? I am being serious. No Luna I don't want to be rogue, but you don't understand the treatment Devon and I have been getting by other members of the pack and we have told our Alpha and he has not done anything about it. What kind of treatment have you and Devon had to deal with that your Alpha should be taking care of and hasn't? Well Josh, Hugh, Franklin, and Ben have all tried to go after our mates and have their way with them. We have had to fight them to get them away from our mates and our mates are not wanting to be with those mutts. They will also destroy our personal property and nothing is being done about that either. The list just goes on and on. Well Alex, I will talk to Jax and then we will have a talk with your Alpha and things will change. But you and Devon have to do your parts with the pack and do what your Alpha says. We should not have to leave our pack to come out here to get you into shape. I understand Luna and I am truly sorry that you and Alpha Jaxson had to do that. It's fine Alex, it's actually a nice change. Don't get me wrong I love the pack Jax and I have, but everyone needs a change of scene once in a while. Alex, you do know that if things don't change and those things keep happening that you and Devon can put in for a transfer to another pack don't you? I don't think that our Alpha would let us transfer. Well if it doesn't stop Alex just try and see if your Alpha will put in for a transfer you can put in for more than one pack and see which one will accept you. Wouldn't that be much better than being sent away and becoming rogue? Yes Luna it would, and thank you. After a couple of hours of training with the guys Jax comes over to me and Alex and tells Alex to go ahead inside and wash up for lunch. He said that he had already sent Devon inside. As soon as Alex was far enough away from us Jax said he wanted to talk to me.

Jaxson 🐺

Hailey I need to talk to you about something. What is it? Devon was telling me things, things that no pack members should have to deal with and that an Alpha should handle if need be. Alex told me too. Hailey said. We need to talk to Alpha Joseph. I agree, we should do that right after lunch. Hailey said. Yes my love, I am sure you are as hungry as I am. Hailey laughed and said, I don't know about that babe even though we are both wolves you can still eat more than I can. I had to laugh at that because she is right. Race you to the pack house? Hailey asked. Sure. I don't know where Hailey gets all her energy, but she beat me to the pack house. As we were going up to the porch I see Hailey's eyes change like she is in mind linking with someone. As soon as her eyes change back I asked her what was going on. Nikola mind linked me and said she needs me to call her. She said it's nothing bad but she has something that she really needs to tell me and that she cannot wait until we get back home. Do you want to call her now? No I told her since everything is okay at home that I would call her right after lunch. Okay well let's get inside and eat.

Nikola 🐺

It has been only a couple days since Jaxson and Hailey left for New York. But I miss my best friend so much. I have Dorian here and he is amazing, but I had been feeling funny for the last week or so and when I told Dorian he suggested that I have the Pack doctor to check me out. I put that off until earlier today but I couldn't put it off any longer because I started getting sick all the time and Dorian said that if I didn't go see the pack doctor or have him to come to the pack house he would carry me to the doctor himself. So I got a hold of the doctor and he came here first thing in the morning. As soon as he was done he talked with Dorian and I. All I wanted to do is talk to Hailey and I couldn't wait so I mind link her and ask her to call me asap. She asked if everything was okay at home and I said yes that there was nothing to worry about that I just needed to talk to her about something important. So she said she would call me after she was done eating lunch. She also told me that she and Jaxson had just finished up with one of the training sessions with the pack members that they went out there to train and get back into pack member shape.

Dorian

I have been so worried about Nikola and she is so stubborn, but I know she is just like Hailey and I did say that when I find my mate I was hoping she was like Hailey, strong and stubborn. But she had not been feeling well in over a week. I could tell something was wrong, but she kept saying that she was fine. But the last couple of days she was getting worse so I told her that if she did not get the pack doctor to come here to the pack house or if she did not go on her own free will to see him that I would put her over my shoulders and I would make her go see him. Well she got the doctor to come here first thing this morning and after he was done checking her out he said he wanted to talk to you both of us so we went into the Alpha office so we would have privacy. When the pack doctor told us what was going on with Nikola I thought I was going to fall over out of my seat. Of course Nikola mind links Hailey right away and told her that she wanted Hailey to call her. I knew Hailey and Jax would think something would be wrong here at home, but

Nikola assured Hailey everything is fine she just had something she needed to tell her. So Hailey is going to call after lunch which reminds me. Nikola and I need to go eat. Babe come on let's go see what the cooks had made for lunch. I will be ahead of you to the table my love. Nikola said with a smile.

Hailey

I cannot believe how much I ate, I guess I was hungrier than I thought I was. But as soon as I was done I asked Alpha Joseph if I could use the phone in his office so I could talk to Nikola privately. He allowed me to use his office phone. It did not take me long to get in there and dial the number to the pack house. Nikola answered on the second ring. What's going on at home? I asked as soon as she answered. I told you through the mind link everything is fine here at home. Then what is so important that you wanted me to call instead of telling me through mind link? Well I haven't been feeling quite right for about a week now, but I didn't think anything about it. Nikola, you should have told me. Jax and I could have worked something out to where someone else could have watched over the pack house while we were gone since you didn't feel well. No, just listen to me Hailey. Okay go ahead. Well finally Dorian told me because I have gotten worse the last couple of days that if I did not have the pack doctor to come to the house or if I did not make an appointment to go see the pack doctor then he would put me over his shoulder and take me himself. Well I don't blame him, but Nikola seriously I can have Jax find someone else to watch over the pack since we won't be gone much longer so you can get some rest and feel better. Hailey if you would just listen you would realize that even if you got someone else to watch over the pack which Dorian nor I want you to do that because me getting rest to get better would not do me any good at this point. OMG Nikola what is going on with you? I could feel the tears start to form in my eyes and Jax walked into the office just then and seeing that I was getting upset so he came over to me and kneeled down in front of me. What's going on babe? What is going on? Do we need to go home? I mouthed that I didn't know yet. All I thought about was when I lost my friend Page to cancer. I could not handle losing Nikola especially now that I finally got her back. HAILEY!!!! Would you just shut up and listen to me. Nikola laughed. Why are you laughing Nikola? This is not funny. Oh stop freaking out Hailey it is something great at least I hope you will be happy. What do you mean you hope I will be happy you're sick Nikola why would I be happy about that? I'm actually not sick. You just told me that you had to see the pack doctor. Why would you have to see the pack doctor if you are not sick? As I said that I seen Jax get a smile on his face. Hailey, I'm pregnant not just pregnant with one pup, but I am going to have three. My mouth dropped, my eyes got great big and I believe I almost dropped the phone. You're what? I'm going to have three pups, Dorian and I are going to have a house full. OMG Nikola I am so happy for you! I wish I was there so I could give you a big hug, oh I cannot wait to come back home so we can go shopping. I know and I cannot wait for you to be back here because I want you and I to go shopping too. As soon as we get back home I am going to start planning a baby shower for you. So you now have my good news. How is everything going with the two in the New York pack? It's going pretty good actually, not as bad as Jax and I thought it was going to be. But I cannot say much yet because there are some things that need to be discussed here that have not been yet so I will tell you about it when we get home. Are you sure everything is okay they're at home? Is everyone on their best behavior? Yes

Luna everything is fine and everyone is on their best behavior. Nikola I told you we are best friends and we always have been, there for you do not have to call me Luna. I know, I just know how to get your attention. Oh funny. Well I better go we have some things to take care of here. But I do miss you and I cannot wait to be home. We miss you too and be safe on your way home. We will. When I get off the phone with Nikola Jax ask me if what he thought was right. Is Nikola pregnant with more than one? Yes she is. Her and Dorian are going to have three babies. That's awesome, speaking of babies. Jax has a big smile on his face. When are we going to start our little family? He asked me while holding on to my hips. Looking down at me and kind of slowly swaying with me. Well we will have to see about that when we get back home won't we. As for now we have duties to attend to. You are right as always. Let's go find Alpha Joseph so we can find out from him his version of what is going on. Sounds like a plan to me. We find Alpha Joseph in the dining room, or what they like to call it the eating room. They don't call it the kitchen, or breakfast, or lunch, or dining room because we all eat every meal in one room.

Jaxson

Alpha Joseph, can Hailey and I have a talk with you in private please? I asked him. He looked a little surprised, but said yes. So Hailey and I went into the office with Joseph. Once we all sat down I started the conversation. So there are things going on among your pack members that you do not know about, or do you know about what has been going on and just not doing anything about it? What do you mean Alpha Jaxson? Well it seems that there are some problems with a few of the other pack members doing and saying things to the pack members that Hailey and I are here to work with that is causing them to be the way they are because they feel like you are not doing anything to prevent what is going on. Hailey and I both seen Alpha Joseph sink back into his seat. Why did they not come to me? Alpha Joseph asked under his breath. They said that they did come to you, but that nothing was being done. Well Alpha Jaxson I am very glad you brought this to my attention and while you are here I want to take care of this that way you and Luna Hailey can see that it is being taken care of. Well Alpha Joseph, you know you can take care of this without us here. But we are willing to be here so someone beside you knows it was taken care of. Thank you Alpha Jaxson. I am sure you can tell me which ones are the actual problems. Yes I can Alpha Joseph. They are Josh, Hugh, Franklin, and Ben. I thought Alpha Joseph's whole face was going to fall off when I told him which ones were causing the problems. Have these members always cause problems with other members of the pack? It's not that Alpha Jaxson, it's that Josh and Hugh are my Beta's. Oh well sounds like we are going to have to take care of this now. Yes Alpha Jaxson. Alpha Joseph called for Josh, Hugh, Franklin, and Ben to the office. As soon as they were all there they sat down. Hailey and I stayed standing, but behind Alpha Joseph's desk while he sat in his seat. Hailey and I could tell that Alpha Joseph is pissed but this matter needs to be taken care of.

Alpha Joseph 🐺

Josh, Hugh, Franklin, and Ben do you all know why I called this meeting with you all? They all just sat there and looked at me like children caught playing somewhere they were not supposed to be. I called this meeting because there are some issues that have been brought to my attention that cannot be let go. We are all family here in this pack. We are supposed to look after each other. Isn't that right? I asked all of them sitting there. Yes Alpha. That's when I slam my fist down on my desk. Then WHY IN THE HELL are you all doing things that is not acceptable around here? What are we doing Alpha? I looked right at Hugh. Are you FUCKING KIDDING ME RIGHT NOW? Making moves on another pack members mate, giving other pack members hard times. None of that is okay. Do you all want to be going through what Devon and Alex is going through right now? Do you all think this is fair to Alex and Devon to have to be going through this extra training with Alpha Jaxson and Luna Hailey. I said screaming at them. You two I pointed to my Beta's You two are supposed to be my Beta's, how the hell am I supposed to be able to trust you to if I cannot trust you two right now, at least not until you two can show me that you can be trusted again. I had to pull these two (I pointed to Hailey and Jaxson) from their pack to come here so I didn't have to pull myself away from the entire pack to take care of Devon and Alex. Do you all realize that I can take the Beta title away from you and turn you all out and you all would become rogues. Is that what you all want? Do you all not like our pack, or family unit that we have here? Franklin spoke up just then and said, I am truly sorry Alpha. I myself and the rest of us do love this pack and we love the family we have here. Thank you Franklin, I will tell you and the rest of you that if things do not stop and if I have to keep Luna Hailey and Alpha Jaxson here longer you four will be thrown out and become rouge's. I think Luna Hailey and Alpha Jaxson are going to finish out the week here and then they will be going back home. So I expect you and everyone to still treat them with respect as they will be here helping with the training exercises. Yes Alpha, we understand and we will treat Alpha Jaxson and Luna Hailey with the up most respect. Thank you all and I will be watching to make sure you all keep your word. You are dismissed.

Hailey 🐾

The next few days went as normal as normal can be with wolf pack's. Just two nights before Jax and I were to leave to go back home to our pack I kept getting a very weird vibe. It wasn't anything I could explain, so I kept it to myself but my wolf Casey was very uneasy all day and no matter what I did I could not get her to settle down. I tried to block her, but that wouldn't even work. So I ended up going through the day as I normally could having breakfast with the entire pack, helping with the training exercises. Everything seemed to be falling into place. Devon and Alex were doing much better and seemed to be in much better moods than they were when Jax and I first arrived here. Jax and I got ready to go to bed as we talked about the day just like we always do every night. It wasn't until after we were fully asleep that it happened. Jax and I both woke up to smelling smoke. We both jump up and heard everyone else scrambling to get out of the house. The house was on fire. We had to make sure that we get everyone out of the house. Things were crazy but once outside we started doing a head count. There was only one person we could not account for. It was Ben. Ben is not out here. I seen Alpha Joseph start to run inside to look for Ben, but Franklin pulls Alpha Joseph back. I go to run back in the house and I feel pack members trying to grab me but I am really fast. I run into the house looking in all the rooms, yelling out for Ben. I don't know, maybe the roar of the flames were too loud for him to hear me. I ran up the stairs opening all the doors yelling for Ben and trying to look for him in the rooms I could get into. I could hear people yelling my name, but

I needed to find Ben. Is he is trapped in here I would feel so bad if something happened to him and I had not tried to help him. I could feel Jax behind me, I felt him grab my arm. Jax I have to make sure Ben is out of here. Hailey we don't have time we have to get out of here. Jax leads me down the stairs. As we start out the door a rafter cracks and falls. Jax turns around as the rafter knocks me to the floor. I can see Jax trying to get the burning rafter off of me and I see the others coming to help him but the smoke from the fire was getting to me and everything was going black. I hear Jax calling out to me. Stay with me Hailey, please stay with me.

Jaxson 🐾

Once we did get Hailey out of the house the fire department had arrived and so had a few ambulances. The only thing about this situation is these paramedics are probably part of a regular hospital and we can not really go to a regular hospital since we are not human, at least not fully human that is. I talk to one of the paramedics and explain how important it is that I get Hailey back to our hospital back home. He said that once we get to the hospital they would do what they could there to get Hailey stable and once she is stable they would transport her by helicopter to the hospital in Kettle Falls. It took about twenty to twenty five minutes to get from he New York pack house to the hospital. It took a few hours for them to get Hailey stable, but once they did the doctor came out to get me because they were about to load Hailey back up into the helicopter and take her to our hospital in Kettle Falls.

Nikola 🐾

OMG Dorian we need to get to the hospital NOW!! Babe is something wrong? Is something wrong with the babies? No Dorian, it's Hailey. She's in the hospital and all I know right now is that it is BAD!! But Nikola if it is something that is going to upset you and cause harm to our babies even though Hailey is our Luna and Jaxson is our Alpha I don't want anything to cause harm to our babies. Dorian it is causing me to be upset not knowing and not being there for my best friend. I thought I was your best friend now. Dorian said to me with that cute smile he does. You know what I mean. Hailey has been my best friend since childhood. I need to be there for her and if I can not be there for her like I should be that's really going to upset me and how's that going to be good for our babies? You have a point my love, okay let's go. Thank you sweetheart. I said to Dorian as I wrap my arms around him and give him the kiss that I always give him when I get my way.

Jaxson 🐾

I can not lose her. I told the doctor that was helping to rush Hailey back to the ICU. Please take good care of her? Alpha Jaxson you know I will do everything in my power to take good care of our Luna.

All that kept going through my mind is that rafter falling and I tried to pull Hailey faster so we could get out of the house. Why did she have to go back in there? Why? Why did she have to be faster than me? I tried to stop her from going back in there to look for Ben, but she is so fast. If I ever find that Ben he is going to wish he had never been born. He had better hope that my mate makes it out of this. He already knows the punishment for the crime he committed and he will be lucky if the elders get to him before I do because what I will do to him will be so much worse. I can feel myself wanting to shift and run, but I knew I could not leave the pack hospital, not at least until I know Hailey was going to be okay. It seems like it has been hours. All I can do is go over everything that happened from the time we woke up smelling the smoke to when Hailey was knocked down and the only other thing I can do is watch the clock just slowly tick by. I can not handle this, the not knowing is driving me crazy. I want to get a hold of Ben and slowly, painfully torture him. I want him to feel Hailey's pain, my pain, Lauren's pain, our pack's pain. I want to be in there with my mate. Our pack is doing so good at handling what is going on. The guards are on high alert looking for Ben and for Lena. DAMN!! I haven't mind linked Dorian yet and told him what has happened. Dorian, I need to talk to you and it is VERY important. I said to him through mind link. Yes Alpha. He answered right away. That is another reason he is my Beta. He always answers me right away. I don't want you to freak out and I don't want Nikola to freak out, especially because she is pregnant. Alpha does this have anything to do with Hailey being in the hospital over the fire at the New York pack house? How did you know about that? Hailey mind linked Nikola and told her. We are pulling into the parking lot of the pack hospital as we speak. I hope Nikola is okay and not to freaked out. She is fine, just like Hailey they are both very strong woman. We are walking in now Alpha. I closed the mind link and greeted both Nikola and Dorian as they came in. Thank you both for being here. You are very welcome Alpha both Dorian and Nikola said at the same time. Can I go in with her? Nikola asked. Her mom is in there with her right now and they are only allowing one person at a time in with her. That's ok Alpha, they probably need each other right now. Yes I am sure they do. I said with a worried smile. So can I ask you what happened Alpha? Dorian asked. Of course. I know the entire pack needs to know since we are on high alert and the guards are on watch for Ben from the New York pack and for Lena. By the way, has there been any sightings of Lena since Hailey and I have been gone to New York? I asked Dorian. One of our guards saw her somewhere near the land and went after her, but she did get away. Dorian told me. DAMNIT!! I feel all eyes on me so I turned around and told everyone it's okay and I am sorry for shouting. It took several hours, but finally the doctor came out. I thought I was going to jump out of my skin when I seen the doctor. How is she, please tell me she is going to be okay. I should have never of taken her when I had to go to New York. Alpha, calm down. The best thing you can do right now is to be calm. How can I when I don't even know how my mate is? She is going to be fine. It's going to take some healing. Her legs were burned pretty badly. Her mid to lower back was burned pretty bad too. But she is a wolf there for she will do some healing on her own. She is a very lucky girl. Once we see how much she can heal on her own then we might have to do some skin grafting, but that is a last resort. She could very possible completely heal on her own. I have seen wolves burned worse than Luna Hailey and not have a single scare on their body from self healing. We of course put some ointment on her burn's and we had to give her some pain medicine for the pain of the burn's. I am sure the worst of the pain is when she had to be scrubbed, but that has to be done before the ointment goes on so there is no infection. Other than that she is going to be fine. She does want to see you now though, so I am sending her mom out here so you can go in Alpha. She has been asking for you this whole time. I want to see her too. She is the love of my life. Some other pack members should be here soon too. That's fine Alpha. I will instruct my nurse to let them know where they can wait. We don't want to many in with Luna right now. Will you have the nurse to let me know when they get here? Yes Alpha, I will do that. Thank you doc. Your welcome.

Ben 🐺

It is a lot harder than I thought it was going to be especially by myself. I can not believe that Franklin and the others backed out. I just need to make it to Canada and I will be fine. I am sure they have some of the pack guards on high alert, but at least I got away before everyone got up. I have a great head start on them all. Just sucks that I have to keep the mind link off, I can't risk anyone at all to be able to hear my thoughts.

Hailey 🐺

The ointment that they put on me was cooling the burn's on my legs and my back. I am not sure what all they put into my I.V. but I feel really drowsy. I see Jaxson walk in and I reach out for him. Hi baby, please come over to me. I know this is probably a really dumb question right now, but how are you feeling? I can not feel any pain right now, but I am so sorry for going back into that house. You thought Ben was still in there and I know you felt that you needed to find him. Yes Jax that is how I felt. Was he ever found? I put my head down not really ready for the answer, but I needed to know. No he was never found, not even a body. I could see that Jax was getting really irritated. Hailey, we all really think he is the one that set the pack house on fire. But why? Why would he want to kill the pack, why would he want to hurt all of us? I asked Jax. I don't know the answers to those questions babe. But he better hope that someone such as the elders find him before I find him. But let's try to get off of this subject for now. Jax said to me. I could tell the more he talked about Ben the more pissed off he was getting. The doctor said it is going to be a little bit, but you should heal up. He wants to wait and see how much you heal yourself before doing anything he said that if you don't completely heal. The most important thing right now is that you and I made it out of the fire and I hope the rest of the pack made it out too. I said to Jax. We did a full head count just before you ran back in the house last night. Don't you remember that? That is how we knew that Ben was not there with us. Oh that's right. I said to Jax as I looked up at him and I could see the sadness in his eyes. Why are you so sad babe? You're here in the hospital Hailey. I feel that this is my fault, if I had not had you to come with me to help with the New York pack this would have never of happened to you. Jax stop, you know that I would have went with you anyway. That is part of my job as Luna. I am supposed to be right next to you and help you when ever need be. I love you Hailey, and I know that the moon goddess did right by choosing you as my mate. Just then a nurse walks in. There are some others here now Alpha. Okay I will be right there to see who is here. The nurse walks back out. Hailey I love you and I can not wait for you to heal so we can go home and get our wedding planned. I love you too Jax and I look forward to us planning the rest of our lives. Before Jax walk out he bent down and kissed me so lightly as to not hurt me because of the burns. But the burns are only on my back and my legs. But Jax is always so careful with me.

Lauren 🐾

I thought I was going to die when I got the news that my baby girl was stuck in a fire and had been hurt. I could feel my heart almost leave my body. All I could remember is someone grabbing a hold of me because my knees went completely weak and I could not hold myself up anymore. It is going to be okay. I heard Kaden say. Which hospital is she at? I could not hear the answer that the police officer gave Kaden, all I know is I felt Kaden putting my jacket on me and walking me to the passenger side of the car and helping me to get in. He drove me to the hospital. When we got there, Jax was in the waiting room. Where is my daughter? I asked Jaxson. They are only letting one at a time go in there. Just then the doctor came into the waiting room. I run over to him. Where is she? How bad is it? Is she okay? What happened? I need to see her. Jaxson walked me over to a seat with me and helped me sit down. She is okay, a lot better than what I expected her to be. She has burns on her back and on her legs. But whatever doesn't heal on its own we will do skin grafts to fix but I am very certain that she is going to completely heal herself. I want to see her, I need to see my baby. I will take you back there and show you what room she is in, but you cannot be upset when you go back there. I want anyone who goes back there to be calm so Hailey will stay calm. I will, I don't want to upset her. The doctor showed me what room Hailey is in an I held it together as I walked in. I wanted to hug her, but I know I cannot do that because of the burns. Hi my precious baby girl. How are you doing? As soon as I asked her that I see the tears roll down her face. Oh Mom I am so sorry. Shhhh don't be sorry for anything. You are a brave girl, and you care about everybody you have such a kind heart and I couldn't be more proud of you. I have to ask you though Hailey, what happened? Why did you get stuck inside the house? Were you just the last one to get out? Mom I had gotten out, and we did a head count there was one person missing. It was Ben, one of the pack members. Being a Luna I could not let anyone be left in the house so I went running back in. I was searching all the rooms upstairs and down. I was yelling out his name and each room I went to. I was upstairs when I felt Jax come up behind me. He started pulling me out of the house. We were almost out of the house, we were right at the front door when the rafter broke and knocked me to the ground. I remember Jax, and some others coming to get the rafter off of me, or trying to pull me out. But that is all I remember. The next thing I know I woke up right here. As Hailey was telling me what happened and how she ended up here in the hospital I could feel the tears rolling down my face. I was trying to be brave for my daughter, but I could not help picturing everything that she was saying as it happened. I could have lost my daughter, my only child. Hailey I am going to go out and see who all is here. I may send Jax back and depending on who is here. Okay mom, I love you. I felt Hailey reach out and grab my hand. I squeezed her hand and said, I love you too Hailey. As I walked out of her room and shut her door I lost it. If she didn't find that Ben kid inside the house and he wasn't outside during the head count, did that mean that he had left before anything happened, or is he the reason for the fire? I need to talk to you Jaxson. I head for the waiting room and it was full. Everyone from the pack and more was here for my daughter. Nikola I know Hailey would like to see you. Okay, Mrs. Moran I will go see her now. Jaxson I need to talk to you now.

Jaxson

When Hailey's mom walked out from seeing Hailey she had Nikola to go in and see her, then she said she wanted to talk to me. Let's talk down this way. She followed me down the hall away from the waiting room and away from Hailey's room. Jaxson I need to know how the fire started. Hailey said that there was a head count when everyone was outside and that there was one person missing, someone named Ben. Yes Ben was missing and that is why Hailey ran back in and I tried to stop her but she is so fast she is faster than me and she slipped through my hand. I know how fast she is, she was hard to catch when she was just a little girl. I said to Jaxson as a memory of Hailey when she was little popped into my mind. I was trying to catch her for some reason and I couldn't. She was always so fast. So no one found Ben? I asked Jaxson. No I am sorry to say that no one has found him and I have my guards on high alert and so is the guards of the New York pack. He better hope and pray that the elders get a hold of him before I do I promise you that Mrs. Moran. Jaxson I have told you many, many times either call me Lauren, or call me mom. I don't like being called Mrs. Moran. Well maybe after the wedding I can call you mom. I said to her with a smile. I can tell that made her feel a little bit better. The wedding? Lauren asked me. Yes the wedding. As soon as Hailey is out of the hospital and better we are going to start planning our wedding. We are going to plan it when we got back from New York and we were going to announce our engagement to everyone when my parents throws my coronation. Oh Jaxson I am so happy for you and Hailey. With everything that has went on I had completely forgotten that you and her are already engaged. Lauren gives me a big hug and she finally has a smile on her face. That will give Hailey something to look forward to and a great reason to heal and get out of this pack hospital. Yes that is what I am hoping for as well. Sorry would you give me a second. What is it Daniel? One of my pack members mind linked me while I was talking to Lauren. We got a tail on Ben. One of the guards picked up his scent. He is getting close to the Canadian border. Tell all the guards, even mind link Alpha Joseph. Yes alpha. I close the mind link. Lauren that was Daniel, one of the pack members of our pack. Yes I know who Daniel is. He said one of my guards got a scent on Ben and he is close to the Canadian border. I told him to mind link all of the guards and even the New York pack guards and let all of them know. They will get him Jaxson and when they do he better hope that the elders do get to him before we do. That is what I have said too. I told Lauren. I will torture him to the point he would wish he was dead and then more before I will kill him. Jaxson I need to go for a little bit, but I will be back. I have some people I need to talk to you. I will let Hailey know that you will be back. Thank you Jaxson. You're very welcome.

Nikola 🐾

When I was told that I could go see Hailey it was all I could do not to run to her room. When I got in her room she looked tired. How are you feeling Hailey? I know that is probably a very stupid question. I am not feeling any pain at all if that is what you were talking about. That is good. The doctor said that I should be able to heal up on my own, but if it doesn't all heal up that they can do skin grafts, but they are very sure that they won't have to do all of that. It only hurts when they put the ointment on, but that was before the pain medication kicked in. Well I am glad you are not feeling any of the pain. Hailey look up at me. Nikola can I ask you something and you answer me honestly? Of course. Has anyone caught Ben yet? Not that I know of Hailey. Who is Ben? He is or was part of the New York pack and possibly the one that set fire to the pack house. But Nikola I don't want you to worry about all of this. I want to talk about you since I have not seen you in a while. Hahahaha Hailey it's not even been 2 weeks, but I have missed having my bwff around. How is the babies doing? Hailey asked me. As far as we know everything is good with the little ones. Dorian and I are so excited. I'm excited too Nikola. Well then you need to get better so you can get out of here. I looked Hailey right in the eyes, my babies are going to need their godmother. When I said that I saw tears in Hailey's eyes roll down her face. Really Nikola? You want me to be your babies godmother? Of course I do, who else do you think I would have for their godmother. Dorian said that he wants Jaxson to be the godfather. So that means that you need to get better and get your ass out of here. You know that if anything was to ever happen to me and or Dorian you would be raising our babies. Nikola nothing is going to happen to you or to Dorian. Well I just want to be prepared for anything and everything when it comes to these babies. I know you do and you are going to be a great mother Nikola and Dorian is going to be a great dad. When Hailey said that to me I felt the tears. I am sorry for crying Hailey, but my emotions are all over the place. Well just get some rest and get better so you can come home because we have a lot of different things that need to be planned out. I am most definitely going to do that. I said to Nikola. Well I want you to get some rest. I know Jaxson has been in here to see you and your mom and now me too so I know you have got to be tired. But I will be out in the waiting room if you need me. Thank you Nikola. For what? For being my best friend, for being here, for just being you. You're welcome and we both know that we probably would not be best friends if I was not the person I am. Yes I know. Hailey said as I lean down and gave her a hug before I left the room.

Jaxson 🐺

When I seen Nikola come out from Hailey's room I was going to go back in. But Nikola said that Hailey was resting so I didn't want to wake her. Then I see Lauren coming back into the waiting room. How's my baby girl? She is fine and resting now. Good. Lauren said. Jaxson can I talk to you again? Of course Lauren. We walked back over to where we talked before she left earlier. Jaxson I got the pack that Hunter and I was in for a while back together and I gave them the info I had. They are going to mind link Alpha Joseph and get the rest of the info on Ben. I thought the more we have out looking for him the better. Thank you Lauren. I just want Hailey to get better so she can go home. You look like you need to go home and take a shower Jaxson and maybe get some rest. I can sit here in case she wakes back up. No I am not leaving here until she can go home. If someone catches Ben I will go see what I decide to do and come back but other than that I am going to stay right here. I cannot be at home without her. I understand and I am glad that she has you. Is there anything you want us to do Alpha? Dorian asked. You are already doing enough, just being here and having the guards to be on high alert. I think I am going to sneak back in her room and try not to wake her. We will sit out here in the waiting room. Nikola said. Thank you both. As I walked back in her room she was sleeping so peacefully I went over and sat down in the chair. I hate being away from her for even a second. I got a mind link from Joseph as I sat down. What's going on Alpha Joseph? Has there been any word on

Ben? Yes there has Alpha Jaxson. I hate telling you this but from what I was told by my guards he made it across the Canadian border. I wanted to smash something when Joseph told me that Ben got across the Canadian border, but I knew that I would wake Hailey up so I didn't want to do that. Thank you Alpha Joseph. I promise you Alpha Jaxson I will have my guards to stay on alert in case he tries to make his way back across the border. I really appreciate that, you have no idea how much. How is your mate doing? She is doing okay, she's resting now. The doctor says she should be able to make a full recovery, but if they need to they will do some skin grafts. Well just know that I am hoping that she makes a full recovery and I am glad that she is able to rest. I am truly sorry for what happened to her. I feel so bad. You both were here helping me with members of my pack and that happened. It is not your fault Joseph. But I am glad you are thinking of Hailey and hoping she gets better. If there is anything and I mean anything you, your mate, or your pack needs at any time please let me know. Thank you. After that I cut the mind link. I seen Hailey moving a little bit so I wanted my full attention on her.

Hailey 🐺

Two weeks in the hospital I think is my limit doctor, but I want to thank you for everything you have done. Well Luna you have made a great recovery. We did not have to do any skin graft at all since you completely healed on your own. I am glad about that. If I would have had to stay any longer I probably would have went crazy. Nothing against you or the staff, but I just really don't care for hospitals at all. I understand Luna. I will get your paperwork printed out and your prescription for the ointment, and pain medication printed and have my nurse bring that to you and wheel you out and then you will be on your way home. That sounds good to me, going home. Don't worry doc she is going to be very well cared for when she gets home. Jaxson said to the doctor. Yes I will, I am sure you seen all the people that were here around the clock for me outside of the staff here. Yes I did. Oh doc I wanted to ask you, how soon can I start training again? I miss doing that and my workouts. Well if you feel up to it you can get back to your workouts and the training when you feel up to it, but don't overdo it. I will make sure she doesn't overdo it. I just smile at Jax when he said that to the doctor because he knows as well as I do that he isn't going to be able to stop me from doing as much working out and training as I want to. The reason I said to be careful working out and training Hailey is because you're "new skin" even though it is your regular skin it's still tender and cannot take to much sun exposer. I will be safe and smart about it doc. If you need anything else you know you can call for me or send for me. We will and thank you again for everything. Are you ready to go home? The nurse asked me as she came in with the paperwork, the prescriptions, and of course the wheelchair. I just rolled my eyes at the wheelchair. I did not need to be pushed out. But I know that Jax isn't going to allow me to walk out of here. He and my mom are so much alike when it comes to babying me. It's sweet, but at the same time it drives me crazy. Are you hungry babe? Jax asked me as we got in the car. I'm starving. I asked the cooks to make you something special for when we get home. I noticed you did not eat much while you were in the hospital. Well have you tasted that food? Jax just laughed. You got me there babe. But you will eat very well when we get home. Of course and I cannot wait to see what the cooks are making for me. I cannot wait until we go to our home so I can lay in our bed and be more comfortable. You don't want to stay at the pack house babe? No I want to be home where it is quiet and I'm very comfortable. Okay, okay I won't try to argue.

Jaxson 🐾

As Hailey was being wheeled out to the car I sent a mind link to Dorian to let him know that Hailey was being released from the hospital and we are on our way home. If you could would you please make sure that the cooks have the meal done that I asked them to make and would you please send one or two of the pack members over to the house to make sure it is all clean and fresh sheets, and blankets are on the bed. Already done Alpha. Nikola and one of the girls went to your and Hailey's house and made sure it was all cleaned up and the cooks are finishing up. I will let everyone know you are almost here though. Thank you Dorian, thank you for everything. You and Nikola have been such a great help.

Hailey 🐾

When Jax and I got to the pack house there were more than normal the amount of people there, but it was so wonderful to see all the faces that I know and love. When we walked in my mom was the first to greet me. She gave me the biggest hug ever. Mom? Yes sweetie. I can't breathe. My mom started laughing. I am sorry Hailey I am just so happy that you are out of the hospital. I know and so am I. Then there was Kaden. Welcome home Hailey. He gave me an easier hug than my mom did, which I was glad. It is so good to see you Kaden. It seems like forever. I was just thinking the same thing. Then there was Jace, Vondra, and Corbin. Jax's brother, mom, and dad. They all gave me a hug and told me how happy they were to see me back and better. Then of course there was Nikola. Are you starting to get a belly? I said to Nikola and I kind of laughed. Yeah right. I am not getting a belly yet, but at the rate that these little monsters are growing it won't be long. I just cannot wait to meet them. Dorian chimed in. How are you doing Hailey? I am doing better now that I am back, thank you for asking me Dorian. Then I hear Jax. Okay everyone, please let my mate make her way into the dining room so she can eat. She did not like the hospital food. We all went into the dining room and sat around the table. There was so much food. There was lasagna, Texas toast, meatballs, ham, mashed potatoes, green beans, cornbread, salads of different kinds and so many other foods I cannot remember them all. I want to thank all of you for your love and support during my time in the hospital and of course now that I am back I want everything to go back to normal I do not want anyone and I mean anyone to go out of their way for me. The doctor said I will be fine. That I can go back to regular exercise and that I can go back to training. But he also said that he doesn't want you to over do it. Jax chimed in. I just looked at him. My point is that I do not want extra special attention. I hope everyone can understand that. Now let's all eat this amazing meal. I know I am hungry. After I was done eating I wanted to go back to mine and Jax's house, I wanted to be home. It just seemed like it had been forever since we had been home. I wanted to take a shower in my own shower and I wanted to sleep in our bed where I am comfortable and hopefully I won't have the nightmares like I was having in the hospital about the fire and me getting stuck in the house. I would wake up screaming but of course Jax would always be right there to comfort me. I went to walk outside, but I felt Jax right behind me, so I turned around. What are you doing? Are you following me around. I said with a smile. I just want to make sure you're okay. I am fine babe. I was just going outside to get some fresh air. But I would much rather go home. We can go anytime you are ready. Jax said to me as he came up to me and put his arms around me. I cannot live my life without you Hailey. I am always going to be here Jax. I was so worried though Hailey. I was so worried when that fire happened and you ran back in the house, and then when that rafter fell. Shhhh Jax. I am fine, and I am right here. I just want to go home and relax the rest of the day. Whatever you want to do Hailey. I just want to make sure you are okay and that you are happy. Let me go tell Dorian that we are going. Okay I will wait for you outside on the porch. As Jax went to talk to Dorian I went outside. I didn't even hear or see you go out from the dining room area let alone go outside. I said to Nikola. I did not want to disturb you and Jaxson. Are you okay? I asked her. Yes of course I am okay. I was so worried about you though Hailey. I want everyone to stop worrying, I am fine. We just care about you and we don't want anything to happen to you. You are my best friend and my only best friend since childhood. I would just die if anything happened to you Hailey. I know, I just want everything to go back to normal. Hopefully that will help me to push that memory away and help me to not have the nightmares I've been having. I am sure everything will get back to normal very soon. Nikola said.

Jaxson

Dorian I want to let you know that Hailey and I are going to head home. She wants to be in a comfortable surrounding and relax. She is saying she wants to lay in her own bed. I thought she would want to stay here to be around everyone, but I want to do what makes her happy. I know Alpha and that is fine. If you and Hailey need some time to yourselves Nikola and I can handle things with the pack however long you two need. Thank you Dorian, I will let you know what is going on. I know Hailey wants everything to go back to normal as soon as possible so we will see. Just focus on our Luna. I knew you would understand Dorian. You make me realize everyday how right I was in making you my Beta. Oh and speaking of me being your Beta, I am not trying to rush anything but do you know when your dad is going to be doing the coronation and officially passing the Alpha position over to you? That is something that he and I have not had a chance to talk about yet. But I will be talking to him soon I am sure and you will be in on that meeting as well. Okay Alpha I will see you soon. Thank you Dorian. You're welcome Alpha. Hi ladies. I said to Hailey and Nikola as I walked outside and seen them engaged in conversation. Hi Alpha. Hello Nikola, how are you doing? I am doing very well Alpha, thank you for asking. You are welcome. How are the little ones? We have only seen the pack doctor once, but so far so good. If they keep growing at the rate they are growing we will have full grown new pack members hahaha. Well that is a good sign that the babies are growing that well. I don't want to disturb you ladies, I was just checking to see if my mate is ready to go home but no rush. I actually am very much ready to go home. Hailey said to me. We both said bye too Nikola and as soon as the girls were done giving each other a hug I helped Hailey into the car and once I was in the car we headed home.

CHAPTER 6

THE CORONATION

Corbin

Well Vondra, now that we are home and now that Jaxson and Hailey are home I think it is about time to arrange the coronation. I think you are right my love. We could use a distraction from everything that has happened in the last few weeks and I think it is a very good idea and great timing. Okay then I will mind link the boys and set up a day and time to talk to them about when would be a good day for them. Okay sweetie. I hope Hailey is okay I know we have not seen her since she was in the hospital and I feel so bad about that. Vondra said. I am sure if there was anything going on with Hailey Jaxson would have contacted us by now. I know how much you worry about everyone in our pack family. I just cannot help it, I guess it is the mother wolf in me.

Jaxson, and Jace I need to ask you both an important question. I said to them through mind link. Yes father, what is it. They both responded fast. I would like to know when you both would be able to come meet with me. We have some important things that we need to go over. I can meet anytime you need me there. Jace said. Me too dad, I can clear anything that needs to be cleared or have Dorian to take over if need be. Can you both come over here to the main house tomorrow? Yes. They both said at the same time. Okay I will see you both tomorrow and Jaxson give Hailey mine and your mother's love. I will dad, and thank you. You're welcome son.

Jaxson

Is there anything you need me to get for you babe? I wish you could do a back rub on me, but we both know that cannot happen. I could tell that Hailey was feeling down. That was the first time she had said anything like that since the accident. Babe I know this is a hard time for you but I am here for you. I just want to do whatever I can to help you feel comfortable and to help you relax. I know, and I'm very sorry for saying that. It just sucks that I thought Ben would be in the house possibly stuck in the fire, it sucks that I got trapped and that my back and legs got burned. But you did heal up, so maybe I can give you a back rub. At least a very gentle back rub. Or I could run you a soothing bath. That would be nice babe. I will get right on that. Thank you babe. Once I got Hailey's bath ran I helped her upstairs and into the tub. Let me know when you are ready to get out and I will come help you babe. Oh and my dad sent a mind link wanting us to come over to the main house tomorrow, I hope that is okay he said it is important. Of course it is okay. I would love to see your mom and dad, it seems like it has been forever even though they are at the pack house when we got there from the hospital. But it isn't the same as just getting to see them, visit with them with everything that has been going on. Well let's not be in any hurry to get up, I want you to get as much rest as possible. The next morning I got up kind of early, but Hailey was still asleep and I did not want to bother her. I know she needs as much rest as possible. I did however mind mink a couple of the pack members that do the cooking and ask them to make something special for Hailey and bring it to our house. Then I mind linked Dorian. Hey Beta, good morning. Good morning Alpha. I hope everything is good with you and our Luna this morning. Yes it is, thank you for asking. What I wanted to talk to you about is my dad has asked me and my brother Jace to come to the main house today so I am thinking that he might want to talk about the coronation. If he does I will have him or I will mind link you and ask you to come over. Okay Alpha I will be ready whenever you mind link me. Like I said I think that is what he wants to talk about, so if you and Nikola have any plans and go ahead with whatever you want to do today. Oh we are just at the pack house having breakfast we don't have any thing else planned. Okay I will let you know and thank you Dorian. You're welcome Alpha.

Jace 🐺

Hey big bro I hope you are awake and up. Yes I am, what's up? Just wanted to see when you are going to Mom and Dad's. I had to mind link Jaxson because I stayed out with some buddies last night and I wanted to make sure that I was back home when Jaxson and Hailey gets there too. Are you not home little bro? Jaxson ask me in his joking big brother self. No I'm not at home. Me and the guys stayed out late so I crashed at Donnie's. Well how adult of you bro. Yeah I thought so too. So do you know when you will be at Mom and dad's? No I don't know actually, I am letting Hailey sleep in a little today. I think she needs it after everything she has been through. Yeah she probably does. How is my future sister-in-law? She is doing really good, but I need to be focused in case she wakes up. I also have a couple of the cooks bringing some food over to our house special for Hailey. I am trying to take notes from you bro on how to treat my mate. Oh yeah Jace you are soooo funny hahahaha. How is Abby? She is great, and I am seeing her later today. Okay little brother like I said I need to get off the mind link and get ready for when Hailey gets up. Okay see you soon.

Corbin 🐾

I am glad you too could come over here today. I think that after recent events we all could use a distraction from everything that has went on. I couldn't agree more. Jaxson said. Me too dad. Jace chimed in. Okay well since you both agree with me on that I think it is about time we made you Jaxson the official pack Alpha. I would be honored. I would like to ask you something first dad. Jaxson said. Of course whatever it is. Before we decide on something I would like to mind link Dorian and ask him to come over here for the rest of this meeting. Yes of course. It won't take him long to get here, he and Nikola are at the pack house. Yes, yes go right ahead. Jace while Jaxson is talking to Dorian I will go over a few things with you. Okay dad. You know that Jaxson is having Dorian to be his Beta, but that does not mean you are off the hook. I could see Jace giving me a really weird look. God forbid but if something was to happen to your brother you would have to step up which means you are going to have to step up anyway. You are going to have to make it to all of the training sessions and all of the meetings. I will dad. I mean it Jace. I know I have allowed you to slack, but since your brother is taking over as Alpha it is time for you to step up and help out. Okay, Dorian should be here any second. That is good, I will be glad to see him again. Is he bringing his mate Nikola? I believe so, especially since Hailey is here. They have always been best friends. Jaxson was right, it only took Dorian a few seconds to get here from the pack house. I like that he is very prompt. Welcome Dorian. Jaxson told me that you wanted to be here for this meeting. I was telling Jaxson and Jace that with the recent events that have went on that I feel like we could all use a distraction. That I would have to agree with sir. So I am wanting to plan the coronation to pass the Alpha title and duties on to Jaxson and Jaxson said that he would like for you to be here. Yes sir that is true. Well I already know that he is going to name you as his Beta, and I know you will be a great Beta. Thank you sir. Dorian you and Jaxson have been friends all these years you do not have to call me sir, you can call me Corbin especially now that I will no longer be the pack Alpha. Now let's get to the important part. When would be a good day and time for you three for the coronation, I was thinking maybe this weekend. Jaxson said. The sooner the better. He added I think that is a good idea too. Dorian said. Well how about you Jace, you have a say in this too. This weekend works for me as well. I have nothing planned. Then this weekend it is. Which day would you three like. I would say Saturday. Jaxson said. Then Saturday it is, how about we get everything going that afternoon or early evening that way everyone has a chance to hang around and unwind. That sounds good to me. All three said at the same time. Then it's official. I will let Vondra know and we will get the details handed out to the pack members. Now where is Hailey and Nikola? I would like to see them and say hi to them. It has been a while since I have been able to comfortably sit down and just chat and relax. They are out there with Mom somewhere. Jaxson said. Well let's go out there.

Vondra

Hailey has been a great help with helping me get everyone their duty roster. We have a lot of work to do before tonight's coronation. It is so exciting to finally be having the coronation. I know that Corbin loves being the pack Alpha, but it is time for him to pass that along to Jaxson and for Corbin to take a break. Jaxson is young and he is very wise. He always had listened when Corbin was teaching him things and showing him things

I used to watch Jaxson, Corbin, and Jace When Corbin would work with the boys and Jaxson was always the one that was eager to learn. Mrs. Carter? OMG dear, I almost jumped right out of my skin. Oh I am so sorry I did not mean to scare you. Oh no sweetie, I was just in deep thought. Is everything okay Mrs. Carter? Well it will be dear, once you start calling me Mom or Vondra. I seen Hailey get a big smile when I said that to her. Yes of course Vondra, but don't worry because I will get into the habit of calling you Mom after the wedding is done. I really do look forward to marrying your son. I think the goddess did a great job of making Jax and I mates even though I didn't think it would happen because of the way he was when I first met him. I know what you mean Hailey. I did not raise my son to be that way, but I guess when you know that you will one day become Alpha then your head starts to swell some hahaha. Oh but please Hailey do not tell Jaxson or anyone else I said that. It is our secret. Hailey said to me with a smile. I hope everything is set up and already in time. Alpha's do not like to be late for anything at all. Oh I am finding that out since Jax and I have been together. Hailey you are going to make such an amazing Luna. I also wanted to tell you that I am sorry for all of the hectic things that have went on here since you have joined our family unofficially. I seen Hailey have a confused look on her face when I said that. Oh dear I don't mean anything bad by that. It's just you and Jaxson have not marked each other yet. Oh Jax has already marked me. I move my hair so Vondra could see that Jax marked me. Oh and it has the crescent moon in the middle. I said so excited. Yes it does. You two are going to be closer than you ever thought possible. Thank you for making me already feel that I am part of your family. You are very welcome Hailey. If I would have been lucky enough to have had a daughter I would have hoped that she would have been just like you. Thank you Vondra. You don't have to thank me Hailey. I mean every word I have said to you. Will you please excuse me Vondra, Jax just texted me and asked me to come to the office. I hope nothing is wrong, but yes go on ahead and see what he needs.

Jaxson 🐺

Tonight is going to be so much more than everyone is expecting. Hopefully when Hailey gets here and I asked her to marry me she will say yes. Then at the coronation tonight we can announce our engagement. I don't know why I am so nervous, I know she is going to say yes. I have already asked her once when we first went to our house right after it was built. I know she loves me, and I know we are meant to be together. When Hailey came in she nearly caused me to jump right out of my skin. I was still going over in my head how I was going to ask her again to marry me. Hi babe, you wanted to see me? Is everything okay? Yes of course it is, I wanted you to come up here because there is so much going on at the pack house and around the grounds at the pack house I just wanted us to have a few minutes alone before everything gets underway. Is something wrong Jax? No babe, everything is actually perfect I said to Hailey as I walked over to her and put my arms around her. Hailey, I know we have not known each other our entire lives, but I also know that the moon goddess has had a plan for us our entire lives. When I seen you for the first time I knew without a doubt that you are my mate just like you knew that I was your mate. We are destined to be together, but I want to give you everything not only as what we should have and do as wolves, but I also want to give you everything as a normal human as well. (Getting the ring out of his pocket and getting down on one knee) Hailey Marie Moran, I know I have already asked you once before but would you do me the honor and make me the happiest man/wolf on earth and become my wife? As soon as I asked Hailey to be my wife her head dropped. What's wrong Hailey? I don't know Jax, I have waited and waited for this moment and now that it is here and after all the crazy things that have went on in the past weeks I am not sure if now is the right time for us to be doing this but if we wait for the exact right time I know it may never happen so I know there is no better time than now to say yes, yes Jaxson Alexander Dravin Carter I will marry you, yes I want to officially become your wife and live the rest of my life with you. Oh Hailey you scared me, I really thought you were telling me no this time and mean it. Now how could I tell you no you goofball? The moon goddess made us mates long before we even knew we were alive. We are meant to spend the rest of our lives together and there is no one at all on this Earth or any other planet that I would rather spend my life with than you Jax. We will announce our engagement tonight right after my dad officially passes the title of Alpha over to me. I think that is a perfect time to let everyone know. For now I think we should start getting ourselves ready for the coronation, what do you think? Hailey asked me. Yes babe I think you are right.

Corbin

HI EVERYONE! CAN I HAVE EVERYONE'S ATTENTION PLEASE (everybody starts to quieten down as Corbin starts to speak). Hi everyone. I am so glad to see so many familiar faces out here this afternoon as this is a very important day for not only my family, but the entire pack family as well. Vondra, Jaxson, Hailey, Jace, Abby, Dorian, and Nikola I would like for you all to join me up here please. It has been a great honor to watch our family grow and when I say our family I don't just mean mine and my wife's family I mean our pack family. I was handed the title of pack Alpha by my father. May his soul and wolf rest in peace. I can still remember the day of my coordination happened. It was exactly 57 years ago today that it happened for me and now here I stand with my mate/wife, our sons Jaxson, and Jace, and with Hailey, Abby, Dorian, and Nikola. Dorian even though you are not my biological sign, you are still my son and Nikola as Dorian's mate that would also make you my daughter in the goddesses eyes and no disrespect to your biological parents at all which I am sure they know that too and they also know that is how this goes in the coronation (we could see Lily and Todd shaking their head in agreement.) Dorian and Nikola you are wonderful mates for each other we have all seen that so now comes a time since you Dorian will be the Beta for the new Alpha that you and Nikola shall mark each other to signify that you shall be each other's mates for life. Everyone's attention turns to Dorian and Nikola. Now that Dorian and Nikola have marked each other it is time that the second Beta Jace, Jaxson's little brother and Abigail shall do the same and mark each other. Everyone's attention turns to Jace and Abby. Now that Jace and Abby have also marked each other everyone will respect Dorian, Nikola, Jace, and Abigail and know that they are now officially mated to their mates and no one in the pack will disrespect the bond of the mates. I am pretty sure everyone here knows the degree of punishment for disrespecting the Beta's and their mates. But that is not what we are here for, we are not here to talk about rules. Now, (Corbin turns to Jaxson and Hailey) Jaxson, my first born child, my first born son. It has come time for me to hand over the title of Alpha of the Golden Sun pack. I know that you will be a good Alpha, I know you will lead this pack with pride, but not so much pride that you lead wrong. I have trained you for this day since the day you were born. I know you are going to be a strong leader as you have already shown that in my absence when your mother, brother, and I were taken by Alaric. you made me very proud, you made your mother and brother very proud as well. Even though it is very hard for me to let go of my title, I know it is time and you are ready. Once I hand you the title and the plaque you will mark your mat Hailey and then Hailey will mark you. So now Jaxson Alexander Dravin Carter I hand you the title Alpha of the Golden Sun pack. Everyone stands and cheers for their new Alpha. Jaxson mark's Hailey, then Hailey takes her turn and mark's Jaxson.

Jaxson 🐺

Everyone as soon as you all calm back down I have something I would like to say and I want everyone to hear it. Thank you everyone for being here and sharing this amazing moment not only with me, but with Jace, Dorian, Hailey, Nikola, and Abby. But that is not the only thing I want to say. (Jaxson grabs Hailey's hand). Today while everything was being set up for the coronation I had the chance to ask this very beautiful lady right here for the second time to marry me. At first she scared me, I thought she was going to turn me down but she did not turn me down she actually said yes and made me and my wolf very happy. I never want to be without you Hailey and I promise to love you and to do everything I can every single day to make you very happy. So not only do we have this happy amazing day to celebrate, but there is going to be another celebration coming up the day Hailey and I get married and I promise everyone that day will not be far off. Now I think my father, and myself have taken up enough time so I want you all to party and have a very good time.

Craidon 🐺

Alpha Jaxson!! Yes Craidon what is it? There was a rogue that come up to us guards and had a note we were asked to make sure you got the note immediately and that it is very important. Thank you Craidon. You're welcome Alpha.

The Note

Jaxson, I am writing to tell you that I still love you. I am so sorry about what happened with Hailey. I never meant to do anything to hurt you or upset you. I know in my heart that I should be the one by your side, and I should be Luna. I never want to be harmful to anyone I never want to be violent. But I know that if we are not together and I cannot help rule the pack I will have no choice but to bring war. I really hope it does not come to this I hope you make the right choice yours always love, Lena

Jaxson 🐺

Craidon. Yes Alpha. If that bitch EVER comes anywhere, and I do mean anywhere near this land or anyone in my pack, or the Midnight Moon pack I want her dead!! Do you understand me? I do not mean bring her to me alive, I do not mean put her in a cell, I mean I want her dead!! This bitch is NOT to get near here ever and I mean that. I understand Alpha and I will make sure all the guards understand as well. Thank you for bringing me the letter, you did right by doing that. Now please go let the other guards know that Lena is not allowed to get near the pack land, the main house, mine and Hailey's house, or anywhere that is associated with any member of our pack or Midnight Moon pack. Yes Alpha I am leaving now to do that.

THAT BITCH, HOW DARE HER!! WHO THE HELL DOES SHE THINK SHE IS, WHAT FUCKING RIGHT DOES SHE THINK SHE HAS!!

Babe, are you okay? Hailey asked me as she walked in my office. Yes babe I am okay, just something I read but I am fine now. What was it that you read that made you so upset? I am concerned babe, and since I am your Luna I think I have this right to know when things go on. You are right babe. You remember Lena? How could I possibly forget her she attacked me. Well she sent me a note that said if I don't make her Luna she would get rogues together and come to start a war with us. Well just let her try babe, we will all be ready for her and if I get my hands or paws on her.........Babe she will not get anywhere near the border of our land, I have the guards on high alert and I told them that I want her dead. No one, and I mean no one makes threats like that on any pack. But we do not need to focus on this anyway, we have a wedding to plan. Hailey smiled at me when I said that. Yes we do, but for now let's go out and enjoy the party with everyone else. That sounds like a very good idea. I decided to send a mind link to Dorian. Hey, Craidon brought me a letter just after the coordination was over. It was from Lena, and she was threatening the pack because I will not take her back and make her Luna. I have all of the guards on high alert, but I am thinking you and I should have a meeting with the guards as they do actually know the seriousness of the situation. I just wanted to get your input on that. If you think a meeting with the guards needs to be called then let's do it. I cannot leave the grounds unprotected though that would be a perfect time for Lena to get in here. That is very true. I can go with you to the border and help you with the meeting. Yes that would work, we will do that after we get up tomorrow. Meet me there when you are on your way to the pack house breakfast. I will.

The next morning, it was hard to get out of bed because the party lasted well past midnight, but I had to get myself up. Hailey looks so beautiful laying there I just want to lay there with her, but I know I have to get to work. After my shower and I get dressed I mind link Dorian to see where he is at. I am on my way. Okay I will head out there then, see you soon.

Listen everyone, and listen up very well because I am only going to say this once. Lena is making very serious threats against not only me, but my mate Hailey. I am not taking this lightly at all. This border is to be protected at all times, we are on the highest of high alerts. I do not want any of my guards away from their position. YES ALAPHA! All of the guards said together. Okay, now I have to go back to my mate so we can start making our wedding plans. If I hear of anyone of you guards leaving your post you will have to deal with me. I will make sure you live out the rest of your days in a cell. We understand Alpha. As I go back to the house Hailey is up. Good morning beautiful, I say to her as I go over to where she is sitting at the dining room table. Good morning babe. Did you sleep well? I did. Hailey said back to me. Should I call up a cook to come make some breakfast? Well since you won't really let me do anything still either you can cook, or I can, or you can call for a cook, or we could go to the pack house and eat with everyone

LOVING MY ALPHA MATE

else. I looked at Hailey when she says something about going to the pack house to eat with everyone else. That's the first time you have wanted to go to the pack house to eat. No my love this is the first time you have not already had one of the cooks already here cooking before I get up. I laugh a little. You are right about that. Well then I guess we will be heading over to the pack house then. I am ready when you are. Hailey said. After you babe. Once we got out to the car I open Hailey's door for her and once she was in her seat I shut the door and go around to the driver side and get in. It doesn't take long to get to the pack house.

Dorian 🐺

Hey babe, I got a mind link from Jaxson. What did he say? Nikola asked me. He said that him and Hailey are coming here to the pack house for breakfast. That's really unusual, is everything okay? Nikola asked me. Yeah everything is fine. Jaxson said that he didn't have a chance to have a cook come to their house to make some breakfast and he didn't want Hailey doing all the cooking so they are coming here. Well I'm glad that they are coming here because that will give me and Hailey a chance to hang out. Yes it will. I walk over to Jace. Hey Jace, Jaxson and Hailey are on their way here. They are coming here? Jace looks surprised as he says that. Yes, Jaxson wants to talk to all of us about something. I told Jace. Do you know what it's about Dorian? Let's just wait until they get here. Oh speak of the devil.

Hey Alpha, welcome to breakfast at the pack house. I say to Jaxson with a laugh. Hailey, you are looking beautiful today. Thank you Beta Dorian. Hailey says back to me with a smile.

185

Who are you calling beautiful besides me? Nikola says as she walks up to all of us. My other girlfriend according to you sweetheart. Nikola just laughs and smacks my arm playfully as she walks past me to greet Hailey with a hug.

Nikola 🐾

HAILEY!! I scream just as I always have done when I see my BWFF. NIKOLA!! Hailey screams back. We both laugh. I think we are going to have to do that a lot quieter once the babies are born. Yes I think you are right. Hailey says. I'm actually surprised to see you and Jaxson here at the pack house for breakfast. Doesn't Jaxson normally have one of the cooks come to your house? Yes, but he was busy this morning and didn't have a cook there in time and he doesn't want me doing anything still even though it is driving me crazy not being able to do anything. So I told him that I wanted to come here. Besides I miss hanging out with you. We were never apart before you had to move away because of your dad being in the military and being transferred. I remember, it was the good old days when we were in Indiana and always together. Oh and these are not good days now? I heard Dorian say from right behind me. I almost jumped out of my skin. Babe you scared me. Hahaha, you must always be on guard Nikola. Dorian says. I guess so. I hear Hailey laugh. Babe, Jaxson wants to talk to me and some of the other guys outside so I will be back in a few. Okay babe, I will hang out with Hailey. Sounds good. Dorian gives me a very sweet kiss before going outside with Jaxson.

So BWFF, we need to go shopping. These babies are growing so much that nothing is fitting me anymore. Hahahaha it wasn't that long ago I asked you if your belly was starting to stick out there and I thought you were going to bite my head off. I just laughed when Hailey said that. Stop being so dramatic Hailey. We both laugh. So a shopping day is for sure needed. I am sure we could go today. I know I have nothing planned and Jaxson hasn't said anything to me about us doing anything so if you are free......... well it looks like Dorian is going to be doing pack stuff with Jaxson so I am free. Then you are mine for the day, and if Dorian has a problem with that he can take it up with me. Hailey said and laughed. I mind link Dorian. Hey babe, Hailey and I are going shopping after we are done eating if that is okay. Of course babe. But make sure to come give me a kiss before you leave. You know I will. I close the mind link and tell Hailey that it is all set.

Jaxson 🐺

Okay guys and lady guards. I really need you all to be on the highest of high alerts. Are we still watching for Lena? Yes and anyone that she might send to try and throw us off. I have said this once and I will say it again I want that bitch dead. I don't want her brought to me alive, I don't want her to be put in a cell alive, I want her dead. She has made threats against my mate, your Luna, she has made threats against our pack. That goes against everything we believe in. Also I think we have a traitor in our pack. That's when everyone's eyes got big and mouth dropped. A traitor? Dorian said. Yes Beta Dorian I have not even told you about this because I didn't want anyone to know that I had figured out that we have a traitor until I was sure. But Lena knows way too much for someone who is not in our pack. For someone who was sent away and is a rogue. Alpha Jaxson, is it safe for Luna and Beta Dorians mate to be going out together without some sort of security? No, I want to have

187

one of you guards go with them if they go out. Ummm Alpha Jaxson. Yes Beta Dorian. The girls are going shopping right after they are done with breakfast. Lita and Stella I want you to go with your Luna and Beta Dorian's mate Nikola and Hailey to town. Yes alpha. Two of our female guards say at the same time then they go towards the pack house and wait outside for Hailey and Nikola to come out so they can drive them to town and watch over them. Now for the rest of you guards. I want you all to be on full alert, and I want you all to do this in shifts. The last thing I need is all my guards to be trolling the grounds and getting tired. There is no way all of you can be on top of everything if you're tired. So you all need to do this in shifts. Yes Alpha.

Katie 🐺

I slip out the back door of the pack house and run as fast as I can into the woods. I hope that no one sees me. By the time I make it to the woods my heart is pounding so hard it feels like it is going to jump right out of my chest. But it is not only beating that fast and hard from running to the woods but also from the thought of someone seeing me going to the woods. It takes about 20 minutes to get to the cave that Lena stays in. I don't know why she has not made a house, but to each their own I guess. I get to the edge of the cave and I stepped just inside Lena……..Lena……..WHAT! I hear Lena yell. I step a little more into the cave and I see a light so I go on in. Lena. Yes Katie. Hailey and Nikola are getting ready to go into town. They are going just the two of them? As far as I know they are. Jaxson has never sent anyone with Lun…..I mean Hailey before. Also that Nikola is already pregnant with Dorian's pups. I wanted to be back with him before that happened, I wanted to be the one to be pregnant with his baby. Oh stop whining Katie. WADJET!! What? Wadjet says to Lena. I need those potions. I will get them for you Lena. Then Lena turns back to me. Do you know where they are going shopping at, a specific store perhaps? No, but I know that they are going shopping for Nikola because she is complaining that since she is carrying three pups that her clothes don't fit. Lena rolled her eyes. The slut shouldn't have gotten herself knocked up if she couldn't handle it. I should be the one having Dorian's baby or babies. Good Lord Katie stop carrying on about that Dorian. Lena says to me. But he is the love of my life and you know that. I think the entire world knows you feel that way by now. Lena said. Just then Wadjet comes in with several vials in her hand. Here you go Lena here is the potions that you asked for. These better work. Oh believe me they will work just the way you requested. Wadjet told Lena. Katie go back to the pack land before anyone realizes you are gone. When Lena says that I turn around and leave.

Justa 🐺

Ummm Alpha Jaxson. Yes what is it Justa? Alpha Jaxson says to me. Is there something going on in the woods? Alpha Jaxson looks up at me. What do you mean? Well I have seen Katie go in there for a second time in a few days. Katie? She is a Omega isn't she? Alpha Jaxson ask me. Yes she is. Then she shouldn't even be leaving the pack house. That is what I thought, but I thought I would check with you Alpha. Thank you Justa. You're welcome Alpha Jaxson. I start to turn around to walk out of Alpha Jaxson's office when he spoke again. Justa can you show me where you seen Katie go into the woods. Yes Alpha Jaxson. I walk Alpha Jaxson to the woods where I seen Katie go in at. Thank you again Justa. You're welcome Alpha

Jaxson. Justa will you go tell Beta Dorian and have him come here as well. Yes sir. I run back to where Beta Dorian is at speaking to some of the guards. Beta Dorian, Alpha Jaxson has asked me to come let you know what I have seen and have you to join him. What is it Justa? I have seen Omega Katie going into the woods over there on more than one occasion so Alpha Jaxson ask me to show him where. I walked him to the exact spot I seen her go in and now he is there I think he is waiting for her to come out from the woods but he has asked me to come and ask you to join him. Thank you Justa I will go there now.

Jaxson

When Dorian got here I told him that if what Justa has told us is the truth when Katie comes out of the woods we will find out why she is going in there when she is not even supposed to be leaving the house. Maybe she is the one who has been telling Lena everything that is going on. That can be so dangerous for our entire pack. Dorian says. Not just our entire pack, but for Hailey and Nikola as well. This is the side of the woods where Lena has been cited before. This is not good, not good at all Dorian. I know, believe me I know. We are probably going to go to war. Well our pack is ready anytime it happens Alpha. Dorian and I just look at each other. About that time we hear one set of footsteps and out comes Katie one of the house Omegas.

Alpha Jaxson, Beta Dorian. I am surprised to see both of you here. I am sure you are Omega Katie. You will be coming with us. Dorian and I take Katie by her arms and lead her into my office. What were you doing in the woods? I was just getting some air, I have not been feeling well Alpha. DO NOT LIE TO ME!! I could feel Cain wanting to come out. I could see

Katie shaking. She lowers her head. I was meeting with Lena. WHY? She told me that if I help her that she would help me get Dorian back. Dorian laughs. You will not ever have me back that ended a long time ago Katie. You know that. Dorian said to her. It would not matter if it ended a long time ago or not. I said to both Dorian and Katie. You are an Omega and Dorian is a Beta. Now you will live the rest of your life in a cell. I mind link Justa. Justa I want you to go with Beta Dorian to take Katie to the cells. Yes alpha. Dorian make sure the cell is locked and hurry we need to get to town. Yes Alpha.

Lena 🐾

When they come out they are not going to know what hit them. Hahahaha. I laughed just thinking about how happy Jaxson and I will be while that bitch suffers in a cave the way I have all this time. Here they come. I walk across the street. Hey slut. I yell at Hailey and Nikola as they come out of the store, and they look right at me. I wish I could have gotten a picture of their faces when they looked over at me. Yeah you know that you both are sluts don't you. Lena!! Hailey says and sounding very surprised to see me. Yes that's right I am right here and I have a little something for you. I raise my hand to hit them with the potion that Wadjet made just for this moment. As I am about to throw it someone grabs my arm. I turn around to see who the hell is grabbing me.

Lita 🐾

I am so glad that Alpha sent me as one of the guards to protect Luna. I am so glad that I work hard at our training because it feels so good to be the one to catch this bitch just as she thinks she is going to get away with what she has planned. The look on Lena's face is priceless. Yes Lena it is me, the one guard you thought you were going to get rid of when you thought you were going to be Luna. That didn't happen for you and now this is not going to happen. Hailey is our Luna, her and Alpha Jaxson were meant to be together it was the moon goddesses choice. Lena spit towards my face and that is when I dragged her behind the building and broke her neck. I mind link Stella. Can you bring the car around? I have some trash to throw in the back of it. I am on my way, I'm just finishing up getting Luna and Nikola safely in your car. When Stella brought her car around she pops the hatch and I throw that bitch in the back. Once I was in my car and I see that Luna Hailey and Nikola are in fact safe, then I open the mind link to Alpha Jaxson. Alpha I wanted to let you know that Lena will never be a problem again. Is she dead? Alpha Jaxson ask me. Yes sir, I broke her neck. She came for Luna Hailey and Nikola. It was a good thing you had us to come with them when they went shopping because I guess that was when Lena was going to try something on Luna Hailey and Nikola. Very nicely done. Alpha Jaxson says to me. Thank you sir. I close the link.

Hailey

When we got back to the pack house I see Jaxson and Dorian run out to meet Nikola and I at the car. Babe are you okay? Jaxson asked as he wraps his arms around me. Yes babe I am fine and so is Nikola. Oh thank god. When Lita told me what had happened I was so worried about you. Jaxson I told you that Lena will never get to me and she didn't. What happened? Jaxson asked. Nikola and I were in a shop, when we came out Lena walked across the road. I seen her right away but I was trying to hurry with Nikola to get back to the car which was in front of the store we had been in. Lena had something in her hand and she raised her hand like she was going to throw whatever she had and that is when Lita grabbed her and went around the building with her. Stella got me and Nikola into Lita's car and then Stella went to her car, got in and drove around the building. Not but a couple of seconds later Lita came back and got in the car and drove us back here. I am just so glad that you and Nikola are safe. We are fine Jax. I am ready to go home though, I am tired. Then let's go home. I want to make sure Nikola is okay first though. Okay babe, I will go get our car. As Jaxson goes to get the car I walk over to Nikola and Dorian. Nikola, are you sure you are okay. Yes Hailey, I am just so glad that we had Lita and Stella there. Who knows what would have happened if they had not been there. I know, but let's not think about that. We are safe.

Nikola 🐾

When Hailey and I got back to the pack house Jaxson and Dorian came out and met us at the car. Nikola, Dorian said as he wraps his arms around me. OMG babe are you okay? Are our babies okay? I can feel the tears falling down my face as I bury my face into Dorian's chest. Yes I am okay and our babies are okay. I was so afraid when I seen Lena coming over to Hailey and I. All I could think about was you and our babies. I will never let anything happen to you or our babies. Dorian said to me. But how, how did she know where we were at? Dorian takes a deep breath. One of the Omegas named Katie had been keeping Lena informed of everything that has been going on with Jaxson and Hailey. Why would she do that? I asked Dorian. Dorian put his head down. I dated Katie when I was younger but she was becoming to possessive I ended it with her. I guess she never got over it because Lena told her that if she helped Lena by keeping her informed about everything that was going on with Jaxson and Hailey then she would help Katie get me back. But babe I am in love with you, you are my mate, we were meant to be together. Dorian said to me. Dorian I wish you would have told me all of this about you and Katie before. But what matters now is that we are together and everything is okay.

Dorian 🐺

All I wanted to do was to get Nikola home and make sure her and our babies are okay. I mind link the pack doctor and ask him to meet us at our house. Babe we need to go, I have the Pack doctor on his way to our house. Why? I want to make sure everything is okay with you and our babies. I want to say bye to Hailey. Okay babe, I will be right there with you. Nikola and I meet Hailey as she is walking over towards us.

Nikola 🐺

Hailey are you okay? Yes I am fine, I just hope you and those babies are okay. Dorian has the pack doctor on his way to our house so we have to go. Please let me know how everything is once the doctor is done. I will I promise. I will see you both later. Hailey says as she gives me and Dorian a hug by. Dorian make sure Nikola let's me know how everything is. I will. Please tell Alpha Jaxson bye for us. I say to Hailey. I will.

The doctor was waiting on the porch when we got home. Hi Nikola and Beta Dorian. Hi doctor, please follow us into the house. Dorian says. Once inside the doctor asked me to go into the bedroom and get comfortable on the bed. I could hear the doctor and Dorian talking about I may have to go to the pack hospital for more of an exam, but he will do what he can here. Then they both walk into the bedroom. Everything seems to be fine. The doctor says to us. I can tell more with an ultrasound, but I would have to do that at the hospital. How do you feel Nikola? I feel fine. No pain or discomfort? No none at all. Well maybe if you just stay in bed and rest hopefully there was no trauma done to the babies. But if you feel the slightest bit of discomfort or pain I want you to mind link me and meet me at the hospital. I will make sure of it Doc. Dorian says.

CHAPTER 7

ANOTHER SURPRISE

Lauren

OMG Kaden!! What is it sweetheart? I need to go to Hailey and Jaxson's now. Why what is wrong? Just take me or I will go myself. Okay, okay love I will take you. I run out to the car and get in. Kaden get's in on the driver side. When we get to Hailey and Jaxson's I get out and run to the door. I knock until Jaxson opens the door. Where is she? Hailey is upstairs in our room. I run up the stairs. OMG my baby girl are you okay? Mom, what? Are you okay? Yes Mom I am fine, why? Hailey I know what happened. I know that Lena almost got to you and Nikola? Hailey sighs. Jax was not supposed to say anything. What do you mean he was not supposed to say anything. Hailey I am your mother and I need to know when things go on, but it was not Jaxson that told me. Hailey looked at me in surprise. Then it had to be Dorian or Nikola. No Hailey it wasn't anyone. What do you mean mom, someone had to have told you otherwise how would you know? There is something I have not told you Hailey. She takes a deep breath and looks at me. Mom I asked you a long time ago to tell me everything that I did not want any more surprises or secrets. I know, and I should have told you this but not only am I a wolf, but I am a Caladrius. I can turn into a snow white bird, but I can also see things that are going on with you and any part of the pack family. The only thing is that sometimes I can see it before it happens, or as it is happening, and sometimes after it has happened. Like today when Lena try to attack you and Nikola. I seen it after it happened because you were well protected. If you had not been then I would have been able to see it before it happened. But Mom if you can see things like that then why did you not see what was going to happen to dad? I did not have this power at that time. Well you don't have to worry mom, I am safe. Yes

I know you are, but I still have to come and check on you. I still have a very uneasy feeling like something is not right just yet but I cannot see what it might be. Well Mom don't worry, Jaxson is here with me so I am fine. Well you know I have always been protective of you. Yes I know mom. But I am very tired. So I am going to lay down for a little while. Okay sweetie. I will go downstairs and talk to Jaxson and Kaden. Rest well. I gave Hailey a hug before walking out of her room.

Hailey 🐺

Finding out that my mom is a Caladrius is really weird, but I guess I should be used to weird by now. Actually weird should be normal to me by now. I mean I find out not only are werewolves, vampires, and fairies, and all other mythical creatures exist but I found out that I am a werewolf and that I have been one my whole life. I just didn't know because for one no one had told me, and for two I hadn't phased yet a least not until that first rouge attack that happened after I had gotten here. Everything is so much to take in, but it is something that is my life now.

Hey babe. Yes Jax. We still have some planning to do. Planning? Ummm yes, we still have to plan our wedding. You are right, we do have a wedding to plan. I just have a lot more work to do than you do. I said to Jax. Babe I am going to help you every step of the way. But Jax you can not see my wedding dress until I am walking down the aisle. Well you got me there. I laugh when he says that. I can have Nikola help me with picking out my wedding dress since she is going to be my matron of honor. Instead of just because she's my best friend that she would want that job. Oh I am sure she will be very happy. Jax she is pregnant with triplets I am sure that is taking a lot out of her. You got a point there babe. Maybe you should ask her. I'm already on that. I just asked her if her and Dorian can come over because I have something important I want to talk to her about and I know Dorian is not going to let Nikola out of his sight until those babies are born, and probably not even then. I know that I would be like that with you. Hahahaha babe you already are already like that. Jax smiles when I said that to him. It's because I love you and I never want anything to happen to you.

Nikola

I can not wait to have these babies. Carrying three of them is a lot more than I expected. How are you feeling babe? I'm tired, my back hurts and I am hungry. Dorian laughs. What is so funny? Your just so cute. How is looking like a beached whale cute? You don't look like a beached whale sweetheart, your beautiful, and your glowing. Yeah, yeah, yeah. What would you like for me to make you to eat? I think for a minute. How about a steak, rare. That and some fruit. You got it babe. Dorian goes and gets started on my food. Hey Nikola. Hailey says through mind link. Hey BWFF what's up? I need you and Dorian to come over it's important. Is there something wrong? Hailey laugh's. No silly. Does something have to be wrong for me to want my BWFF to come over? I know Dorian isn't going to let you come over by yourself that's why I asked if you both could come over. Dorian is making me some food so we will be over after I eat. Being pregnant with these triplets is driving me crazy. I am sure it is but it will all be worth it once they are born and that won't be much longer, right? Well honestly it could be any day now and I would love to hurry them along. Oh Nikola they will come out when they are ready. I know, believe me I know. I will see you soon. I close the mind link just in time because as soon as I close it Dorian yells from the kitchen that my food is ready. Babe you are going to have to come in here and help me up. I can hear him laughing in the kitchen. It's not funny. Hailey asked if we can come over once I am done eating. She said it is important. Is there something wrong that we need to hurry for? No I have time to eat first.

Wadjet

Balthazar, the new king of vampires I need you to awaken. I have to get Alaric's son to wake up so he can help me destroy these mutts. I guess Katie was caught because I have not seen her in a while and now that Lena is dead I am going to have to have someone to help that has more natural power's and strength than I do. I have the wolf bane ready just in case we need to use it. Now I just have to come up with an awakening spell. Yes this one, this is the one I will use.

I call upon the magical energy around me. Hear me and obey! Reveal yourself and awaken to the fullest and obey. This is my will. This must be.

It takes a few minutes. I was beginning to think my spell was not working, or that Balthazar had been sleeping way to long. Maybe I wouldn't have the help I needed. I guess if Balthazar doesn't wake up with the spell I used I can always use a sleeping spell on those mutts and then once they are all asleep I can kill them all?

Jaxson

I asked Hailey to let me know when Dorian and Nikola get here. I have to get some work done. I have a lot of paperwork to go over with the transfer request, and information on incoming newbies. Do you need me to help you babe? That's sweet, but no. I want you to focus on our wedding. Yes my love. I am so excited about marrying you and becoming Mrs. Jaxson Carter. Babe I have been thinking about that for a while now and he takes me so seriously. Yeah babe, what are you thinking? I was thinking that I would just keep my last name the same as it is now. Jax stopped right in his tracks and turned around to face me. What Hailey? You don't want to have my last name? Why would you not want to have my last name? I start laughing. Babe you are way to easy to mess with. You are going to have to lighten up especially since we are going to be married. I am Alpha of this pack, if I lighten up no one will take me seriously. Babe I am talking about between you and I. You know that I love to joke around and you are such an easy target. I can not wait to become Mrs. Jaxson Carter. Jax walks over to me and picks me up in his arms and kisses me. Wow babe you have not kissed me like that for a while now. I know and for that I am sorry, also I would have you to help me with the paperwork but since Dorian and Nikola are coming over I want to give you the time you need so you can talk to her about being your matron of honor. Wait, are you two going dress shopping today too? I want to, but if Dorian won't let Nikola out of his sight because she could give birth any time now I don't know if he will let her go shopping just her and I. Well as his Alpha I will tell him that he has to stay here and that Nikola is in good hands with you. Besides I will be sending Lita and Stella with you two again. They are now unofficially your body guards. Plus if anything happens you two can just mind link us and we can meet you at the hospital. I hope Dorian goes for that. He won't have a choice.

Balthazar

Who dare awaken me from my sleep? It is I Wadjet, I need you Balthazar. Why hag? Well I knew you would want to know that your father Alaric was killed. When that hag told me that my father was killed I jump up from where I was laying. WHO KILLED MY FATHER? It was the wolves. The mutts from the Golden Sun Pack that killed your father. I will gather a clan together and we will rip apart those mutts. Balthazar we do have some wolves on our side. Sadly the one that had the pack together that was helping us was killed too by this wolves. A pack killed another wolf? I asked the hag. Well she was what they call a rouge. She was turned away from the pack when the Alpha was done with her. I see, and they killed her? Yes because she had went after the Alpha's mate. I would kill someone too if they went after my mate. Speaking of mate I could use a mate of my own.

Lauren

Hey sweetie, what are you doing today? I asked Hailey through mind link. Well Jax reminded me that I need to start planning our wedding so I thought I would go dress shopping when Nikola gets here which by the way her and Dorian just pulled in. Do you mind if I go? I would love to see the dress you pick out. I would love for you to be there mom. Okay just let me know when you are leaving and I will head to town too. Okay I will. Love you mom. I love you too.

Dorian 🐺

Babe, are you okay? Why? You have been very quiet all the way over here. I was just thinking about what it is going to be like once the babies are born. I was also thinking about how we have not even picked out names and it's not like we are only having one, but we are having three so we need at least three girl names and three boys names. Well one name that comes to my mind, but I don't I know if you would like it or not is Alexander. Of course you would think of a boy's name first. Okay how about Alexandria. Hahahaha oh my love you have a one track mind. What do you mean by that? Alexander for a boy and Alexandria for a girl? Really babe? You don't like the name's? I didn't say that. I do like the name's, but I think we should try to come up with more name's. Your right babe. Well here we are at Jaxson's and Hailey's.

Hailey 🐺

Hey you two come on in. Hey Dorian, Jax is in his office you can go in there. I think he has some things he would like your help with. Okay, thanks and hi Hailey. Once Dorian was in the office I turn to Nikola. Hey BWFF how are you feeling, how are those babies doing? Well I think I might be going into labor. WHAT? Shhhh I don't want Dorian to know yet. What do you mean you don't want Dorian to know yet, you need to go to the pack hospital. Not yet the contractions are not that bad. But Nikola you're having three pups. I know, believe me I know. But still I don't want to go yet. So you said you had something important to talk to me about? Yes, but I want to make sure you are okay first. I'm fine Hailey. Okay, okay. I wanted to ask you something important. Well ask away I am here now. I wanted to ask you if you would like to be my matron of honor. Omg! Nikola screened. Babe are you okay? Dorian asked as he comes running out of Jax's office. Yes I am okay. Hailey just caught me off guard by asking me if I would be her matron of honor. Will you scared me when you screamed like that. I'm sorry babe. Nikola said to Dorian with a big smile. Then she turns back to me. Of course I want to be your......OUCH......Matron of...... OMG. Nikola are you okay? Do you want me to get Dorian? No don't get him yet. Damn that one hurt. But yes I would love to be your matron of honor. Maybe we should talk about this later. I think you should get to the pack hospital. Hailey really this could take hours. I'm sure it could, but you're in pain and they can give you something there to ease your pain. I run into Jax's office. Dorian.

Dorian 🐺

When Hailey came running into Alpha Jaxson's office I knew that she was coming to tell me that Nikola is in labor. As soon as Hailey said that Nikola is having contractions she ran right back out. Jaxson and I both run out into the front room where Nikola and Hailey are at. I had a feeling that you were in labor, I said too Nikola. Well the pain wasn't this bad on the way over here. But that was why you were so quiet in the car wasn't it? Yes it was. Nikola said as she started feeling another contraction. I have already contacted the doctor through mind link and he said to bring you in, so let me help you out to the car. We are coming too, but we will follow you in my car. Hailey and Jaxson help me get Nikola out to the car and once she was in the front passenger seat I got in the driver's seat. It wasn't no time before we were at the hospital.

Hailey 🐺

I am so excited that Nikola is going to have the babies. I hope everything is okay with her and the babies. Everything is going to be just fine. Jax said in his reassuring way. It didn't take long to get to the pack hospital because Dorian was driving really fast, but I am sure he is a very nervous dad to be. But Jax had to drive fast to keep up. I'm surprised we didn't get pulled over. But then again Jax is pack Alpha so no one really messes with him. So if the police officer did see Dorian speeding down the road they would have seen that we were right behind him doing the same thing and that would be why no one got pulled over.

Nikola 🐺

Dorian slow down. I don't want to crash before we get to the hospital. Babe you're in labor, I want to get you there as soon as possible. Well we are not far from there so, OUCH, damn that hurts. Are they getting closer together? Dorian asked me. I think they are. They are also getting stronger. That's why I am speeding. I don't want anything going wrong with you or our babies. That's sweet babe, but PLEASE FOR THE LOVE OF GOD......OMG. Jesus freaking Christ that freaking hurts. I am sure they will give you something for the pain. Yeah well that is not helping me right now. We are here at the hospital now sweetheart. I will come around and help you out of the car. Once we were inside the hospital Hailey went to the nurse's desk and started getting me checked in while Dorian and Alpha Jaxson went with me and a nurse to the room I was going to give birth to my babies in. Hi Nikola. The pack doctor says to me when he comes into the room. Hi doctor. Hello Alpha Jackson and Beta Dorian. They both said hi back to the pack doctor at the same time. We all watch the doctor as he goes over to the monitor and checks the printout. Is everything okay? I asked him. Let's take a look and see how everything is going. I will wait out in the hall. Alpha Jaxson says before the doctor checks me.

Jaxson 🐺

I see Hailey walking down the hall as soon as I step outside of the door to the room where Nikola and Dorian are. How is she? Hailey ask me. The doctor is in there now checking her so I told Nikola and Dorian I would step out here while he checked her. Just then I also see Nikola's parents coming up the hall. Alpha, how is our daughter. She is fine. The doctor and Dorian are in there now and the doctor is checking her. I am sure you will be able to go in as soon as he is done.

Pack Doctor 🐺

What I seen on the monitor didn't look good to me, but normally when a female is carrying more than one pup she usually ends up having to have a C-section and I am thinking that is what I am going to have to do with Nikola. I am glad that Beta Dorian is a little more level-headed than Alpha Jaxson is.

Okay Nikola how are you feeling? Well my epidural has already kicked in so I am not really feeling any pain. Is there something wrong doc? I think one maybe two of the babies is in distress, so we may be going for a C-section which is not uncommon when a female is carrying multiples. Doc, please take care of my beautiful lady here. I will Beta Dorian. If I have to do a C-section I can have all three babies out in under a minute, so don't worry. Just make sure that our babies and Nikola are okay. I will do everything in my power Beta Dorian, you have my word on that. Thank you doc. You're welcome and everything is going to be fine.

Lily 🐺

As soon as I seen Nikola I go over to her and give her a big hug. How are you doing sweetie? I am fine mom. What did the doctor say? He said that one, maybe two of the babies might be in some distress so I may have to have a C-section. Oh my poor baby. Lily she is not a baby anymore. Todd said from behind me. She will always be my baby girl. You know I will be right here for you either way Nikola. If you have to have a C-section your father and I will be in the waiting room. We will not leave until I see you and those babies are okay. Nikola smiles at me. Thank you mom. You're welcome baby. Your father and I will go out to the lobby and get some coffee so Hailey can come in if that is okay with you. I know she is worried about you. There is no need for anyone to worry, I am perfectly fine. Nikola says to me. It is because we all love you. I will check on you in a little bit dear. Thank you mom. I love you both. Nikola says to me and Todd as we are walking out. We love you too sweetie. I said back to her. How is she? Hailey ask me as soon as the door closes. Well the doctor thinks she might have to have a C-section because one or two other babies is under a little stress, but the doctor can have all three out in under a minute so everything should be fine. Can I go in and see her? She is waiting on you. I said to Hailey.

Hailey 🐾

I peek my head inside the door. Is it okay to come in? I asked when I seen Dorian hugging Nikola. Dorian stands back up. Of course BWFF you can come in. Nikola says to me with a smile. Your mom told me what the doctor said. I am going to be right here with you Nikola as long as you want me to be and until they have to take you for the C-section. We really hope that I don't have to have a C-section, but I have also been thinking that it might be safer since the doctor can get them out faster that way then I can push them out. I don't know what I want to do Hailey I am so scared. It will be okay Nikola, you are in good hands with this doctor. As I see a tear running down Nikola's face Dorian walks over to her and puts his arms around her. Try and think about positive things. I said to her. I will. Just then the doctor walks back in.

CHAPTER 8

THE NEWEST PACK MEMBERS

Nikola 🐺

Well doc what's it going to be? Nikola I really think we should do the C-section. Things are not changing the way I would like for them to so I want to get your babies out as fast as possible. Will Dorian be able to be with me? Yes of course. A nurse will be here in a couple of minutes to get you Beta Dorian. I am ready whenever the nurse gets here. Okay I am ready I guess. I will see you after while. I said to Hailey before she leaves the room. I will be waiting to see you and those beautiful babies. I will see you very soon sweetheart. I said to Dorian as a nurse starts getting everything unhooked and getting ready to take me to the surgery room. I am terrified right now. Not only have I never had any kind of surgery, but I am going to have three babies very soon. When is Dorian going to be here? I asked one of the nurses. One of the other nurses just went to get him so he should be here very soon. We just have to get you hooked up to the monitors and get some medicine going in you so that the numbing doesn't wear off before the doctor is done. Just then I see Dorian coming in. He looks so good even in hospital scrubs and surgery cap on. Babe I am so terrified right now. You are going to be just fine sweetheart. Dorian says to me. I am going to be by your side the entire time and I am not going to leave you even after the babies are born.

Pack Doctor 🐺

Okay you two are you ready to meet your first baby? Yes we are. Beta Dorian says. Okay and here is baby number one and it is a boy. I hand the first baby off to a nurse so she can show Beta Dorian and Nikola. Here is baby number two. You have a girl.

Dorian 🐺

When the nurse brought our first born, our son over to us I could feel my heart beating so fast. He is so amazing. I said to Nikola. I see tears going down her face. Then our second baby is brought over to us by another nurse. She is absolutely beautiful, she looks just like her mom. When I said that I seen Nikola's smile get bigger. Then our third baby was brought over to us. Wow all three are crying. I laugh as I say to Nikola. We are going to have our hands full if they all three decide to wake up at the same time for their feedings. Hahahaha yes we are but we will manage it somehow. Nikola said. Just then I see everyone get real still and the warning beepers start going off. What is going on? I asked the doctor as nurses rush to put the babies down. One of the nurses comes over to me, has me to stand up and she walks me out of the surgery room. WHAT IS GOING ON? I shouted. I don't know, but as soon as I do I will come back and tell you. It seemed like forever before the nurses came back with any kind of information for us. By this time I was in the waiting area with Todd, Lily, Alpha Jaxson, Hailey, Lauren, and Kaden. I feel like I am going to lose my mind. I was pacing back and forth in the waiting room. Lily asked me to sit down a couple of times but how could I sit down when my mate is in surgery and I have no idea what is even going on. One minute everything is going fine, our babies were born and nothing seemed wrong with them, then the next minute I am being pushed out of there and told to wait. Finally a nurse comes and tells us that Nikola had started losing too much blood and that is why she passed out. But luckily the doctor caught it in time and has fixed it, and that Nikola is doing fine, she is in recovery. I asked if I could go be with her. Once she is awake I will come get you. Where is our babies then I want to see them. They were taken to the NICU as a precaution since there was three and we had to do an emergency C-section that is just policy that they be taken there instead of the regular nursery. But yes you can go see them. But only a couple of people at a time. I will go with you Dorian. I heard Hailey say. I just nod my head at her and we follow the nurse as she shows us where the NICU is.

Hailey 🐺

I could tell that Dorian is very upset that something happened right after Nikola gave birth. But once we were at the NICU and he could see his babies a whole different vibe came over him. She is going to be fine Dorian. I know Nikola and she is a fighter. Besides nothing is going to happen to her especially now that you two have these very beautiful babies. Wow two girls and one boy. I see Dorian smile. Yes we have been blessed and they all have sets of lungs on them. Dorian kind of laughed as he said this. Well I have known you for a while now and I know you can howl pretty loud so they must have gotten their lungs from both you and Nikola because she can be loud too. It used to drive my mom crazy when Nikola would come over and scream my name through the house until she would find me. Then Dorian laughed when I told him that. I know Nikola well and it won't be long until she is on her feet again. Then these little girls and that little boy will start training to be part of the pack. I look forward to them training. They are going to be great fighters. Dorian said.

Nikola 🐺

OMG I could feel the pain as I was waking up. I must have made some kind f noise because the nurse came to my side as I was opening my eyes. How are you feeling dear? The nurse asked me. I feel like I have been sliced open. She kind of laughed. Well you have been and you have three very beautiful babies as a result. Where are they? They are in the NICU. That is just policy because they were born by C-section. Where is Dorian? He is with the babies, but I can have a nurse to get him if you like. Yes please and thank you. Your welcome, can I get you anything. Can I have something for this pain please, it really hurts a lot. I will get you some pain medicine right now. I see the nurse put a needle in my I.V. and only about a second later I am feeling so much better. Hi sweetheart. Dorian say's as he enters the recovery area where I am at. Hi babe how are you feeling? Well I was feeling like whatever the doctor used to slice me open was still in me, but the nurse gave me something for pain and I am feeling much better now. Have you seen our babies yet since they took them to the nursery? Yes, Hailey and I went to see them and they are absolutely perfect. Your mom and dad are in there with them now. I can not wait to see them again and hold them. Well you need to get rest first sweetheart, you gave me a real scare. I am sorry babe I didn't mean to scare you. I said. What happened to me anyway? All I remember is seeing our babies and then I woke up in recovery feeling like I was still being sliced open. Well you started bleeding into your belly area and then you passed out. But the doctor fixed everything. I was scared because I didn't know what was going on and they made me leave the surgery room. It seemed like forever before the nurse came to tell me what was going on. Well the important thing is that I am okay now. I'm just ready to see our babies and hold them. I feel so empty now that they are no longer inside of me.

Nurse 🐺

I could hear Nikola telling Beta Dorian that she is ready to see her babies, so I page the doctor to come and make sure she is ready to be moved.

Pack Doctor 🐺

Hello again Nikola and Beta Dorian. Hi Doc. Dorian say's. So Nikola I hear you are ready to see the babies. Yes I am, how are they doing? Well the second and third one are very strong, but they have a little bit before they are completely out of the woods yet. We want to make sure they can eat before we move them out of the NICU. But baby number one is already in the regular nursery. Can I be moved to my room now doc? I would like to see my babies, at least the first one. Yes, I will have the nurse to unhook you so you can be moved. Thank you doctor. Both Nikola and Beta Dorian say to me.

Nikola 🐺

Once I was inside of my room and settled a nurse brought the first baby to me. I looked down at her. She is so perfect. I said as tears start rolling down my face. Yes she is. Dorian say's. Babe? Yes sweetheart. I want to name her Gabriela. Dorian looked at me kind of funny. What made you think of that name? Well she is very strong obviously and I wanted to name one of our daughter's after your grandmother since I have heard that she was a strong fighter. Dorian smiles down at me. Yes she was. I can remember her very well and I remember seeing her training no one could ever get her down. Just then Hailey,

Alpha Jaxson, my mom, my dad, Chad, Abby, Jace, Lauren, and Kaden all come just inside my room. I look at them all and say don't be afraid come on in and meet our first daughter Gabriela. They all walk over and surround my bed. I look up at Hailey. Would you like to hold your goddaughter? I see the tears in Hailey's eyes. Really? You want me to hold her first? Well I figured the godmother could hold her then hand her off to the grandmother. We are going to make it official very soon that you and Alpha Jaxson are the godparents of all three babies. I tell both Hailey and Alpha Jaxson. Just make sure you get plenty of rest and when you two are ready we will be ready. Alpha Jaxson says to me. I will, that's a promise.

Lily 🦊

I can not believe my baby girl is a mommy. To me she still looks like my baby.Ummm I think it is my turn to hold my granddaughter and yes I am using the grandma card here. Everyone laughs when I said that. But Hailey hand's Gabby over to me. How did you two come up with her name? I wanted to name her after Dorian's grandmother. Well it is a very good name but have you two come up with names for the other two babies yet? I want to name the boy Alexander and one of the girls Alexandria. But Nikola didn't like giving them names that are so similar so we haven't picked out names for the other two yet. Actually babe, I think you should be able to name the other two if you want. Nikola says to Dorian. Then they will be called Alexander and Alexandria. We can call the kids Gabby, Alex, and Andi.

Jaxson 🐺

I was about to see if I could hold Gabby when I got a mind link from Donovan. Well everyone if you will excuse us, I think Hailey and I are going to go and let Nikola and Dorian enjoy their new family and get some rest too. Everyone said bye and then Hailey and I were out the door. Jax babe, what is wrong? I know something is going on because you wouldn't have had me to leave too if something wasn't wrong. I got a mind link from Donovan he said that he needs us to come to the pack house there's something important he needs to tell us. Once Hailey and I were at the pack house and I meet up with Donovan. What is it? I asked him. We got news from another pack the Light Moon Pack lead guard came to tell us that there have been some rouge's attacking and that they have vampires with them only this time it is Alaric's son. WHAT? I yelled. I thought he was sleeping. I was told that Wadjet cast a spell to wake him and he is looking for vengeance against the pack that killed his father. Donovan told Hailey and I. Thank you Donovan. We will be ready. How long do we have? I was told that they probably will be here by the end of the week. Okay, well high alert again for all guards. Takes shifts. I want one set of guards on duty during the day and the others here at night. Yes Alpha. Donovan said.

Hailey 🐺

I will help you get everyone trained for this babe. I'm going to need your help in a different way this time. Jax said to me. What do you mean? Well since Nikola and the triplets will be just getting home by the time the rouges arrive I will need you to be with the woman of the pack that has young children this time. But Jax. No arguing with me. I really need you to help the woman and young children Hailey. I think Jax could tell I was not happy about this, but he was not backing down. I loved being outside helping with the training and fighting beside Jax. I hate that he is wanting me to be inside this time. I also need you to help me with the paperwork since Dorian is at the hospital with Nikola and I do not want to take him away from her right now. I turn to go back to the car and Jax follows me. Once we were home we both go into the office and start going over paperwork. We both make phone calls to sister packs and talk to the Alpha's of those packs. We let them know that we are going to need all the help we can get. I hear Jax tell one of the other Alpha's that we could take these young rouge's, but one of our Beta's may not be able to help since his mate just had triplets. So how many pack's are coming? I asked Jax when he was off the phone. Four, all four are coming to help. But we are going to be moving the woman and young children to an undisclosed location.

Jax 🐺

I could tell that Hailey was not happy that I was not letting her train and fight this time. But it is really important to me that she is safe. Balthazar is a young very strong vampire and I don't know his plan of attack yet. So I am not taking any chances with Hailey or anyone else getting hurt. Since it is late I decided to try and make this up to my beautiful mate. When I get up and walk over to her she looks up at me and I can see that she is really upset. Babe I just want to make sure you are okay, I always want to keep you safe. I know, I just enjoy training and I enjoy fighting by your side. I know you do. But for now,

I bend down and pick Hailey up in my arms. Jaxson what are you doing? Hailey screams out. I am taking what is mine. Oh you think do you? Hailey says with a laugh. I carry her all the way upstairs to our bedroom.

Balthazar 🐺

I think Instead of just killing all of these mutts I think I will get my revenge maybe, I will get my revenge another way. What do you have in mind? Wadjet asked me. Do not worry about it hag. I know what I plan to do I will get what I want. Balthazar you know you could be my mate. Hahahaha don't flatter yourself hag. I don't like werewolf and I really don't like witches. Are the cells in the dungeon still in tact? Mmmmmm Balthazar if you have not noticed we are in a cave. The werewolves burned the houses down that your father had. A deep roar escaped me when Wadjet told me those mutts burned down my father's houses. What if I had still been in one of them sleeping? They would have killed me too. Oh they are going to pay for that and I mean they are going to pay.

Nikola 🐺

It has been a couple of days since the triplets have been born. Alex and Andi are doing really well. They are both eating from a bottle and they are both breathing very well. The doctor said if all goes well they should be able to go home by the end of next week. Oh Nikola that is great news. Hailey said back to me as we talk through mind link. So what news did you have for me? Well I don't want to freak you out since you are about to bring Gabby home but I know you would want to know this. What is it Hailey? There might be an attack. WHAT? We got the news from another pack that some rouge's and a few vampires are attacking packs. It is Alaric's son Balthazar. Jax said that he is young and he is very strong and that he is taking revenge on his father's death. Oh yeah. I say back to Hailey. That is all we need now that we are about to bring at least one of the babies home. How much training have we missed? That's just it Jax isn't allowing you or I to train this time. WHAT? Yeah, my feelings exactly. I was so pissed when Jax said that he didn't want me fighting this fight. Instead he wants me to help with the woman that have really young children. I guess all of these woman with young children which by the way includes you too, are coming to the pack house so me and some of the other woman can care for them until Jax figures out where to move us. I know you are upset about this Hailey, but honestly since I can not fight right now I would rather you help me than some stranger that I don't know. I know and you know I will be right there with you. Okay, well I better get back to packing up everything in my hospital room so Dorian and I can take this little bundle home and get her settled. I will be at your house when you get there. I've been decorating all day for yours and Gabby's home coming. Your so sweet Hailey thank you. Your welcome Nikola. See you soon.

I was really happy to get Gabby home, but at the same time I'm sad that Alexander and Alexandria have to stay at the hospital longer. Babe, do you think we could come back later today and spend some time with Alex and Andi? Of course we can. We just need to get Gabby settled and find someone to watch her. Oh I don't think we will have a problem getting someone to watch her. I said with a smile. I think you might be right. About that time the nurse sticks her head in the door. Is someone ready for their ride out? Yes I am. I said back to her. I will pull the car around. Okay babe I will see you outside. I gave Dorian a kiss before he went to pull the car up to the door.

Hailey 🐺

Okay everyone they are about to leave the hospital so let's finish up and be ready when they pull in. But remember not to be to loud when they walk in we don't want to scare sweet little Gabby. Everyone agreed with me. It didn't take long to finish up the decorating and it's a good thing because as soon as we were done I heard Dorian and Nikola pull in the driveway. Okay they are here. Places everyone. When I heard them come up to the door I open it and we all said WELCOME HOME. It was good to see Nikola come home from the hospital. As much as I love my best friend I hated seeing her in the hospital even though it was only because she had the babies, but still I am glad she is home and I know she can't wait until she can bring the other two home.

How are you feeling Nikola? I am so glad to be home. I bet you are. I am glad you are home. I have a question to ask you Hailey. Sure, what is it? Dorian and I want to go back to the hospital after everyone leaves after while. Would you like to watch Gabby for us? Are you kidding me? I would love to watch her. Thank you Hailey. It's my honor.

Todd 🦊

EXCUSE ME EVERYONE CAN I HAVE YOUR ATTENTION PLEASE. Everyone got quiet. I want to welcome

Nikola, Dorian, and my sweet granddaughter home. I know I still have another granddaughter and a grandson in the hospital and I am sure that just like me and my wonderful mate Lily, Dorian and Nikola can not wait to have their entire family home. Dorian and Nikola, I want to thank you both for giving us such beautiful grandchildren. Dorian, you are well aware that I was not to happy about you and Nikola being together even though you two were chosen to be mates by the moon goddess. Every father is very protective over his daughter. I also was not thrilled with the idea that you got Nikola pregnant. But I have accepted it and I accept you as part of my family. So congratulations Nikola and Dorian. You two are going to be wonderful parents.

Jaxson 🐾

Dorian can I talk to you for a moment? Of course Alpha. Excuse me for a minute sweetheart. Yes, I will be right here with our little bundle of joy, and with my BWFF. Okay babe.

We have a very serious situation going on that I wanted to talk to you about. What is it Alpha? It has come to my attention that Balthazar has been awaken. WHAT? Yeah that was my reaction exactly when I found out. Why didn't you tell me sooner? Well I didn't want to disturb you since Nikola had just given birth and with the situation of the two little ones. Well yeah and I appreciate that Alpha, but still when something like this happens I am still here for you no matter what. I know and that is why you are my Beta. So what is the plan Alpha? Well Hailey is kind of pissed off at me because I want her and some of the other woman who have young children to be sent to an undisclosed location so they are safe. I agree with that. I knew you might not want to be away from Nikola, but right now this is the safest thing for them. I agree. I will tell Nikola. Dorian said. I know it will be better coming from you.

Dorian 🐺

Hey babe, I need to talk to you about something. Is everything okay? Well I'm not sure right now but I need you to stay with Hailey for the time being. But I thought we were going back to the hospital to spend some time with Alex and Andi? Right now is not the best time. What is going on Dorian? Well there is no easy way to say this, but Alpha Jaxson found out that we are going to be under attack by Alaric's son Balthazar. He is a very young and very strong vampire and he has a team of rouge's helping him. He is seeking revenge on the pack that killed his father. Oh god and that was this pack. Yes it was. That is why I want you to take Gabby and go with Hailey to the pack house. That is where all the woman with young children are going. Okay, I will go talk to Hailey. Oh and babe, Hailey is not to happy with Alpha Jaxson right now because he won't let her train and fight. He wants to keep her safe. She will be, she loves Alpha Jaxson a lot. Alpha is going to have Nick, Jeb, and Jordan to stay at the pack house with all of the woman in case anything happens. Okay babe. Tell Alpha not to worry about Hailey, she might be a little upset with him but she will get over it soon especially since I will be with her. I will let him know that. I love you babe, and take good care of our baby girl. We will go see our other two as soon as it is safe. Okay, please be careful Dorian. I love you too. I give Nikola a kiss before I head out with Alpha Jaxson.

Nikola 🐾

Everyone was starting to leave. I said goodbye to everyone as soon as the last person left Hailey and I went upstairs so I could pack. I wonder how long we will have to be gone. I have no idea. I wish Jax would let me stay to train and fight along beside him. I know you do, but he wants to keep you safe and besides that I am going to need you too. Hailey looked at me really surprised. Nikola you know that you can handle this. Hahahaha Hailey I have never been a mom before and you know that. I have no idea what I am doing and since I won't have Dorian there to help me I will need my BWFF. I guess that will be the only thing that will make me happy about having to be somewhere and not be here. You guess, you guess. I picked up a pillow off of my bed and I hit Hailey with it. NIKOLA what are you doing? The same thing I did when we were younger and you would be all upset about what ever. I can't believe you just did that. Hailey said as she stood up and grabbed the other pillow and before we knew it we heard Nick was at the door asking if we were ready. We were laughing so hard because there was feathers floating all over mine and Dorian's bedroom from Hailey and I hitting each other with the pillows and the pillows busting open. But that is a mess I will have to clean up whenever we are allowed to come back home. We are almost ready Nick. Okay I will wait at the bottom of the stairs. Nick said back to Hailey and I.

CHAPTER 9

LEAVING HOME

Guard Nick, Jeb, and Jordan 🐾

Ladies you two and the baby will be in the SUV with us. Alpha Jaxson wants us to make sure you three are well protected. Nick said. Aren't we going to the same place the other woman and children are going? Hailey asked. No ma'am we are taking you three somewhere else. But we can not say where do to the mind links. Jordan said. Of course not. Hailey rolled her eyes. Now remember Hailey you will be with me and Gabby, we will have fun and the time will pass by so quick and it will be like we were never gone. I am glad you can stay so positive about this Nikola. You are used to your dad having to move you all around a lot, I'm not used to that. I'm also not used to being away from Jax especially when we have no idea as to when we will be able to go back home, or God forbid but if something happens to Jax. Hailey your letting things get to you that we both know is not going to happen. Alpha Jaxson and Dorian are both very strong fighters. They are both still very young as well so they both have a lot in their favor. But Nikola, remember my father was also still pretty young when he died in that rouge attack. Yes but wasn't it Alaric with a knife covered in wolf bane that got your father? Yes. Hailey said sadly. Alpha Jaxson and Dorian will be fine, we have to believe that. Nikola said to Hailey. I really thought it would make you at least a little happier that you and I are going to be together with my new little Gabby. I'm sorry Nikola, of course I am happy that we are in this together and that we have Gabby too. It seemed to take a while before we got to the location. We pulled down a long driveway to what seems to be a cabin, but it was as big if not bigger than the pack house. We carried the ladies and the babies stuff inside and got them settled in. Luna Hailey. Jeb said. Yes Jeb, what is it? Alpha Jaxson is on the phone for you.

Hailey 🐺

Hi babe, I wanted to make sure you and Nikola made it safely. We did, you have nothing to worry about now that I am out of the way. Hailey don't be like that. I love you and it is my main job to make sure you are safe. I would have been safe being right there with you. Well at least I know you are safer where you are at. How long do I have to stay here? I don't know yet babe, but it will be until everything is safe here. Well I am sure Nikola would like to be back soon too so she can check on the other two babies. I know she would. But even Dorian is okay with you both being where you are at for now. I'm sure it will be no time before you are back home. Yeah. That is all I said to him before handing the phone back to Jeb.

Jaxson 🐺

Just make sure they stay inside and keep all three of them safe. Yes Alpha. You know they will be very well guarded 24 hours a day. I know and I trust you three. That is why you are the ones that drove them where you all are at. I will check in as much as possible until it is all clear here. We will wait for your call Alpha. Thank you Jeb. Your welcome Alpha.

Alright everyone it is training everyday until we have to fight so let's go. We all go over to the training field and start going over everything. Then I pair people up. Okay I want you to do the attacks in your wolves. We will not fight the rouges and the vamps as human we will not do all the training as human. Everyone phased into their wolves.

We didn't have an entire week before the attack happened. It was only two days after Hailey and Nikola left with the baby that Balthazar, some vamps, and several rouges showed up. I charged after them with my pack with me. I could hear other pack's showing up. As we started fighting I could see some of my wolves getting hurt, but they didn't go down they kept on fighting. I try to help as many of my pack as I can. I run up and knock vampires off of wolves. The one I want to get to is Balthazar but I don't see him anywhere. That's when I felt myself go flying through the air. I crash land against a big tree and I feel some of my ribs break. It takes away my breath for a few seconds, but I get right back up and run after Balthazar but I feel a wolf on me. It is one of the rouges. As the rouge was about to take a bite out of me I felt it fall off. When I look I see a snow white wolf, Lauren's wolf. She knocked that rouge off of me and she must have stabbed the wolf with some wolf bane because that rouge died instantly. But I still need to get to Balthazar, I want him I want to kill him so that I know my pack will be safe. But I don't see him anywhere and that can not be good at all.

Lauren 🐾

I got a feeling that Hailey is not safe, that she is in great danger. I can not get away to go find where she is and to defend her. Leaving now would be stupid and it would put everyone in danger. These rouge's are a lot stronger than the last ones that attacked and I had to come help. But at least Jaxson has trained his pack very well. Most of the rouge's are either dead, or running back to where they came from. Jaxson we need to get to Hailey she is not safe. I see Jaxson's body movements start changing when I sent him that message through mind link.

What do you mean she is not safe where she is at? I had them take her to the most remote location and we have not talked about where she is at all. I know, but someone has picked up on her tail or her scent because I just seen that she and Nikola are not safe. Just then Jaxson takes off running. At this point the pack can handle what rogues are left. The vampires as far as I know are all either running back to where they came from or they are dead. I can see that Jaxson is hurt, but I cannot see how badly. Jaxson, are you okay? I'm fine I just need to make sure Hailey and Nikola are okay. But you seem like you got hurt in the fight. It is nothing I will have the doctor to look at it when I get back.

Hailey

I got a feeling that something is not quite right, but I didn't know what it could be. I talked to Jax earlier and I know my mom is okay. Nikola hasn't said anything about something being wrong with Gabby and she hasn't gotten a call from the hospital. I have no idea why I am feeling like this. Maybe it's just because I am not with Jax and fighting alongside of him. But my wolf Casey is so jumpy, like she is wanting to come out. But everything is fine here. Maybe I will calm down if I get something to eat since I haven't really eaten all day. Hey Nikola I am going to go down to the kitchen, do you want me to get you anything? Maybe just a glass of juice. Okay I will be right back. I looked down at the sleeping peacefully Little Gabby and smile thinking about how I cannot wait to have children. As I start down the stairs that uneasy feeling grows more and more.

Balthazar 🐺

I seen that the rogues that I got on my side and my little family of vampires are doing a good job. I decide to go find that mutts mate and cage her for a while. But then one of the mutts come running at me and I just swung my arm at it and it crash landed against a tree. That is when I took off running. I knew that was a perfect time to get away and go find his mate. I know if I capture her and cage her I will have what he wants then I will be able to get what I want, all that my father wanted. But not without taking the life of the mutt that took my father's life. I don't care which mutt it was either I just want to feel the bones of their neck cracking in my hands. That will give me some satisfaction and I will not only get the one thing my father wanted which was more land to hunt on but I will have avenged my father's death as well.

Nikola 🐺

Being here with Hailey does take my mind off of what is going on back at home, but it doesn't stop me from worrying about Dorian. I have not heard from him all day and that is not like him. Even though I know he is out there fighting against the vampires and the rogues he would normally still send me an I love you through mind link just to let me know that he is okay. I know I have to stay calm for Gabby, but it is really hard to do. Just then I hear Hailey scream. I jump up and go running to the stairs.

Hailey 🐺

When I got downstairs there was a trail of blood on the floor. But I hadn't heard anything down here and there are three guys.

The trail of blood leads to the front door. So I walk over there very slowly. I feel someone's hand touch my shoulder and I just about jump out of my skin. When I turn around I see that it is Nikola. OMG you almost made me jump right out of my skin. I'm sorry but when you screamed like that I came running. Where is Jeb, Nick, and Jordan? I don't know. I seen that trail of blood and that is when I screamed and followed it over here to the door. Go back upstairs with Gabby and keep her safe. I don't know what is going on here but I don't have a very good feeling. Okay, but keep the mind link open between you and I let me know everything you see. I will. After Nikola goes back upstairs I open the front door. It is freezing cold out there but I have the heat of my wolf to keep me warm. I really wish that Jax was here with me. I have never felt so scared in my life. I find Jeb laying on the ground, blood coming from his neck. My whole body starts trembling at the sight of one of our best guards laying dead on the freezing ground. Where the hell is Nick and Jordan just then I feel another hand on my shoulder. Nikola you are not going to scare me again with that. I told you to go......my words trailed off as I turn around and I am staring into the eyes of a vampire. Not just any vampire though this one is the son of Alaric. The vampire that Nikola's dad killed in the last attack.

Jaxson 🐺

I can feel it, something is not right. I cannot get Jeb on the mind link but I talked to Nick. He told me that him and Jordan are checking the outside of the cabin while Jeb stays inside to guard the girls. Good thinking I told Nick. Keep me posted. Lauren and I along with Todd, Kaden, and Dorian are on our way there now. Balthazar got away and I am worried. Oh don't worry Alpha we completely covered up any scent that would be picked up. Well you know how rogues can be. Some of them can tap into mind links and if any of them have then Balthazar might know where you all are at. That is one of the reasons we are on our way there now.

Nick 🐺

After Alpha told me that Balthazar got away I got a really bad feeling. I know we are good at covering up any scent, but Balthazar knows a lot about how to track, and a lot more than his father knew. He is also a lot harder to take down. But if he comes here he will have the fight of his life on his hands. Once Jordan and I were done checking all around the cabin we decided to go back inside. That's when we saw Hailey outside. Hailey what are you doing out here and where did that blood come from? Just then Balthazar comes out from around the corner of the cabin. GET INSIDE HAILEY! Hailey takes off inside of the cabin and I jump towards Balthazar and I shift into my wolf in mid jump. Jordan goes after the two wolves that came with Balthazar. They had killed Jeb and I was not going to let them get away with that. Jeb had been my best friend for as long as I can remember and I feel really bad about leaving him alone to protect the girls while Jordan and I went and walked the grounds around the cabin, but he was a great guard and a great warrior when it came to fight. Plus none of us thought that anyone would come here.

Hailey 🐺

I run as fast as I can up the stairs and into the bedroom where Nikola and Gabby are at. Get Gabby and hide. What?

Why? What is going on Hailey? You have me scared. No time to really explain, but Balthazar is outside right now. Jordan and Nick are fighting him and the other two vampires off so I need you to hide with Gabby until it is safe. What about you Hailey? You need to hide too. I will be fine, but I don't want anything to happen to you or that precious baby. Now stop procrastinating and do not come out until me, Jordan, or Nick comes to get you two. As I run back down the stairs to go outside so I can help fight off Balthazar and the other vampires I shift into my wolf Casey. The two other vampires were nothing to take on when I got there, but I was jabbed from behind and I felt something poke me. I howled and that was all I remember.

Jaxson 🐺

I seen Balthazar running off when I got to the cabin with Lauren, Todd, and Kaden. There were a couple of rogues still there but were easily taken out. I got a hold of one, snapped its neck and Todd got the other. After that we all went behind different trees and change back to our human form. I look at Jordan and Nick. They had taken a beating, but they were still in good shape. They didn't need any medical attention. Alpha are you okay? I heard Nick ask. Yeah I am fine. Just then I went to move my right arm and the pain from that and trying to breathe just about knocked me off my feet. I guess I'm not as okay as I thought, but that doesn't really matter right now where is Hailey? I want to see my mate. So do I. I heard Dorian say. I turn around. I did not see you with us when we were coming here Dorian. I knew that the rest of the pack could handle the stragglers that were left behind so I decided it would be safe if I came with you besides I couldn't wait any longer to see

Nikola and Gabby. Speaking of where are they? They are hiding upstairs Beta.

Nick

I seen Balthazar grab Hailey as he took off running. I hate that I have to tell Alpha that his mate our Luna has been taken. But I am going to have to let him know. Where is my mate? Beta Dorian asked Jordan and I. She is upstairs hiding with the baby. Beta Dorian took off into the cabin. Then Alpha looked at me and Jordan. Where is Hailey? Is she upstairs with Nikola? Ummm Alpha I hate to tell you this, but Balthazar took off with our Luna. I could see Alpha's eyes changing color. HE WHAT? I am sorry Alpha, I will go after him. NO STAY HERE, HE IS MINE! I AM GOING TO BREAK HIS FUCKIN NECK!

Jaxson

When Nick told me that Balthazar took off with Hailey I was instantly pissed. I am going to kill that vampire. I am going to break every bone in his body before I snap his neck and burn him. We are right here with you Alpha. I heard Lauren tell me through mind link. I cannot pick up on Hailey at all. I told Lauren. He better hope that she is okay when I find them.

CHAPTER 10

THE ESCAPE

Hailey 🐾

The last thing I remember is looking straight into the eyes of a vampire, after that everything went dark. Now my entire body hurts so bad. I cannot stand up. I have no idea where I am at but it stinks really bad like burnt flesh and blood, urine, and other things I don't even want to think about. Hello sleepyhead. I hear a voice I do not know. Who's there? Who is that? I am Balthazar, and you are in my dungeon. I tried to laugh so he knows I am not afraid of him. I won't be here long. Jax will come find me. Balthazar laugh's. Silly girl, he has no idea where we are at. He will track your scent and find me that way. Oh I hope he does. I will enjoy feeling his bones breaking between my hands as I squeeze the life out of him. I could feel tears rolling down my face when that vampire said that to me, but I am not going to let him get to me. You are no match for Jaxson. He will kill you and anything that gets in his way.

Lauren 🐾

That stinking vampire better hope that my daughter is okay. He has no idea what he is in for when we find him. Hailey, are you okay? I asked Hailey when I was able to open the mind link to her. Yes Mom I am okay. My entire body hurts so bad I cannot stand up. We are on our way. Jaxson, me, and Kaden are coming for you. Dorian and Todd are with Nikola and the baby. Are they okay mom? Yes they are fine. We just want to find you and make sure you are okay too. Do you know where you are at? I knew that was a long shot asking Hailey if she knew where she was at. Even though she and I both have lived here long enough now that she should know where everything is I am sure she does not know where that vampire took her. I have no idea mom, I am so sorry but I was knocked out before he took me. It is okay sweetie, we will find you. Please hurry mom. We are.

Hailey 🐾

When Mom closed the mind link I tried to get up again. It hurts so much, but I was able to stand by holding on to the bars of this cage that monster has me in. Who's there? I smell a familiar smell. It's Amee. I am going to try to help you Luna. Amee? I said in disbelief. What are you doing here? Balthazar grabbed me not to long ago. He thought I was you and he was going to keep me caged until Alpha came looking for me, but once he found out that I was not you he let me out. But I am not able to leave because he has an invisible leash on me. I am only allowed around the house and just outside of the house. I am so sorry Amee. Well Alpha is on his way to get me and I will make sure he knows that you are not here on your own free will that you are a prisoner just like me. Thank you Luna. You're welcome Amee. Now go before you are caught talking to me. I do not want anything happening to you. Yes Luna. As soon as Amee was gone I opened the mind link to Jax. Hi babe, I know you are trying to find me. I am sorry I do not know where I am at. Like I told Mom I was knocked out. It is okay I will find you babe, Balthazar kidnapped Amee. He thought at first she was me, but when he realized she was not me instead of killing her he is keeping her and using her. It's okay Hailey I will get you both out of there. I will be here waiting for you.

Amee 🐺

I see Balthazar and some of the other vampires leave. As soon as they were out of sight I go back down to help Luna escape. Hi Luna I am back. Balthazar and some of the other vampires just left so I am going to help you get out of there. Oh Amee I just don't want you to get hurt. If you cannot get me out or if Balthazar catches you I am afraid he will kill you and I would not be able to live with myself knowing you were killed trying to help me. Luna I have to at least try to help you out of here. Once you are out I hope you are able to find Alpha. We together will find Alpha Jaxson, I will not leave you here if you can get me out without you. I have the key to all of the cages down here I just have to figure out which one it is. Oh please hurry Amee. I don't know what I would do if you were caught. I finally find the key that fits the lock. Once I got Luna out we hear noises coming from above us.

Jaxson 🐺

I see a house with very dim lights. I get a feeling that is where the vampires have been staying. Okay everyone, I think this is the house that Balthazar has Hailey in. But we have to be careful vampires as you know are sneaky bastard's. I said to everyone through mind link. We all walk up to the side of the house slowly and I peek around to the front. So far so good. I hear noises coming from inside. I want all of you to be on high alert. Keep your guard up. I start walking slowly towards the front and I feel something hit the back of my head. I look and see Wadjet. The witch that works with the rogues. I let out a loud growl as I run towards her. Then I see Lauren and Kaden fighting rogues. I send Dorian and Todd mind links letting them know that we are being attacked and need their help. I told Dorian to have Nikola stay at the cabin with Nick and Jordan. Dorian agreed and said that him and Todd are on their way to help.

Dorian 🐺

As soon as Alpha Jaxson said he needed mine and Todd's help we were on our way. I hated leaving Nikola and Gabby, but I had no choice and Nikola understood. I gave her a quick kiss and took off shifting into my wolf Demetrius. When we got close to where Alpha Jaxson, Lauren, and Kaden are at I can see what is going on and that is they are all fighting. I hate that witch Wadjet and I can see her trying to help other rouges get the better of Alpha so that is when I run up to first knock her off her feet. She is no match for me though, I am waiting for her to land and when she does I grab her by her neck and start to bite into the flesh. Just then I feel something hit my eyes and I drop the witch.

Wadjet 🐺

I seen them mutt wolves were coming. I was trying to help the rouges so that these others would not get into the house. I know Balthazar would not be happy at all if I allowed the mutt that killed his father to get away. When I seen that mutt run over to help the others I knew what I needed to do. I was not expecting one of the mutts to knock me into the air but that gave me the time I needed to reach for the potion that I had made up earlier today. I was going to use it in case any of those mutts got out of the cages. It was to be thrown into their eyes. When I landed this mutt thought he was going to harm me. But I have a surprise for him. I throw the potion and yes it hit him right in the eyes he let go of me and started howling which that gave me a chance to get away.

Jaxson 🐺

When I hear Dorian howling I knew something was wrong. I ran over to him. What is this? That bitch through something in my eyes I cannot see anything. I will get someone to help you. I will not let anything happen to you, I promise. I ask Lauren to come over where Dorian and I are since the rest of the vampires are laying on the ground dead. What is it Alpha? That witch put some sort of potion in Dorian's eyes and now he cannot see anything. It burns too. Dorian said between growls. It is okay Dorian, Lauren is here and she is going to help you while I try to find Hailey. Go Alpha I will be fine. I hated leaving Dorian. I am his Alpha and I should be there with him, but I do have to find my mate. Don't leave him Lauren. I won't, now go find our girl. I jump up and start for the house. I see the front door start to open as I approach the house and I get into defense mode.

Hailey 🐺

I can hear all kinds of things going on outside. That has to be Jax, at least I hope he found us. I tell Amee. Stay down and I will look outside. I waited for Amee to get into a safe spot then I look outside. I see Dorian, he has Wadjet by the neck and I see Jax ripping the head off of one of the vampires. Then I see Jax run over to where Dorian and Wadjet are at. Next I see my mom's wolf run over to where Jax and Dorian are at in their wolf form. I see my mom doing something too Dorian. I really hope he is okay. I know Nikola would be upset if anything happened to Dorian. I opened the front door and started to step out onto the porch and I see Jax coming towards me in defense mode. Jax, it's me Hailey. He stops for a second as if he needs a second for his brain to register who I am. JAX LOOK OUT! I scream as I see Balthazar run full force towards Jax, they both fall to the ground. First I see Balthazar on top of Jax and that scares the hell out of me. But then I see Jax getting out from under Balthazar. I see something reflecting and I see Jax fall. MOM! I scream and she looks up. Jax need your help. As my mom goes towards Jax, I shift and run in the same direction. I jump onto Balthazar. I am going to KILL YOU. I say as I grab a hold of his head. I feel something sharp in my leg and I let go and fall to the ground. When I hit the ground I let out a loud howl and I see Jax and my mom come running for Balthazar. After Jax reach Balthazar all I see is a huge cloud of black smoke rise up from where they are. Then I see Jax looking towards where Amee is at. JAX NO! I yeah and he looks over at me. She is the one that help me. Remember I told you that when I was talking to you through mind link. I also told you that Amee had been taken by mistake by Balthazar because he thought that she was me. Oh that is right. Jax goes over to Amee and said thank you to her he pushes his muzzle up against her. You're welcome Alpha. I hear Amee say. I go over to my mom and Dorian. How is he mom? He is going to be just fine. I was able to flush out what that witch put in his eyes. His vision might be blurry for a few hours, but after that he will be as good as new. Well what do you say Beta Dorian, would you like to go get your mate and your little one? Yes I would.

Dorian 🐺

I could not see anything once that which Wadjet hit me with whatever that was in my eyes. But Lauren in her wolf form came and helped me. The only thing that really sucked is that it will still take a few hours before I will be able to see anything again. But at least Wadjet and Balthazar are dead and we don't have to worry about them anymore or so I thought. I didn't know that Wadjet got away. But I am still not going to be able to see Nikola and Gabby for a few hours but the important thing is that we will be together. Are you ready to go get your mate and your baby? I heard Hailey ask. I got a big smile on my face and said yes. It was not hard to get back to the cabin that Nikola and Gabby were in. I would have no problem finding them even if I was really blind, all I would have to do is follow their scent. When we got to the cabin we had already phased back into our human form and we all were completely dressed. Nikola came running out and even though I could not see her my senses let me know she was close and I knew that she would jump into my arm so I was able to catch her. I heard everyone else gasp because they didn't think I would be able to catch her just because I can't see. What's wrong, I heard Nikola ask. I can't see babe. What do you mean you cannot see? Well, that witch threw some kind of potion into my eyes which made me lose sight, but Lauren did something and I will have my site back in a few hours. Well I am glad you will not be blind forever. Me too babe, me too. But just know Dorian even if you were blind the rest of your life I would still be by your side every day of our lives. You would also be able to use your senses.

Hailey 🐾

Now that everyone is okay do you think we could head home? I am sick of being here and away from everything and everyone that I know and love. I thought you would never ask. Jax said to me, then he scoops me up in his arms bridal style and started walking towards home. Jax you know that I could walk and we could get there a lot faster, or you could put me down and we could shift and run. You are probably right, but I am not letting go of you ever again. It's going to be a little bit hard to get your work done if you are always holding me. I said and then let out a little laugh. I will manage somehow, you are the one that is going to have to get used to it my soon to be Mrs. Jaxson Carter. Oh yes, we have a wedding to plan. Yes we do and we are going to start on it as soon as we get home. Oh I don't know if I will be wedding planning we will be doing as soon as we get home I say to Jax with a shy little grin. Oh yeah, and what exactly do you have in mind future Mrs. Carter? Jax asked me. You will have to wait and see Mr. Carter.

Once we were all home my mom gave me the biggest hug, I am so glad you are back here where you belong Hailey. Then Jax chimes in. I feel that was somewhat my fault everything that happened with Balthazar having access to kidnapping Hailey. No Jax this was not your fault, I said. It was those rogues and vampires that cannot get it through their thick heads that we cannot be beaten. Everyone cheered when I said that. Okay since you all want to listen in anyway. I laughed. I have an announcement to make. Now that things should calm down, Alpha Jaxson and I are going to make it official and have a wedding. Everyone cheered even harder when I said that announcement. Even though I have already asked her once

I would be truly honored if Nikola would be my matron of honor. I would be honored to be your matron of honor. Then it is carved in stone. We all laughed. Once we got home I felt so much more comfortable. I want to take a shower. I said to Jax. Can I take one with you? Well you are the one that said that you don't want to let me out of your sight. Did I say that? Hmmm. I slap him playfully and we both just laugh.

Jaxson 🐻

When Hailey said that she wanted to take a shower I asked her if I could take one with her and she playfully slapped me I started acting like I didn't remember that I had said that I would never let her out of my sight ever again. Hailey you really are the most important person to me, you are everything I have ever wanted in a mate and I would die if anything ever happened to you. I am to protect you in any and every way I possibly can. Jax why are you getting all emotional on me now? I am here and I am fine, nothing is going to happen to me. I know, but when you were taken by Balthazar I thought I was going to go crazy. My heart has never ached the way it did when I was looking for you. You are my everything. Jax, listen to me. I am here, we are together, nothing or no one will ever come between us and nothing is going to happen to me. We are going to have a very long life together. We are very lucky because we found each other while we are still very young. Your mother told me that some mates do not find each other until much later so we have a lot to look forward to and a lot to be thankful for. Hailey said to me looking me straight in the eyes. You are right babe. Now I will get our shower going. I know Hailey is my mate and I know it is natural for me to have the feelings for her that I am feeling, but I really cannot keep my hands off of her tonight. It's like on her 17th birthday when she was…………….. As I was washing her back I asked. Hailey are you in heat again? What are you talking about Jax, it has been months since my last heat and I think by the way you are acting you can tell that I am in heat again. We are going to have to be careful I do know that especially if we want more time to ourselves before we start a family. Well then what do you suggest that we do? Because I know when I went into my first heat you couldn't hardly stay off of me. I didn't think we would get through our training session. Well there is something we can do about what it does to me when you go into heat but we are going to have to figure something out to keep you from getting. Shhhh Jax whatever happens, happens. We have to let everything run it's course naturally.

Hailey 🐺

I am starting to wonder if Jax even wants a family the way he is talking about being careful so that I don't get pregnant. I hope he wants a family we are going to have someone to pass the title of Alpha onto like it has been for centuries.

I wonder when Nikola and Dorian are going to be able to bring the other two babies home. Maybe you should check in with them tomorrow. I know that would bring some happiness to the pack if they were able to come home soon. Jax said. Jax? Yes babe. Do you want us to have children, or at least a child? Jax turned around and look at me. I thought you knew that I do want children. Well I thought you did, but the way you talked about us being careful so I don't get pregnant. Jax walk over to me and put one finger over my lips. I want us to have children, why else would I have two of the bedrooms in our house turned into nurseries? I hope that they have your eyes, your nose, your lips. I only said that I want us to be careful so you don't get pregnant is because I want us to have more time together before we start our family. There is so much I want us to do together and so much I want to show you that you have not seen since you have moved here. After everything we have been through with me being in heat right now I had to have him. I jump into his arms but naked. We spent the rest of the night satisfying each other's desires. It is probably a good thing we don't live in the pack house because no one would have gotten any sleep.

CHAPTER 11

NEWEST MEMBERS COMING HOME

Nikola 🐺

DORIAN I yelled as I got off the phone and I go running through the house. Dorian. What babe, what? The babies. I try saying as I'm trying to catch my breath. What about the babies? Did something happen, is something wrong? No everything is perfect. What do you mean Nikola, what are you talking about? I just got off the phone with the head nurse at the hospital, since we have not been able to go over to the hospital for the last couple of days to be with Alex and Andi because of everything going on here I wanted to call and check on Alex and Andi. Yes of course. Dorian said. So what did the nurse say? She said that they are both at 100% and that we could come get them today and bring them home. I could feel the tears running down my face because I am so happy that my family is finally going to be complete, my other two babies are coming home. Oh babe that is great news. So when can we go get them? Now, all we need to do is go get ready to go.

Hey girl I wanted to touch base with you and see how Alexander and Alexandria are doing. Hailey said through mind link. OMG Hailey we are going to get them and bring them home today. Oh Nikola that is great news. So......Yes Hailey you can come over. Well I know that I am not going to be the only one that is going to want to be there to see the babies. Well let's keep it limited to a few people I don't want to overdo it with the babies. Of course. Okay well give them kisses for us and I will see you all very soon. Oh wait who is going to watch Gabby while you two go get the babies? Well I was going to ask you if you wanted to watch her. You know that I do. Well then I suggest you get over here because we are getting ready to leave for the hospital. After that I closed the mind link so I could get ready to go pick up my babies. Babe? Yes. Hailey and Alpha Jaxson are coming to watch Gabby while we go to the hospital and pick up Alex and Andi. Yeah what else are they going to do? Dorian asked with a laugh. You already know don't you. I told Hailey to keep the number of people small I don't want to overdo it with the babies on their first day home.

Hailey 🐾

JAX! I'm right here babe. OMG you scared me, I didn't know you were behind me. I'm sorry babe. So did you talk to you Nikola? How are the babies doing? They are doing good, actually they are doing better than good. What do you mean? They are getting to come home today. Oh that is great news. Yeah and we have to get going because we are watching Gabby, and we are getting a few people to welcome Alexandra and Alexander home. So we need to send a mass mind link. I can contact your mom, my mom, Nikola's mom. It sucks that Dorian's parents are not around here to enjoy seeing their grandchildren. I know babe, but maybe one day they will be able to come see them. I will contact my dad, Kaden, Todd, and Jace. Oh then I should have Abby to come too. Well considering that is Dorian's sister I would say she would be pretty upset if she wasn't asked to come over to welcome her nieces and her nephew home. Well let's get going and get on the mind links so we can get to Nikola and Dorian's and we can get everyone together. I'm ready when you are. Jax said to me.

I was beginning to thank you two ended up doing something else and we're to busy to make it over. Nikola said with a smile as she opened the door at her and Dorian's house when Jax and I got there. Haha so funny. We will have plenty of time to work on our own family later. Now where is that precious goddaughter of mine. She is sleeping but she should be waking up soon. Dorian said as he entered the front room. Are you two ready to bring your other two bundles of joy home? We are more than ready, we have been waiting for this day long enough. Well I am going to take my beautiful mate here and get her into the car so we can go get Alex and Andi. Nikola smiles up at Dorian as he says that. Now remember Hailey you promise not a lot of people here when we get back. I don't want the babies overwhelmed. I know, I know and I do promise just a small few. Now go, go get your babies.

Lily

I never thought this day would come. That my baby would be bringing her baby, or babies home from the hospital. I could not imagine what she is going through, to have two of her three still in the hospital and have one at home. Her nerves must be shot. Come on Lily will you please settle down. You act like they are your babies and that you are the new expectant mother. Todd said to me. Well I am the grandmother and even though I have not met the babies yet I still feel and overwhelming feeling of protection over them. Well where are we supposed to go to? The hospital or Nikola's house? Todd asked me. You know it is Dorian and Nikola's house. Just because you don't like the idea of your baby girl being with her mate yet doesn't mean you can act like he doesn't exist. I hear Todd growl when I said that. Well it is true Todd. You have not liked Dorian ever since you found out that he is Nikola's mate and there was nothing you could do about it. Oh there is plenty I could do about it, I just don't think the elders would like it and I would not want the judgment coming down on me for what I would do to that mutt. You know my daddy was not too happy when you and I finally found each other. I see Todd smile when I reminded him of how my father felt when he found out that I had found my mate. Oh and to answer your question we are supposed to go to Nikola and Dorian's and wait for them to get home with the other two babies. We can meet our granddaughter Gabby there. They have Hailey and Alpha Jaxson watching Gabby while they pick up Alexander and Alexandria. Well let's get going. Is Chad going with us? Or is he driving himself? Todd asked me. I think he is driving himself and Abby over there.

Lauren 🐺

Well Hailey just asked me through mind link if we are coming over to Nikola and Dorian's to be there when they bring the other two babies home from the hospital. Well what did you tell her? Because if you want to go over there I will go with you, Jaxson already asked me if you and I were going to be over there and I told him that I would ask you. Of course I want to go, Hailey and Nikola have been best friends so long that Nikola is like another daughter to me. Well then we better go. Kaden said with a smile. I cannot wait to let everyone know our little surprise too. I know you have been waiting for this moment for at least 5 months now. Yes I have. Kaden said.

Abby 🐺

Hey girl what is going on? I asked Hailey when she opens the mind link. Well we are having a little get-together here at Dorian and Nikola's. They have already left to go get Alex and Andi. Jax and I are here watching Gabby and getting everything ready for when they come home. They don't want too many people here so we are only asking you, Chad, Jace, my mom and Kaden, Todd, and Lily Jaxson's mom and dad and brother. We think that might be pushing it a bit, but you all are the closest family members. Well of course I will be there. It won't take me long to get there too. Chad should be here anytime. Okay, well we will see you both when you to get here. Sounds good to me. Do you need us to pick up anything? No we have it all. The Omega's took care of making all the food and I had the banner made about a week ago and I already picked it up and it is being hung now. Okay then I guess you have it all under control then. I said to Hailey. She has been so good as Luna since Jaxson was given the Alpha title. Yes I do. So I will see you soon. Hailey said to me. Yes you will. We close the mind link just as Chad pulled up in the driveway. Well that was very good timing. Why is that? Chad asked me. Hailey just mind linked me and asked if I was coming over to be there when Nikola and Dorian bring Alexander and Alexandria home. Well I know you are crazy about babies so I know you would not miss this for anything. You are right, if you hadn't wanted to go I would have drove myself. I said to Chad with a smile.

Hailey 🐺

Well everyone should be starting to pull in any time now and Nikola is supposed to mind link me when they are leaving the hospital. I just hope that they like all the decorations and all the food. I am sure they will love everything you have done babe. Jax say's to me as he pulls me into him and gives me a very passionate kiss. What was that for? Just because. Well you can kiss me like that anytime. You have done a great job Hailey, I know that Nikola and Dorian are going to like it, and I am sure with three babies at home they are going to really like having this food already done for them. I might even have a cook come here to help out for a while, at least until they have a routine down. I think that would be a great idea Jax.

I went to look out the window because I heard a car pull in. It is Corbin and Vondra. Babe, your mom and dad just pulled in. Then right behind Jax's parents was Todd and Lily, Nikola's parents. If they all keep pulling in like this everyone will be here at once. I said to Jax as we go to open the door together.

Nikola 🐾

When Dorian and I got to the hospital we went straight up to the nursery. The head nurse wanted to go over some instructions with us before we take Alex and Andi home. Most of what the nurse went over with us is common knowledge. Make sure there isn't a lot of people around the babies, make sure everyone that holds the babies washes and sanitizes their hands, and absolutely no smoking around the babies, and make sure that they make it to all scheduled appointments with their doctor's and no going out in the cold. Dorian and I agreed to everything that the nurse said. We are just so happy to be able to have all three of our babies home finally. On the way out to the car I couldn't stop smiling. I was carrying Alexandria and Dorian was carrying Alexander. I can not wait to get them home and with Gabby. I also cannot wait for everyone to see all three of our children. Just don't forget what the nurse said. Dorian said to me. I know, I know. I am just happy that we will have our little family together. So am I babe. We carefully place the babies in the backseat in their little car seat. All the way home I could not stop looking back at them. It just seems like a dream that these little babies are ours. Yeah, just wait until we are waking up at 3:00 in the morning or four in the morning to feed them. Oh Dorian, it will all be well worth it.

Lauren 🐺

Hi Hailey, Alpha Jaxson. I am so glad to see you both. Lily and Todd it is always nice to see you two. Hi Lauren and Kaden, how are you two……. Lily trailed off as she seen my belly. Oh you're pregnant. Yes I am Lily. Kaden and I we're going to announce my pregnancy, but with everything that has went on we just haven't had a chance. Mom, you haven't even told me. Hailey said with a shocked look on her face. Well Hailey you have been dealing with a lot and it's not like me or Kaden was trying to keep it from you. We are hoping you will be happy having a new little brother or sister. Well how are you feeling? Hailey asked me. I am feeling great actually. I thought I would go through hell being the age that I am but surprisingly I am doing great and the doctor says everything is really well and right on track.

Lily 🐺

I cannot wait to meet my grandbabies. They should be here anytime. Hailey said to me. Have you heard from Nikola? I asked Hailey. Yes she told me through mind link that they were leaving the hospital. I know I got to see all three at the hospital after they were born, but it just seems so different now that they will be home. You act as though you have never had children before. Todd said. Oh like you will not melt when you see and/

or hold your grandchildren for the first time Todd. He just gave me a look like he is made of steel. Oh I hear a car. Hailey is that them? Yes it is. Hailey said. Okay. Ok everyone places.

Hailey 🐺

We all gathered around the front door, but leaving enough room for Nikola and Dorian to come in with Alex and Andi.

Everyone
Welcome Home Alexander and Alexandria

Dorian 🐺

Thank you everyone. I am glad you are all here to share with Nikola, and I this happy time as we bring Alexander and Alexandria home to join their sister Gabby. We now feel complete that we have all three of our children home. Now there are some things that we were told before we could leave the hospital with these two. Anyone that wants to hold the babies must make sure that you scrub your hands first and we have a big bottle of sanitizer for anyone that wants to hold the babies to use. Also we don't want to many people to hold the babies right away. We don't want to overstimulate them. They are going to be around for a very long time so each and every one of you will have a chance to hold them at some point even if you don't get to hold them today and yes I am going to be that very protective father of my children. Now with that being said I want to introduce to you all Alexander and Alexandria Jacobs.

Nikola

Now that Dorian has made his speech, I want to make mine. I also want to thank you all for being here on one of the happiest days of my life. I never thought about having children. I actually never thought of myself as being a mom, but now that I am I know that I am also going to be very protective of my babies probably more so than Dorian is. I heard everyone kind of laugh when I said that. I do want to change the baby's diapers before anyone holds them so whoever does want to hold one of them please go wash your hands now and the sanitizer will be right here. I set the sanitizer on the table by the front door oh and one more thing. If I see anyone doing something to one of my babies that I do not approve of I will be kicking you out of my home. You all have been warned. With that Dorian and I took Alex and Andi and went into the baby's room to change all of the baby's diapers. Hailey followed us with Gabby in her arms just like a good godmother. How was Gabby while we were gone? I asked Hailey. She was very good, not a cry or anything you have such great babies Nikola. I cannot wait until Jax and I start a family. Hailey said. I think you probably won't have to wait as long as you think. What do you mean? Hailey asked me. Well there is something that has been a little off about you Hailey, and you have had a different scent about you. Well I was just in heat again. No that isn't it. Babe what are you getting at? Dorian asked me. Well if I am right I believe that my best friend here just might be pregnant. WHAT? Hailey yelled. Then Alpha Jaxson comes running in.

Hailey 🐺

When I screamed WHAT, Jax came running into the baby's room. He thought something was wrong. What are you talking about Nikola? There is no possible way. What is there no possible way of? What is going on? Jax asked. I think your mate might be pre......Nikola thanks I might be pregnant. I said to Jax. What do you mean Nikola thanks you might be pregnant? She said that there has been something a little off about me and that I have a different sent to me. Well she is right about the scent. Jax says to me. You smell a little different, but I didn't think much of it since everything that has been going on and all the places that we have been and all the people, wolves, and vampires that we have been around I just thought maybe I was still smelling some of them on you babe. Do you think I should get checked? I asked Jax. We can go tomorrow to find out if you want. Jax said. Oh Hailey wouldn't that be so awesome if you are, our children would be close in age. Yeah that would be nice. Then what is wrong Hailey? Nikola asked me. Well Jax and I just talked about when we would want a family and we both decided that we want to wait for a while. Nikola kind of laughed. What is so funny? I asked Nikola. You can't control some things Hailey. Sometimes nature takes over at times we may not expect it to. I know. Well there is no reason to get upset and spoil this great occasion. Dorian said. You all won't know anything until you go to the doctor anyway Hailey so why don't we just have a good time and be happy that Alex and Andi got to come home. You're right Dorian. I am happy that you and Nikola got to bring your babies home. Let's take the babies back downstairs and let everyone see them. Sounds good to me.

Nikola

Everyone got to see all three babies, but after about an hour they were getting tired and hungry. Hailey would you like to help me take the babies upstairs and feed them. Of course. What kind of godmother would I be if I didn't help my BWFF out with my God children? Hailey I know you said that you and Alpha Jaxson want to wait before you start a family, but is there something else bothering you? No, nothing that I can think of. I just look at Hailey because I know her very well I know there is more on her mind than her possibly being pregnant before she had planned. Well I wish my dad was still here. With everything that has went on and is going on, it's just a lot to deal with. I know, of course I don't know what it is like to not have one of my parents but I know there has been a lot going on and a lot falling on your shoulders as well as Alpha Jaxson's shoulders. Yeah, but if I couldn't handle it I am sure the moon goddess wouldn't have chosen me for Alpha Jaxson.

CHAPTER 12

QUITE TIME

Jaxson 🐺

It's been about a month now since Dorian and Nikola brought their babies home, and only three more months until Hailey and I have our own little one and we still have not had the time to plan our wedding but so much has went on with the attacks, and my parents and my brother being kidnapped. We have several transfer's coming in, and I have had a lot of emails and phone calls to take care of. But what I would really like to do is to do something to take Hailey's mind off of everything. I think maybe a nice quiet weekend away from everything and everyone would be what Hailey and I need. Just her and I and not thinking about anything but us. I don't know if I want to take her to the cabin because I don't want her to think about when I had to send her and Nikola there to protect them from the last vampire and rouge attack. The only thing is that with Dorian and Nikola having the babies at home I really don't want to put a lot of work and the entire pack on him. Maybe I can get Jace to take over for a little while and get some of the Omegas to watch Gabby, Alex, and Andi. I need to run all of this by Dorian and see what he thinks.

Dorian 🐺

Babe, do you need any help with the babies? Yeah if you could change Alex I already have Gabby changed and ready for the day and I am getting ready to change Andi. I'm here and ready to help. I love being a dad, but I know that Todd would have liked it if Nikola would have been married first before she got pregnant. About that time I got a mind link from Alpha Jaxson. Yes Alpha. Could you, Nikola, and the kids come over to mine and Hailey's house for a little bit? There are some things I need to go over with you. Sure thing Alpha, we are just getting the babies ready for the day and we will be right over. Okay, I will see all of you guys in a little while. Yes Alpha. When I ended the mind link Nikola asked me what was going on. Alpha has asked if we all can go over to his and Hailey's house. He has some things he wants to go over with me. I can see that Nikola is excited about going to Jaxson's and Hailey's. We really haven't been anywhere since we brought the babies home and I know Nikola needs to get out of the house. I think Alpha realizes that we have not really been anywhere since we brought the babies home and that's probably why he asked if we wanted to come to their house instead of him coming here to go over whatever it is he wants to go over with me. Besides I think it would do us all some good to get out of the house. Well let's pack up the bags of what the babies will need while we are over at Alpha Jaxson's and Hailey's.

Nikola

It is so nice that we have a big enough vehicle to be able to haul all five of us. Alpha got a nice SUV as a gift after the babies were born. Dorian and I could have afforded one on our own, but Alpha insisted on getting one for us as a baby gift. Once we got all three babies loaded up in the car we headed over to Alpha Jaxson's and Hailey's.

Hi guys. Hailey said when she opened the door for us. She seemed surprised to see us. Hey BWFF, we decided to come over for a little visit, Alpha Jaxson said that he wanted to see Dorian. Hmmm is something going on that I don't know about? Hailey asked Dorian. No he just said that he wanted to talk about something. Maybe a transfer. I know we have had a lot to go over as far as paperwork on transfers Hailey said to Dorian. Well he is in the office. Once Dorian walked into Alpha Jaxson's office Hailey told me to come sit.

Jaxson 🐺

Thanks for coming over Dorian. Your welcome Alpha. What's going on? Well I was thinking and I don't want to jinx anything, but since it has been really quiet here lately I thought it might be nice if you and I take the girls on a much needed vacation. That sounds great Alpha and I don't want to sound ungrateful, but Nikola and I have the babies. I know and that is why I wanted to talk to you. I was thinking if you and Nikola are okay with this idea maybe we could have a couple of the Omegas to take care of the babies for a few days. Dorian sat there for a few minutes thinking. I really want to do this not just for Hailey and I, but for you and Nikola. I am sure Nikola and you could use the break. That is very thoughtful of you Alpha but I should run this by Nikola before I answer. That is okay with me, of course you should talk with Nikola. Have her come in here and I will have Hailey to come in here too. Dorian got up and went to get the girls. When the girls came in I asked them to sit down. What's going on Jax? Hailey asked me. Is there another rogue attack that we need to get ready for? No babe it's nothing like that. I have been thinking that since it is kind of quiet now it would be a good time for Dorian and I to take you two on a little vacation and before you two say anything just hear me out. I was thinking that maybe we all should go on a little vacation and we could have a couple of the omegas to take care of the babies. I know you and Dorian could use a break, and I want to take Hailey somewhere nice and I know she would love to have you there Nikola.

Nikola

When Alpha Jaxson said that he wanted all of us to take a little vacation I didn't know what to think. It sounds like a good idea, but at the same time I don't know if I'm comfortable leaving my babies. I mean they are only a month old and poor Alex and Andi had a hard start at life. Then Alpha Jaxson through this in. Nikola I can promise you that if for any reason you and Dorian need to come back I will have you both back here very fast. I understand Alpha Jaxson, I just have a hard time with the idea of leaving the babies especially with them only being a month old. Nikola I will have an airplane on standby at all times, and I know without a doubt that Hailey would love to have you there and you two can hang out, go shopping, and do all the things you two use to do. I guess I could try it since you promised that I can come back if something happens, or if I start really missing my babies. Speaking of my babies who will watch them. I know my dad won't let my mom watch them, he thinks there are too many for my mom to handle for a couple of hours let alone overnight or longer. Well that is why I think having a couple of omegas watching them would be good. They have already watched children and they have been around your babies and they know your routine. I look to Dorian to see what his thoughts about this is. What do you think babe? I think it would be good for us to have a break and to get some time in just the two of us. Dorian said. Okay then it's settle we will go with you and Hailey.

Hailey 🐆

When Nikola said that she and Dorian would go with me and Jax on a little vacation I screamed in excitement, and Jax smiled because he knew this made me very happy. As much as I hate using Jax's money which he says is our money I know that Nikola and I needed to go shopping for this vacation. Babe, Nikola and I will need to go shopping to get some clothes for the vacation. That is if Nikola wants to go shopping. I looked over to Nikola. What do you say BWFF? I need to go shopping, ever since I had the babies nothing fits me anymore. Jax handed me the credit card and said that him and Dorian would watch the babies while Nikola and I went shopping. One of the guards pulled a car around for Nikola and I to take.

Once in town Nikola and I went to a little store that had bathing suits. We tried on so many different ones. I wasn't too sure about wearing a bikini. I was starting to get a pooch, but Nikola who just had three babies a month ago looked amazing in the bikini that matched the one that I was trying on. Her belly was flat again and her boobs were enormous but filled the top of the bikini perfectly. Oh Hailey that bikini looks great on you. I'm not so sure, I'm starting to get a pooch. But you cannot even tell that you are pregnant. Come on Hailey get that one and I will get this one and we can match. Even though I was still not sure I went ahead and got the bikini so we could match even though we had no idea where Jax was planning on taking all of us we knew to be ready for anything. Nikola and I spent the entire day shopping and we went out to lunch it was so nice and it was like we were kids again even though Nikola did worry about Gabby, Alex, and Andi while we were out a couple of times. But that was to be expected.

Jaxson 🐾

While the girls were out shopping I thought it would be a good time for you and I to go through these transfer requests. I said to Dorian. Who are you going to get to look after the pack while we are gone? Dorian asked me. Well Jace is second Beta in line so I thought I would give him the responsibility to watch after everyone. He hasn't really had to do anything since I become Alpha. Have you told him your plans for all of us to leave for a couple of weeks? No not yet, but no better time than now to have him to come over so I can talk to him.

Hey little brother, what are you doing? I asked Jace through mind link. Nothing at the moment. What's up? Can you come over to the house I need to run something by you. Sure, I will be there soon. It really seems like Jace has stepped up since I became Alpha. He is always here when I need him. When Jace got here he had Abby with him. Hi Abby, how are you doing? I am doing very well Alpha Jaxson, thank you for asking. Where is Hailey and Nikola? The girls went out shopping. All the babies are getting so big already. Abby said to Dorian. Well I guess baby wolves do grow a pretty fast. Dorian said back.

CHAPTER 13

VACATION TIME

Jaxson 🐺

After the girls got back from shopping it took me and Dorian both to carry in all of the bag's that the girls brought back. What all did you two buy a whole new wardrobe for every season? I laughed at the look Hailey gave me when I said that. No Jaxson. Hailey said. I am starting to get a belly, and Nikola just had the triplets so we needed to get some clothes that actually fit. Babe it is okay. I said to Hailey while laughing. When I gave you the credit card I said to get what you both needed. So while you two were gone Dorian and I went over and looked at some places that we all four could go to. Some of the places we looked at is Cape cod, Dayton Florida, Hawaii, or Mexico. If you two can think of anywhere else you both might like to go just let me know. Or we can go to one place for a certain amount of time and then we can go somewhere else before we come back home. What do you think ladies? I asked the girls

Hailey 🐺

Nikola and I at the same time said HAWAII. I guess that let the guys know that we are serious because we both said it at the same time. I handed Jax back the credit card, but he used a different credit card to book the plane and the hotel that we will be staying in. OMG Nikola we are going on a vacation that I never dreamed would be possible. I know, I really thought that once I had the babies that was it. That taking care of the babies and being the mate of a Beta would be all I would be doing. I thought if I ever got to go anywhere it would have been while my dad was in the military and even then it would not have been any fun because we would have just stay on the military base all the time. Well girls get ready to have some fun. Jax said to us.

Jaxson 🐾

Ok I have everything booked and ready to go. Beta Dorian and Nikola you two better go and get your bag's packed and ready to go because we are leaving in the morning for beautiful Hawaii.

Nikola 🐾

I know that it is going to be sad to leave the babies, but at the same time I think you and I really need this. I said to Dorian. I think you are right babe. I know it has not been very long since we brought our babies home, but you think about it this is going to give us time to ourselves, so when we get back home it will be like a fresh start. Dorian said. I am so glad that Alpha Jaxson decided to invite us along. Me too babe, me too.

Jaxson 🐾

Are you happy babe? Jax, you know I would be happy even if you had not suggested that we go on a vacation. Hailey said to me. I know, but I told you that I am going to show you every day how much I love you. Babe you don't have to buy me things and you don't have to take me on expensive trip's. That is just showing off your money. I do very much appreciate what you do for me and that you include Nikola and Dorian from time to time. I just want to make sure that each and every day that you know without a doubt that I love you babe.

Hailey 🐺

When Jax said that he wanted to make sure that I know each and every day how much he loves me I take Jax by the hand and I lead him up to our bedroom. What are we doing up here babe? Come on now Jax I know that you are a smart man, you can figure it out. But just in case you can not figure it out, maybe this will help. I go over to the bluetooth speaker and put on some sexy music and then I walk slowly back over to Jax and I playfully push him back on the bed. Then I proceed to very slowly, with my back to Jax very seductively do a little dance as I slowly remove my shirt, then I remove my bra and I toss it onto Jax's face. I turn around and I move my hands over my chest, down to my boobs, I slowly move my hands to my nipples, then I start moving my hands slowly down my stomach and I undo my pants, and I slide them down and take them off by that time I hear Jax moaning and I know he is getting very sexually excited.

Dorian 🐺

When Nikola and I got back home I could tell that Nikola is in a great mood and she is ready for this vacation that Alpha Jaxson invited us to go on with him and Hailey. But I could also tell just like me she is worried about our babies. Babe, everything is going to be okay. I would not even called you into Alpha Jaxson's office to ask you about going on this trip if I thought for a second that the babies would not be well cared for and very safe. I know babe, it just makes me sad to think about leaving them already. They are not that old and they can not even tell us if anything happens that we might need to know about. Babe, like Alpha Jaxson said at any time you and I can come back home. Besides we have FaceTime that we can do to see the babies, and we have the cameras that we can look in on at any time to see how things are going. You are right babe. I look forward to this vacation and then there will eventually be the vacations that we will be able to take and bring the kids.

Jaxson 🦊

Hailey I guess decided to take me up to the bedroom. To my surprise she had in mind to do a striptease for me. That was blowing my mind. She had never done anything like that before. I was so excited and so hard that I really thought I was going to explode before I could get her over to me. I grabbed her by her hand and pulled her over to our bed. But she still did not let me have any control. No she had all the control this time. She finished by taking her panties off and they are some very sexy baby blue lace ones too. They look so hot on her, but I need them off of her. Hailey then takes my shirt off of me, then she did not just move down to my pants but she licks and kisses her way down my neck, down my chest, all the way down my stomach to my pants. I have never in my life had a girl actually undo my pants with her teeth before and Hailey was definitely a virgin when I got with her so I have no idea where she learned that move.

Hailey 🦊

I know I am driving Jax nuts with the things I am doing to him right now. He is squirming around, he is moaning and I haven't even touched him yet. It's almost comical how excited I have him in this moment. There is nothing he can really do either to hurry me along because I'm going to take my time and make sure this is one that he never forgets.

Nikola

Babe, do you think I should tell my parents that we are going on this vacation? Honestly babe that is up to you, but if it were me I probably wouldn't tell them. But what if like my mom wants to come and see the babies and we are gone. Good point babe. Yeah you might as well tell them and get it over with. I mean really what are they going to do, tell you that you cannot go on this vacation. You are grown, you graduated high school, and you have three kids now they really cannot tell you anymore what you can and cannot do. You have a point. Now should I call them on the phone, or should I just mind link my mom? Why don't you call them on the phone. We really need to only use the mind Link in case something serious is going on. You're right babe, I will call her on my cell phone.

Hey mom, I wanted to call you for a couple of reasons. One is just to see how you and Daddy are doing. We are doing great sweetie. How are you, Dorian, and those precious grandbabies of mine doing? Alex, Andi, and Gabby are doing good. They are growing so fast. That's how it goes Nikola. One day they are babies and the next they are all grown up going off on their own with their mate. Well mom, there is another reason I called you. What's going on sweetie? Well Alpha Jaxson, and Hailey have invited me and Dorian to go on a little vacation with them. Oh Nikola, don't you think the babies are still too little to be going on a trip? Well Mom that is just it, they are still too little to go besides this trip is just for me, Dorian, Hailey, and Alpha Jaxson. Nikola you know that your father will not let me babysit. I wasn't calling for that Mom. I just wanted to let you know that we are going on a vacation. Well what about the babies Nikola? Alpha Jaxson is having a couple of Omega's to come over to watch and take care of the babies while we are gone. Before you say anything mom they are the Omega's that have been here and they know our routine. Well as long as you think the babies will be okay while you are gone I don't see a problem with you going. Well Alpha Jaxson said that he will have a plane on standby in case I have to come home, or even if I really start missing the babies I can come home. Then I don't see any reason why you shouldn't go. Thank you mom, that makes me feel so much better about going.

Hailey 🐺

I finish undoing Jax's pants with my teeth and I pull them off of him with my hands. His underwear came off with his pants I made sure of that. I slowly kiss him up his legs as I move up between them and I see that he is harder than hard so I slide my tongue down his cock and I slowly move my warm mouth over it as my tongue slides up and down. I wrap my tongue as much around his cock as I can. As I move my tongue all around I move my mouth down then up slowly. Jax is going crazy by now. His hands are in my hair moving with my head. I feel his cock swelling up like he is about to cum, but I am not ready for him to cum yet and I am still in complete control. I slide my mouth off of him and I straddle him. I lower myself on to his hard cock and I start moving on so slowly at first, but I go a little faster each time. Jax is begging me to finish him, he wants to cum so badly but I tell him oh no babe, not yet. I grind myself on him more. Every time he is close to getting off I slow down, or I come to a complete stop. But I finally give in and I ride him like a wild wolf.

Jaxson

OMG Hailey has never done anything like that before, at least not like she did tonight. As soon as we both cum Hailey slides off of me and she lays beside me and I have my arm around her. Babe I don't know where that came from, but damn that was amazing. Your welcome babe. Hailey says with a smile. I was so relaxed after she did that I was ready to go to sleep, but I know we still have to pack for our trip. I also still need to talk to Jace about watching over the pack while we are gone. Babe I need to get a hold of Jace and see if he will come over real quick so I can see if he is willing to watch over the pack while we are gone. So I have to fit in both talking to my little brother in with packing. Okay babe, I can pack a bag for you while you are talking with your brother. How did I get so lucky for the moon goddess to choose you as my mate. It was total fate babe. Hailey said back to me with that beautiful smile that I love.

I mind link Jace. Hey little brother are you busy? Hey big bro, no just hanging out with abby. What's up? Well I wanted to see if you could come over for a little bit. I have something I want to go over with you. Yeah, is it okay if Abby comes with me. She and I are hanging out together all night. Sure that is fine with me. Okay we will be there here in a few.

Jace 🐺

Babe, Jax wants us to come over for a few. He said that he has some things to go over with me. Okay well let's go. I know it's not nice to make that Alpha wait Abby said to me and we kind of laugh. We go out and get into my car. When we got to Jaxson and Hailey's we just walk in. I hope you both are decent. JACE!! Abby says to me. What, I don't want to walk in and see my brother and future sister-in-law naked. I said laughing.

I'm in the office Jace. Hailey is up in the bedroom, but she is decent if Abby wants to go hang with her. Thank you Alpha Jaxson. Abby says to Jax.

Abby 🐺

Hey girl, how are you doing? I asked Hailey as I get to her bedroom. I'm doing great. It seems like forever since I have seen you. Hailey says. Well it was when Nikola and Dorian brought the kids home from the hospital so it has been a few weeks I guess. I said to Hailey. So what are you up to? Well Jax surprised me with a vacation. Oh wow where are you guys going to? Well if you can believe it we are going to Hawaii. OMG Hailey that is so awesome. How long are you going to be gone? That I am not sure of, Jax didn't say. All he said is that if me and Nikola want to spend some time in Hawaii and then if we want to go somewhere else we can spend a week or more in another place. Oh Nikola is going to? Yeah Jax wanted me to have Nikola to hang out with. Well is Dorian staying here with the babies? No we are having a couple of omega's to go to Dorian's and Nikola's to watch the babies while we are gone. Well I hope you all have a good time. Thank you Abby

Jaxson 🐾

So I want to take Hailey, Nikola, and Dorian on a vacation. I want to get Hailey away from here for a while especially after everything that has happened. I don't blame you bro. I am sure that Hailey needs to get away. But what does that have to do with you needing to talk to me? Well you are second in command since you are second Beta I wanted to see if you would be willing to take over and keep an eye on things while we are gone. This will be your chance to prove yourself especially to our dad. Of course I am willing to take over while you're gone. Jace you know you cannot be a hot head while you are over the pack? Yes Jaxson I know I have to keep my cool. I don't want you to make any major decisions while I am gone like kicking anyone out, or to accept any incoming newbies. I will take care of that along with you and Dorian when we get back. Just make sure there is still a pack when we get back. Jace laughs and says yes sir. I can give you all the paperwork on everyone at least that way you have a list of all the names. I know it can be a lot to remember everyone's names. Yeah there are a lot of people / wolves to remember. Jace say's. Well little bro I think that is it. But remember I want a pack to come home too. Don't worry so much Jax, it will make you old before your time. Jace laughs again. I we'll walk out into the front room with you and say hi to Abby.

The girls come downstairs as Jace and I go into the front room. Hi Abby, how are you doing. Hello Alpha Jaxson. I am doing good, thank you for asking. How is my little brother treating you? He is really good to me. That is good I would hate to take him down if he did not treat you right. We all kind of laugh when I said that to Abby.

Hailey 🐾

Thank you Abby for coming over. It has been really good to see you. You too Hailey. Maybe when you all get back we should hang out. I would love that. I said to Abby. Jax and I walk Abby and Jace to the door. Once they were gone I look at Jax.

I am so tired now babe. I have both of our bags packed and ready to go. I packed my new clothes that I just got when Nikola and I went out shopping. Am I going to like the clothes that you picked out? Well I don't know babe you will have to just wait and see. I said with a smile because I know Jax is going to love the clothes I got. I even got something a little special for when Jax and I are alone in our room that I want to wear for him. I cannot wait to see how he reacts to that. Are you ready to go up and take a shower and get ready for bed? Jax ask me. I sure am babe.

Jaxson 🐾

The next morning, the morning of our trip I woke up at 4:30 in the morning. The alarm was set to go off in an hour. I guess I'm just so excited to take my beautiful mate on this trip that I just could not sleep anymore. I look over at Hailey, she is still very much sound asleep and so very beautiful. I go downstairs to the kitchen and make some coffee. I am definitely going to need some caffeine to keep me awake through the whole day. I just really hope that Hailey has a good time on this trip. She has been through way to much not just since she has been with me but before she even met me too. I know she lost her dad when she was very young, then she had to move with her mom from the only home she ever knew to come here. Then there is everything she has been through since she has been here and she has only been here just a little over a year now. I can not wait to relax with Hailey on the beach.

Before I knew it an hour had went by. I had just finished my third cup of coffee when Hailey came downstairs. Good morning my beautiful mate. She is beautiful even when she wakes up and still looks very sleepy.

Hailey 🐺

I hear the alarm go off, but I was waiting for Jax to turn it off. To my surprise Jax was not in the bed when the alarm went off. I shut it off and got up. First I went to the bathroom because I had to pee really bad. Of course Jax was not in the bathroom either. I wonder why he s already up so damn early. I grab my robe and put it on but left the front open. I have on pj shorts and a T-shirt. When I get downstairs I can smell coffee. Good morning babe. How long have you been up? I woke up an hour ago. Jax told me. I am just to excited about our vacation that I could not go back to sleep, so I decided that instead of tossing and turning trying to go back to sleep and possibly waking you up that I would just get up, come down here and have some coffee. He told me. Well is there any coffee left? I might have to have some to be able to stay awake all day. Jax laughed and told me that is exactly why he wanted to have some coffee. I wonder if Dorian and Nikola got sleep last night or if the babies kept them up. Well I sent the two Omega's over there yesterday so they would be there to help out. So I am hoping they were able to get some sleep. Do you want to mind link Nikola, or would you like for me to mind link Dorian and see if they are at least up? Go ahead and mind link Dorian because Nikola is very grumpy in the mornings if she has not had enough sleep. Jax just kind of laughs when I told him that.

Jaxson

Hey Beta Dorian, are you and Nikola ready? I said kind of joking. I was at least hoping he would be awake, but I am not expecting him to be completely ready? Yeah I am totally awake and ready. I am dressed for Hawaii, I am wide awake. I even already have mine and Nikola's bags in the car. If Nikola isn't awake yet when we end this mind link I will be waking her up. Well sounds like you are ready to go. Do you want to come over here when Nikola gets up, or are you meeting us at the airport? I ask Dorian. I thought we could all ride together to the airport so that way we all get there at the same time and no one is waiting on the other. Good idea, you think things so we'll through Dorian and that makes me even more proud that you are my number one Beta. Well thank you Alpha. Yeah we will be over here in a bit. Ok we will see you both when you get here. I ended the mind link then.

Dorian

After Alpha Jaxson and I got done with the mind link I very quietly go upstairs to mine and Nikola's bedroom. I can not help but to admire how beautiful Nikola is. I have thought she was the most beautiful person in the world when I first met her, and now that she is also the mother of our children I really think she is even more beautiful if that is even possible. I mean she is so beautiful I hate even waking her up, but I know she would be so pissed off at me if we missed out on this trip.

So I lay partly on the bed and I very gently start kissing Nikola on her face. I see her start to stretch, and then that beautiful smile creeps across her face. Before she even opens her eyes I hear her say. Good morning my love. It makes my heart melt just hearing her voice. Good morning beautiful. Are you ready for today? More than you know. Well then all you have to do is get yourself up and ready. I have already taken our bags and put them in the car, and Alpha Jaxson has already mind linked me and we decided that it would be better if you and I drive to his and Hailey's house and then ride with them to the airport. That sounds good to me too babe.

Nikola 🐺

Even though today I am really excited about going on this trip with Hailey, Alpha Jaxson, and Dorian I could definitely sleep a lot longer. It has completely worn me out from having three babies. I really thought I would have recovered by now.

Babe I need you to help me get out of bed. I say while laughing. I am so tired my body won't let me get up babe. Dorian comes back into the bedroom from being in the bathroom brushing his teeth. Give me your hand babe. I put one of my hands up and Dorian grabs my hand and just before he slides me completely off of our bed he reaches down, scoops me up in his arms the gently stands me up? Thank you sweetheart. I said to him. Your very welcome my love. I get into the shower just to help myself wake up more. Once I was done I step out and dry off. I put my lotion on before I get my clothes on. I can hear Dorian talking to one of the babies and if I had to guess I would say that it is Alex. Alex is just like his daddy a very early riser. The girls Andi and Gabby are more like me, they love their sleep. I make sure that Antonia, and Sylvia are awake and they are. They are the two Omega's that are staying here to watch our babies while Dorian and I are gone. Good morning ladies. I just wanted to make sure you both are okay with watching the babies. Yes ma'am. They both say to me. I also want to make you still have all the phone numbers even though you can mind link. Yes, we have everything covered. Antonia says. Now if anything, and I mean anything goes on or happens you make sure to get a hold of myself and/or Dorian. Alpha Jaxson said he will have a plane on standby in case I need to come home early. Of course ma'am. I really appreciate you both for doing this. It is our pleasure. Sylvia said. I go and brush my teeth real quick before getting into the car to go over to Alpha Jaxson's and Hailey's.

Hailey 🐺

While we are waiting on Dorian and Nikola to get here I decided to take a shower so I can feel more refreshed. When I walked into the bathroom to get ready to take my shower I start feeling a little nauseous so I hurry over to the toilet. Sure enough all the coffee I drank this morning came right up and believe me that s really gross to have black coffee come up. Babe are you okay? Jax asked me. Yeah babe, just a little morning sickness I will be fine. Do you think we should put the trip off until you feel better? Believe me babe you do not want to postpone our vacation. You think I am a lot to handle when I get pissed off, you haven't seen anything. When Nikola gets pissed off there is nothing that stands in her way without it going flying. Okay babe I was just thinking of you my love. I know and that is really sweet of you. You know that the only thing that sucks is I am the only one who can not drink on this vacation. Why not babe, it is your vacation as well as it is all of the rest of us that is going. Jax think about it, I am pregnant. OMG babe I am so sorry, it is still very early in the morning and I was just not thinking right. Well you can get the drinks without the alcohol in it. Yeah I guess that is true. About that time we hear a knock on the door. Jax goes downstairs and answers the door. I can hear Jax, Dorian, and Nikola downstairs talking.

Hi you two. I say to Nikola and Dorian as I come downstairs. Hi BWFF. Nikola says back to me. Dorian you definitely look like you are ready for Hawaii. Jax, Nikola, and I all laugh when I said that to Dorian. What? Are you all jealous that you all didn't think to dress Hawaiian style. We all laugh again. I guess I'm just not used to seeing anyone now a days wearing that much Hawaiian style clothes. I'm getting in the mind set. Dorian said to all of us.

So is everyone ready to go? Dorian asked all of us. I just have to carry mine and Hailey's bag's out to the car and then I do believe we will be ready. I can help you with that Alpha.

Dorian

Hey Jaxson, I wanted to show you this while the girls are not around. Dorian pulls a box out of his pocket and opens it up. Damn Dorian I am sure that wasn't cheap at all. Oh it wasn't, but I really think Nikola is worth it. So are planning on asking her to marry you while we are on vacation? Yes I do, as long as the right moment comes along. Believe me Dorian any moment is the right moment when you are asking the love of your life to marry you. I know but I want to make this really special for Nikola. I hear you man, believe me I hear you. Dorian puts the ring back in his pocket as him and Jaxson walk over to Dorian and Nikola's car so they can take the bags out of that car and put them into Jax and Hailey's car. You might want to put that into your suitcase that way you are not stopped at security for setting the metal detector off. You do have a good point there Alpha. Dorian slips the ring in the box into his suitcase just in time because Nikola and Hailey open the front door and start to come outside.

Hailey 🐾

Is everything ready to go? I asked the guys. Yes it is, let's get going. Jax says back to me. Nikola and I get in the back seat while Jax and Dorian ride up front with Jax driving my car that he had gotten me as a graduation gift. I really hope that no one scratches my car while it is parked at the airport while we are gone. Oh babe I am sure the car will be fine besides they have cameras on all the cars there. How are you able to ride in the backseat while you are pregnant Hailey? Nikola asked me. It doesn't bother me at all. OMG I could barely ride in a vehicle let alone the backseat while I was pregnant with the triplets. Well maybe it helped that I already got rid of everything that was in my stomach this morning. By the way Nikola how long did your morning sickness last? Oh it was at least a couple of months. I think it was more like just under four months babe. Dorian said to Nikola. Remember the doctor was going to have to give you some medicine if it hadn't stopped when it did. Oh that is right. I almost forgot about that. God I hope it does not last that long for me. I absolutely hate throwing up.

Lauren 🐾

I woke up around four this morning with the worst pains than I ever had when I was going into labor with Hailey. I looked over at Kaden and he looked like he was sleeping so peacefully so I didn't wake him as I was getting out of bed. I went downstairs and went to sit at the kitchen table. But that didn't last very long. I had to get up and walk around. That was the only way I knew that I was going to make it through the contractions. I look to see what time it is and I realized that Hailey and Jaxson should be on their way to the airport with Dorian and Nikola. I open the mind link to Hailey

Hey sweetie are you all on your way to the airport yet? Yes we are almost there now. Is everything okay mom? Oh yeah everything is fine. I just wanted to say be safe and enjoy your vacation. Mom are you okay? Of course I am okay, why do you ask? Well it sounds like pain in your voice. Oh no sweetie I am completely fine, I'm actually thinking about going back to bed. I just wanted to be up in time to mind link you before you got on the plane. I love you my baby girl. I love you too mom, and remember that Jax will have a plane on standby if any of us need to leave for whatever reason. So if you need me I can come right home. I will be just fine Hailey. I just want you to have a good time. I will, and I love you mom. I love you too Hailey. I closed the mind link as another contraction was coming on and this one is hurting worse than any of them have. I guess I should go and wake Kaden up. I start going up the stairs, I get to about the fourth stair and I have to stop for the next contraction. It really feels like I am going to rip in half. Once that contraction ended I started up the stairs again. I climb four more stairs and I have to stop again. OMG this is crazy. At this rate I am never going to get to Kaden. Okay that contraction is over. I make it up the last few steps. Once I was at the bedroom doorway another contraction comes along. DAMN that hurts. Kaden must have heard me because he woke up. Babe what's going on? I think it is time to go to the hospital babe. Kaden jumps out of bed and puts his clothes on faster than I have ever seen anyone put their clothes on. He helps me go back downstairs. I go to get my jacket because it can still be kind of chilly in the mornings here in the state of Washington but Kaden gets it for me. Babe I could have gotten my own jacket. Lauren sweetheart you are in labor, there for I am going to do as much as possible for you. You are such a sweet man. Kaden helps me into the car. When Kaden gets in on the driver's side I told him that I was going to mind link the pack doctor. I already did babe. Kaden said. He is meeting us at the hospital.

Hailey 🐺

We got to the airport with plenty of time left for us to just sit around and wait for our boarding to be announced. Babe I am worried about my mom. I said to Jax. Why are you worried about her? Well she mind linked me while we were on our way here and she said that she just wanted to tell me to have fun, to be careful, and to tell me bye, but I could hear pain in her voice so I am worried about her going into labor while we are gone. Well she has Kaden there with her. I know she does, but I am still worried about her. Do you want to go back home? No I don't want to ruin this for you, Dorian, and Nikola. I am sure if anything goes on my mom will let me know. I know you are right babe. Besides just like I told Nikola there will be a plane on standby in case any of us need or want to go back home.

Airport Announcer 🐺

Can I have your attention please. For everyone on flight 186 to Hawaii you may no get in line.

Jaxson 🐺

Hailey, Nikola, Dorian and I all get up and go get in line. It doesn't take to long to get on the plane. Once we got on the plane I had another surprise for Hailey, Nikola, and Dorian. We are going to Hawaii in style, we are going first class. OMG babe I am so glad you did that. Hailey said. Now we can all sit comfortably. I smile at Hailey when she said that. Babe I will always treat you as my queen. Besides I will always keep my promise of showing you each and every day how much I love you. We definitely need to be comfortable though since it takes about five hours to get to Hawaii. Well at least we are not stuck sitting the entire time. Hailey said.

Nikola 🐺

I had get my phone out to check in on the cameras and see how my babies are doing. I know that they should be waking up soon for their morning feeding. As soon as the cameras come into focus I could see that Sylvia is getting Alex. He is definitely ready for his morning bottle. I laugh to myself. I could see he was throwing one heck of a fit. Just about that time Gabby wakes up. She isn't as loud as Alex is. I see Antonia going into the babies room and get Alex. Then she gets the diaper, then the wipes. She is good for someone who hasn't had any children yet. About that time Dorian looks over at me. What are you doing babe? I smile and tell him that I was just checking in on the babies. Your not home sick yet are you? No, I just wanted to make sure the Omega's are not just letting our babies cry. They will be fine babe. I know but that doesn't mean that I don't want to check in on them.

*Kaden

As soon as we pull in at the hospital I shut the car off and I get out and go around to help Lauren out. Are you okay sweetheart? I will be so much better once these pains stop. Well I am going to help you walk in and then I will get a nurse to help us. Have you told Hailey? No she's on her way to Hawaii. I don't want to ruin her vacation.

We finally got inside of the hospital and a nurse told us to go on up to labor and delivery which is on the third floor. When we got up to labor and delivery another nurse takes into a room. She gives Lauren a hospital gown to put on. Oh we forgot to grab my bag. Lauren says to me. It's okay babe, I will go get it after the baby is born and you are moved to a regular room. Just then the pack doctor walks in. Well Lauren, how are you doing? I would be doing much better if these contractions were not so damn painful. Well I am guessing you would like a epidural. I definitely want an epidural. Well I will make sure they bring it right up and get you all set. Would you mind if I check you since I'm in here now. That's fine doctor. I don't think anything else could hurt worse than these contractions.

ʠauren 🐾

Well you are doing very well. You are at five centimeters, so about halfway there. I wish I was already done with the pushing. Well the way you are going it won't be long. I would say that I can send a nurse in to put a peanut as we call it between your legs to help the baby come down faster, but I really don't think you are going to need that. Please doctor I am not trying to be rude or mean, but I really want that epidural. Okay I will go get that coming.

Babe had I of known that you would be in this much pain I would not have wanted another baby. Well it is to late to turn back now. I said to Kaden. Just then another doctor looking guy comes in with what looks like a big tool box. I hear someone is in a lot of pain and needs an epidural. Yes, yes I do. Well if you can sit on the side of the bed. Then he looks over at Kaden and if I could get you to come over here and get in front of her and hold her hands. Now I am going to have you to kind of lean over a little. I didn't feel anything so I didn't know when he stuck me with the epidural and I didn't know when he was done until he said he was done. It took a couple of minutes, but it finally took and the pain was so much easier to deal with. A nurse came in after the epidural took effect to check me. Okay Lauren can you give me some practice pushes. Yes, but I don't know if I will be able to tell if I am doing it right or not because I am pretty numb. It's okay just do the best you can. One, two, three push. Okay, okay, okay stop. You did such a good job you almost pushed the baby out. Let me go get the doctor. It seemed like as soon as the nurse walked out her and the doctor walked back into my room. Okay I have been told that it is show time. Okay Lauren show me what you can do. It was only three pushes and our baby was born. It's a very healthy baby boy. Kaden started kissing me all over my face and I could feel his tears of happiness drip onto my face. Well Kaden we have a little boy we need to name. Lauren I don't know how you will feel about this but I would love if we could use Hunter's name in part of our sons name like maybe his middle name. OMG babe, that would make me so happy and I am sure it would make Hailey happy too.

Printed in the United States
by Baker & Taylor Publisher Services